A Trembling of Finches

David M Cameron

ISBN: 9798808798359

ACKNOWLEDGMENTS

My deepest appreciation of Olwyn's work editing my manuscripts and her constant support.

YOU WIN ONE YOU LOSE ONE

Paul was having quite a night. The drinks flowed freely, and the company was good. They had just completed a complex prosecution and won their case. The whole team was in a self-congratulatory mood. One of the most unpleasant and slippery criminals in the city would spend the rest of his days in prison. He had stayed longer than he intended, but he knew Shelley would understand, in the circumstances.

Feeling more than a bit tipsy, he left the rest to a long night, and walked out of the restaurant to get the waiting taxi. His car was back at the offices. He had anticipated not being in any state to drive, and he insisted the others follow suit and provided them with taxi vouchers to avoid any temptation to try.

Despite it being late summer, the air was more than cool and it hit him as he left the heat of the restaurant. At this hour, the streets were almost deserted. A few revellers were wandering in small groups and a couple walked towards a parked car. Paul pulled his jacket collar up and looked for the waiting taxi. He saw it across the road and paid close attention for any traffic, before walking a little unsteadily across. He went around and opened the rear door and got in, pleased to be on his way. This was his first, and as it happened, his only error of the day.

Even in his intoxicated state, he realised his mistake. There was another man in the back. But before he could react, a powerful hand pressed over his face.

He came around disorientated and confused, but quickly realised he was trapped between two large, powerful men, unable to escape. The car sped along the dark streets, and the men on either side remained silent, unmoving. His head throbbed and was not helped by a bitter chemical taste in his throat. A piece of gaffer tape sealed his mouth, preventing him from speaking.

No one said anything. Despite the alcohol, he was now sober, alert, and scared. Today, his team's victory had sent a very bad man to prison. Was this connected? The men and the driver looked like hired thugs. He had sent many to jail. His profession held an element of danger, but like all prosecutors, he had pushed that into the back of his mind. He should have been more careful and understood how much danger he was in.

As if reading his thoughts, the man on the right turned to him.

'Mr Spinx sends his regards. He said his appeal will be successful and told me to say goodbye to you.'

The speaker's manner was unpleasant, but he took no further notice of the man next to him and he stared out into the darkness and the car was in silence.

Paul didn't try to speak. It would be futile. He could only hope for some miracle, but he had never had faith. They drove for about twenty minutes, and Paul recognised familiar landmarks. The car passed through Harehills and continued on towards Oakwood. This was his area. He knew it so well and it was only a short distance from where he lived now in Moortown. They took a turn past the old clock tower and then turned a sharp right along the sides of the Soldiers' Field, the vast area of grass sports fields. He saw they were approaching Roundhay Park, a place he had often visited as a child, and where he and Shelley enjoyed lovely walks and coffees at the Lakeside Cafe. It was late and the park would be deserted.

The car had slowed and now headed down the steep hill towards the carpark. It stopped at the entrance to the Lakeside Cafe. The door opened, and he was pulled out by the man on the left and held firmly, whilst the other two men joined them. They led him through a gate to the storage areas below the cafe. The door of one was wide open and a couple of men were at work, untangling a long, heavy iron chain.

'Ready?' the man who had spoken in the car asked the one with the chain.

'Ready!' was the reply.

There was an old wooden chair, and they pushed Paul down onto it. They tied his arms behind him and to the back of the chair. His legs were taped to the chair legs, to prevent him from making any noise that would attract attention. Paul panicked, struggled and tried to break free, but he was powerless and completely at their mercy. His eyes searched for help, but there was none. He was almost sick with fear, but totally unable to do anything, apart from watch, as his fate unfolded.

There was the sound of oars slapping on the water, and one of the rowing boats appeared. His parents had rowed him in them when he was a child and he had trailed his hands in the dark and mysterious waters.

The boat came alongside the quay and the oars were stowed. Paul's breathing was rapid, his chest heaved in and out, and his eyes darted uncontrollably. Three men pulled him to the side of the boat, still sitting in the chair. They said nothing as they roughly manhandled him, and he and the chair fell into the boat, making it rock violently. He struck the wood with force and almost blacked out. Paul's face was pressed into the pooled water in the bottom, and he struggled to catch his breath. Panic filled his everything, but there was nothing he could do, as the boat cast off from the edge beneath the cafe. One man rowed whilst the others sat silent.

In a short time, the man rocking at their feet ceased his struggling. They reached the centre of Waterloo Lake. There was no moon this night, and a light mist hung in wisps. The darkness hid the drama and anyone on the lake edge would have been oblivious to the unfolding tragedy. A fish jumping or a bird diving? The sound seemed unnaturally loud, but no one heard it, no one wondered, and the water kept its secret.

HOME

It had taken a while to recover, but eventually Gabriela and Gordon both mended physically and with each other's help, mentally. It always surprised Gordon how quickly the world moves on and how the public interest wanes. He remained with Gabriela in her house in old Calpe and when fit enough, Gordon ventured to the local bar and within a short time became accepted as almost a local.

After some initial suspicion, as Gabriela was a well-known and loved resident, they warmed to him when it was clear he was a long-term part of her life. His feelings towards the young Spanish woman were clear, as were hers towards him. The regulars greeted him at the bar. He picked up more of the language and shared in their conversations. They all knew the story of how Gordon and Gabriela had survived the madness, but as time passed and they recuperated, this became less important and soon it was all but forgotten.

The physical wounds left scars. In Gordon's case, they added to his array, but on Gabriela it was obvious, at least to Gordon, and it was a constant reminder of how close they had come to losing each other. In a short time, their bond had become closer, firmer, and he wouldn't put her at risk again. It was the mental wounds that lingered. Gabriela had lost a little of her spark, with the realisation of her mortality, but she pushed that aside and it became a shadow, trailing her, but no longer dominating or threatening.

Gabriela returned to the Morena Bar and Gordon loved to spend time there watching her work, before walking slowly around the bay to have a drink and a meal at Spasso's. The town was its usual buzz of excited holidaymakers enjoying the sun, the sea and the sand, whilst the Ifach looked down: solid, resolute and permanent. Gordon had not returned to smoking, and was better for it. Gabriela said nothing, but he knew she preferred him not to, and he was willing to do anything for her. She had changed his life in the most positive of ways.

He hadn't felt this way in a long time, but there were important decisions to make. Much as he was enjoying just being with Gabriela, he knew he couldn't continue being on holiday for the rest of his days. His two-week holiday to recharge his batteries extended to three months, and his finances wouldn't last indefinitely. He had his flat and office back in England and he hadn't officially closed his business. He knew he would never return to security work, but he had to do something. The first inklings of an idea had begun to grow, but he wasn't sure he wanted to raise it with Gabriela yet.

There was one thing that he needed to do and that he had discussed with her. He needed to return to England to sort out his finances, check his flat and office were not housing squatters or the like, and let those he cared about know that he was well. Above all was the desire to introduce Gabriela to his city and the places that had made him what he was. He didn't want to show her off as some kind of trophy, but he wanted to share his background with her, as she had shared hers with him. He was worried she wouldn't want to, but she beamed with joy and gave him a hug that had hurt his damaged body, but healed his soul. The woman was a delight, and he loved her more than he ever thought he could love anyone.

The only problem was that he still wasn't well enough to make the trip, but a couple of weeks later, he was. Gabriela was at work on her last day at the Morena. She was taking four weeks' holiday, and Eduardo, the owner, was generous in giving her the time, despite it still being a busy latter part of the season. Lucia was relieved that she had fully recovered and would miss her friend, but felt the change of location would do her good.

The flight was in the evening and when Gabriela returned, there was just time to get to the airport.

She had never visited the UK, and she was as excited as a child at the prospect. Gordon couldn't help teasing her, but he shared her excitement.

Strangely, it was Inspector Navarro who had offered to drive them to Alicante airport. The police officer had become quite a friend as they, and the town, recovered from the crime war. He had suggested Gordon return home during the drama, but now appeared almost sad to see them both go.

'Now, you keep out of trouble, Meester Bennet! Look after Señorita Morales in England better than you did in Spain! Stay away as long as you like. It will be nice and quiet without you, I am sure!'

With that, he left them at the airport with their luggage and headed back towards Calpe and the daily tasks of a police inspector. Gordon and Gabriela took one look after the disappearing car, picked up their bags and entered the busy airport, ready for the tedium of check-in.

Alicante airport was quite a building. Catering for the tourist trade, particularly between the United Kingdom and Spain, it was large, full of marble and concrete. The polished road surfaces in the carpark made even the slowest of cars squeal like a Hollywood car chase. Built to impress, it was a shame that checking in luggage and passing through customs proved such a chaotic nightmare. Long queues, frayed tempers, and unhelpful announcements ensured that reaching the other side of the process was a welcome relief. A few stiff drinks provided comfort if you hadn't missed your flight, and were definitely required if you had!

To add to the general ambience were the returning holiday makers. Some were tanned, still drunk, carrying straw hats and duty-free carriers, which clinked regularly. Their holidays in Benidorm had been an alcoholic blur, but they had tales to tell to their envious friends when they returned. Some less fortunate ones were pushed in on wheelchairs, leg raised, plastered, recovering from an accident that had dented, but not spoiled the holiday. Even these returning travellers grasped the obligatory carrier bags of duty-free. There were arguing families, returning pensioners, and they all mingled, trying to find a space to relax before having to board their crowded flights.

Gabriela was amazed and the English tourists, en masse, were quite a daunting experience. She kept a firm grip on Gordon's arm as a group wearing 'Two Pint Steve' t-shirts sang raucously, whilst one of their midst had to down a pint of beer. Gabriela hoped they were not on their flight.

Inevitably, they were. Any hope of a quiet journey disappeared as the flight crew struggled to keep them in their seats and behaving. As it was a budget airline, drinks were on sale, but it only took a short time for the supervising attendant to lay down the law and refuse to serve them any more if anyone got out of their seats or misbehaved.

Fortunately for Gabriela and Gordon, they were at the back, away from Two Pint Steve's associates, and headphones offered an escape. The flight was only a short one and the arrival at Yeadon couldn't have come too soon.

After the usual rigmarole of customs, luggage retrieval and collecting the hire car, the two drove through the countryside before entering the city of Leeds. As if it knew the importance of a good first impression, the weather was at its best. The roads were lined with green hedges, the gardens full of flowers and the sky was blue and dotted with cotton wool clouds.

Gordon and Gabriela had said nothing, but they both shared a sigh of relief, as they had escaped from 'Two Pint Steve's' followers and Gabriela's eyes were wide, taking in her first sight of Yorkshire. Gordon had told her that he owned flat and office above a shop in a place called Oakwood. She had pictured what it might be like, but the road from the airport revealed sights of a countryside that was productive, gentle, and fertile. The houses they saw as they entered the outskirts were solid, old, and stone built. They had a sense of permanence that was reflected in the ancient churches they passed. As they encroached further into the city, the houses became smaller, closer and brick built, but they still held that solid feeling that she was to learn was part of the Yorkshire character.

Gordon drove and was soon passing through the familiar areas of his boyhood. The nostalgia was strong and his heart was squeezed with the powerful emotion of being home. You can take the lad out of Yorkshire, but you can't take Yorkshire out of the lad, he thought. He reached out with his left hand and squeezed Gabriela's and she turned and looked at him, a smile on her face.

'It is so green and beautiful,' she said.

'You are seeing it at its best,' he replied, 'but yes, it is a place of great beauty and contrasts. I will show you some of the countryside. It is quite magnificent.'

She squeezed his hand back, and they continued. They were now entering a busy road, a dual carriageway, and soon they reached a roundabout and approached Moortown Corner. Gordon didn't speak as he wanted Gabriela to see his hometown and district. He turned left at the traffic lights and along Street Lane. Large houses and old trees fringed the road and soon they passed the gates to an extensive park.

'Roundhay Park and the Soldiers' Field,' he said, and she looked at the wrought-iron gates and the gardens within. The sports fields were vast, dark-green, and the entire view opened up.

'Almost home,' he said. 'This is Oakwood coming up.'

Gabriela saw a large clock tower, and shops and restaurants lined the street to the right of the crossroads. Gordon drove straight over the junction and turned a sharp right down a narrow old lane, directly behind the shops. He saw a space to park on the lane, which was crowded with cars parked partially on the flag-stoned pavement. Trees overhung the car and created a curtain of yellow blossoms. The car took a moment or two of manoeuvring, before it came to a standstill and Gordon opened the passenger door for Gabriela and he escorted her through the narrow gateway, up the steps to the old blue painted door. The paint was peeling and in need of some attention, but Gordon didn't notice. His eyes never strayed from Gabriela.

'Welcome to my home!' he said, as he unlocked the door and entered a small, but high-ceilinged hallway.

A door to the right held a small wooden sign above the glass-panel that read OFFICE, and a staircase that led upwards. Gordon took to the stairs and Gabriela followed. The building carried the smell of age, old paint, old carpet, and cat.

At the top of the stairs was another door, and Gordon used another key to unlock it. He ushered Gabriela in and followed, shutting the door behind him. The room held a three-seater sofa, a small dining table, four chairs and an old television. A small kitchen adjoined and there were two more doors that Gabriela assumed led to the bathroom and bedroom. She smiled, as the flat lived up to her expectations. It was much like Gordon himself: rough around the edges, in need of care and had an enigmatic charm.

'It's how I imagined,' she said, and she threw her arms around his neck and kissed him deeply and with affection.

'Is that a good thing?' he asked when he could get a word out.

'Perfect, Mister Bennet! Just like you!'

He smiled, and she smiled back.

'But it could do with a dust and a clean!'

'I'll give you that,' he replied. 'I need to nip round to the shops and get some basics. Will you be alright?'

'I remember what happened last time.'

'I promise no one will kidnap you whilst I'm gone. Have a look around. I'll get some milk.'

He left her viewing his home and was soon on his way back. For the briefest of moments, he held his breath as he entered his flat, but was instantly relieved when he heard her moving around. Gabriela smiled as he unloaded a couple of carrier bags of essentials onto the kitchen surface.

She had located the kettle and was filling it. Two mugs were clean and sitting on the side with a tea bag in each.

'I'll bring up the bags, whilst you're making the tea.'

He vanished, but soon returned laden with bags.

Gordon looked around his flat and he wished that he had cleaned up more before he left for his holiday, but after being left unoccupied for so long, the layer of dust was only to be expected. Gabriela opened the window to allow some fresh air into the room and even Gordon admitted it was smelling better than a few minutes earlier.

Tea was made, and the two sat and were enjoying the moment after the busy day travelling, when Gordon's mobile rang.

He pulled it out of his pocket and answered, 'Hello?'

'Gordon, It's me, Shelley.'

'Shelley, why are you phoning?'

'It's Paul, Gordon. He's disappeared and I'm worried.'

'What do you mean, disappeared?'

'He left for work two days ago, and he hasn't come back.'

'Hold on, Shelley. Have you told the police?'

Gabriela reacted with surprise at the mention of Shelley's name. Gordon had told her all about his ex-wife, and she was the last person she expected to call.

'Of course I've told the police, but they think he's left me and won't do anything yet.'

'Are you sure he hasn't? You don't have a great track record!'

The voice of his ex-wife became hysterical with sobbing for a few minutes, and Gordon waited for the emotion to subside.

'Paul left for work, and they went for drinks afterwards. He walked out of the restaurant to catch a taxi, and no one has seen him or heard anything since. He hasn't been into the office and he is not answering his phone. The messages go to voicemail. I'm really worried, Gordon. You know I wouldn't call you, but I have no one else to turn to. Are you still in Spain?'

'No, I arrived back in Leeds a few hours ago. Just got back to the flat.'

'Can I come round? I need help. I think something's happened to him!'

Gordon turned to Gabriela, who had been listening in with a worried look on her face. She nodded her approval.

'Come round, Shelley. I'm sure there is a simple explanation. You can tell us all about it when you get here.'

'Us? You're not alone.'

'No, I'll introduce you to Gabriela. Will you be long?'

'I'll come right round! Gabriela?'

'Yes!'

The phone clicked dead and Gordon turned to Gabriela.

'It looks like you are going to meet my ex-wife. I'm sorry. This is hardly the way I wanted our trip to start.'

'It's alright, Gordon. She needs your help.'

'Yes, but I'm not sure I want us to get involved.'

'You have to help her, Gordon. It is the right thing to do.'

Gordon heard the truth in her words, but he felt bad.

He moved the luggage to the bedroom, and Gabriela unpacked and hung the clothes in the wardrobe or put them in the chest of drawers. Gordon went back to the shops and bought a few more essentials, which included some wine to supplement his stock. He had barely returned and unpacked when a ring of the doorbell alerted him, and he pressed the button to allow Shelley access. Footsteps came up the stairs and onto the landing, followed by a gentle knock, and the door opened.

Shelley appeared. A tall, slim woman in her thirties, she was immaculately dressed. Her hair was beautifully cut and her clothing was both stylish and professional. She was striking. Gabriela judged her own appearance in comparison, but Gordon held her hand briefly, aware of the tense situation.

'Shelley, this is Gabriela. Gabriela, this is Shelley.'

'Pleased to meet you,' said Shelley, but her expression was one of worry and the words a formality. She barely noticed the Spanish woman, and she turned to Gordon.

'Something has happened to him, Gordon. I know it has! The police are wrong. Paul hasn't run off. He's not like that.'

'Sit down,' Gordon said. 'Would you like a drink?'

'Do you have a whisky?' she asked as she took one of the armchairs.

'I'll get it,' said Gabriela, and she busied herself in the kitchen, glad to get some separation.

Gordon sat on the chair opposite and looked at his ex-wife. She was still stunning, and even in her current traumatic state, her makeup applied immaculately and she projected an appearance that most women would kill for. But Gordon saw through this to the woman who was desperately worried, needed his help and in any other circumstances wouldn't have asked for it.

I have my uses, after all, he thought to himself.

'Tell me what's happened, Shelley. When did you last see Paul?'

'Two days ago. He left for work as usual, but he never came home. He had been working on a big case and it was the day the jury was to report back. They won the case, and as usual, the team celebrated with drinks afterwards. Paul left some of the others still drinking and walked out to get his taxi in the centre of Leeds. He called me to let me know he was on his way, but he never arrived and that was the last anyone saw of him.'

'What was the case?' Gordon asked, aware that this was the most likely link.

'It was a high-profile crime family case. Marcus Spinx, the head of the family, was charged with drug offences and people trafficking. The family was infiltrated by the police, and firm evidence collected. Paul was the chief prosecutor. They proved the case and Marcus Spinx was going down for a long stretch. Paul was really pleased with how it had gone, and with the verdict. I'm scared, Gordon. They could have got him. Marcus Spinx is a very nasty man, high profile in business circles, likes the highlife and publicity, but a real mean piece underneath. I'm really worried, otherwise I wouldn't have contacted you.'

Gordon heard the truth in those words and believed Shelley's concerns were justified. He had met Paul, and the man he had met did not seem the type to disappear.

'The police have not been any help?'

'Help? A complete waste of time. Just wait a few days and he will turn up. Most missing people's cases are people choosing to leave. He wouldn't vanish, Gordon! You know that!'

Gordon knew that, and of the three of them, he was the one most likely to up and go.

'You've tried his phone?'

Gabriela handed Shelley a large tumbler of whisky, and she gave one to Gordon. She walked back to the kitchen and stood there listening, a drink in her hand.

'It goes straight to voicemail, and no one else has been able to contact him.'

'Which station did you report him missing to?'

'Stainbeck, it's the nearest.'

OLD HAUNTS

Shelley explained all that she had done, and all that the police hadn't. They had been polite, sympathetic, but condescending, assuming that this was another broken relationship and that Paul Montgomery would turn up in his own time, and probably with a new partner. They didn't say this, but Shelley thought that was what they were thinking. She was just another jilted lover, in their eyes. Even the female police officer felt the same. It showed, and Shelley felt like screaming.

The reality was if the situation were reversed, she would probably have assumed the same. But that couldn't explain it. She knew Paul, even better than she knew Gordon. Paul was open, clever, honest, considerate, and trustworthy, and those were attributes that her ex-husband couldn't be accused of.

Gordon listened, asked probing questions, and coming to the same conclusion as Shelley, but he didn't express this.

'I understand your worry, Shelley, but the police may be right. But look, I will make some enquires. I have contacts in the local force and they might be able to help. I can't promise anything, but I will see what I can do.'

'Thank you, Gordon. I didn't have anyone else to ask. I'm so worried! He wouldn't do this to me. He would have contacted me if there was anything wrong.'

She took a long drink and put the glass down.

'Would you like another?' Gabriela spoke to Shelley and Gordon's ex seemed to notice her for the first time.

'No thank you, dear. I had better be going. Nice to meet you. You will try to find him, Gordon? You understand I wouldn't ask...'

Her voice trailed off, and Gordon answered.

'I promise I will do my best. I won't say try not to worry. That would be silly. I will contact you if I hear anything. I'll do it straight away.'

Gordon showed her to the door, and Shelley turned to Gabriela.

'You seem to be good for him. I hope he will be good for you.'

'He has already been good for me, but he has made life interesting. I am sure he will find out what has happened.'

'I bet he has, and I hope you're right. Goodbye!'

Shelley left, and Gordon escorted her down to the door on ground level. Gabriela couldn't help but watch as the two stood and spoke on the doorstep, before the woman disappeared and Gordon turned. Gabriela shot back inside, not wanting Gordon to think she was prying.

Gordon looked a little embarrassed and upset when he returned to the flat a few moments later. Gabriela tried to look busy and was washing up the glasses. He walked over to her, put his arms around her, and rested his chin on her shoulder.

'I'm sorry, Gabriela. This wasn't the way I wanted to spend our first day here. She really must be worried and from what she said, she may be right to. I did some security work for Marcus Spinx and he is not a nice man, not a nice man at all.'

'That's all right, Gordon. She really does need your help, our help. She is your ex-wife, so I understand why, and you would do it for anyone, anyway.'

'Thank you for being so understanding. I can't think why I love you!'

'Apart from being fabulous, gorgeous and incredibly beautiful, you mean?'

Gabriela laughed and so did Gordon, and once again, for the briefest of moments, all was right with the world.

'My last holiday to Calpe became a holiday from hell, so I will not let your holiday be spoilt. Come on, I want to show you a local spot and get something to eat.'

The two left the house and got in the car. It was mid-afternoon on a lovely Indian summer day and Oakwood was lush and green with the old trees forming a canopy across the road. Gordon drove along the back of the houses towards a thick wall of dense green. He stopped at the t-junction.

'This is Gipton Wood. I used to play for hours in there when I was a boy. I will show you it properly another time.'

He turned the car to the right and carefully drove down a narrow cobbled lane to the front of the shops and the main road. He turned right, left by the clock tower, and along a wide road that edged the sports fields. The houses were large, grand and had enormous gardens, but Gabriela noted that many had been converted into flats.

The sun was lower in the sky, and long shadows formed. They drove down a steep hill towards a carpark. Quite a few cars were parked, and Gabriela saw some people walking dogs. Gordon parked, opened the door and reached into the back to retrieve the two jackets. The temperature dropped, and they were glad of the light jackets that kept the chill at bay.

Arm in arm, they walked towards the cafe and Gabriela stood for a while, taking in the view. The vista before her was spectacular. The large lake was festooned with ducks, swans and other waterfowl. Some rowers in sculls scudded across the flat water. Around the edges, family groups stood watching younger children toss bread to the ducks and swans. Streamers of white trailing clouds contrasted with the blue and purple tinged sky as the dazzling golden heart of the sun continued its path to the horizon.

They ordered food and drink, and wandered outside onto the veranda whilst they waited for their meals to arrive.

'It is beautiful, Gordon. Truly beautiful!'

'It is, isn't it? It is forever changing, and each season brings its own individual touch. I used to come here with my mum and dad. I have always loved it, and I hoped you would.'

Together they stared out at the placid lake, darkening, pewter grey, full of life on a stunning afternoon. They didn't speak, but seemed to drink in the beauty, and shared the moment where the world showed off.

Their reverie was broken when the waiter arrived, and there were a few moments where plates were placed, cutlery positioned. They focused on eating for the next ten minutes. With the travel and Shelley's worries, they had forgotten how hungry they both were. They wolfed down the first mouthfuls before they relaxed, slowed, smiled at each other with a hint of self-consciousness, and then laughed.

'It's good!' she said.

'It is,' he replied, and they continued to savour their first proper meal of the day.

'What are you going to do about Paul? You promised Shelley you would help.'

'I will call my contacts in the force. See what they have to say. When we've finished, I'll call them.'

They enjoyed their meal, enjoyed each other's company, however the need to help Shelley hung like the sword of Damocles over their heads. It came as a relief when Gordon got to his feet, walked away from listening ears, leaned over the barrier, stared out onto the darkening water of the lake, and made a call.

'Hi, Peter? Yes, it's me, Gordon. Yes, I got back today. No, I'm not on my own. Yes. Gabriela. She's more than gorgeous.'

There were a few moments of silence.

'Yes, I met her about an hour or so ago. No! She has asked for my help. Yes, she is in a bad way. This is serious, Peter. Paul has disappeared.'

There was another moment of silence.

'He's been working on the Marcus Spinx case. He was the lead prosecutor. Yes, she has reported it, but you know what they are like. They suspect he's probably run off, but you and I know he wouldn't do that. She's beside herself, imagining all kinds of things.'

Another tense moment of quiet.

'Could you? That would be brilliant. To be honest, I think she has reason to be worried. Spinx is a bad man, as you well know. Thanks, Peter. Will you get back to me? Thank you. See you soon.'

He walked back to Gabriela, who had been watching and taking in his body language.

'Well?' she asked.

'He knows no more than we do and agrees Shelley has grounds to be worried. He will see what he can find out and let me know. Do you fancy a bit of a walk?'

'Sounds good. I'm stiff from all the sitting on the plane and on the drive.'

The two got to their feet, and she put her arm through his and they walked together out into the evening. They went around to the lakeside and followed the path, passing others strolling on the lovely evening. There was a chill, and the wind was picking up, but it was only enough to create a few ripples on the surface of the lake.

'She is a beautiful woman.' Gabriela's voice was quiet and unsure.

'Who? Shelley?'

'Yes, Shelley. Who else?' Gabriela sounded a little subdued and Gordon stopped, turned to her and put his arms around her for a few moments. He held her at arm's length and spoke in a serious tone that she hadn't heard him use before.

'Yes, she is. But no, there is nothing still between us. You are the most precious thing in the world to me, Gabriela. You have given me my life back and there is no one, no one on this planet that I would rather be with. Do you believe me?'

He looked into her brown eyes, leant forward and kissed her, delicately, but leaving her in no doubt that his words were true.

'You think I'm stupid!'

She laughed and slapped him on the arms playfully, embarrassed at her doubts.

'I'm sorry, Gabriela, this isn't what I wanted. You know that! Sometimes things just happen.'

'I understand, Gordon. You must help her. It is important!'

'Believe me, she wouldn't seek my help unless she was desperate. I'm not sure what I can do.'

'You will do your best, and that will be enough.'

They continued their stroll. The sky was darkening, and the ducks and swans were disappearing for the night, as were most of the visitors. The lights of the cafe were behind them and it was difficult to believe that they were in the centre of a city. Thickets of trees bordered the water and, apart from a distant drone of traffic and the muffled voices of diners in the Lakeside Cafe, they could have been alone in the world.

After a half an hour's walk they returned to the car, now one of few still in the carpark. They drove back the way they had come and found a parking spot near Gordon's office and flat. They were a little weary and Gabriela asked if she could have a shower. Gordon had remembered to put the water heater on before they left, and so Gabriela enjoyed a long, refreshing and relaxing shower, whilst Gordon answered a call from Peter.

'Hi, Peter. Thanks for getting back to me. Yes, I know it. An hour? We'll be there. I owe you one!'

Gabriela reappeared with a towel wrapped around her, hair wet.

'Was that about Paul?'

'Yes. That was Peter. We are meeting him in an hour. It's round the corner. The Pie and Mussels, we can walk there. Can you be ready?'

'I can, but you are not going until you've had a shower.'

At any other time, Gordon would cross the room and the towel would be cast aside, but somehow the thought of Shelley's fear and worry took such thoughts away.

'I am on my way, madam!' He saluted her as he passed, and she laughed and he did too.

The walk to The Pie and Mussels was short, and both of them felt the tension build as they got nearer. Gordon had explained that it was almost the opposite side to his home, on the front parade of shops. It was part of a new movement towards rustic, but trendy, bars: small and intimate facilities and a warm and welcoming atmosphere. Outside, there was a raised section where the smokers could sit and not feel too ostracised.

The place was busy with a majority of young customers, but there were also pockets of older locals. The floor was bare boards and a hotch-potch of assorted and well-worn sofas, coffee tables, tall tables and wooden chairs, and many customers standing in groups, but the common feature was that they were all drinking a range of beers and wines.

Gordon looked around for Peter, but he couldn't see him. He led Gabriela over to the bar and bought a couple of drinks and then he went up the stairs to see if his friend was there. As they emerged onto the first floor, he saw a man sitting at a small table on his own. He had a pint of beer and a whisky chaser. It was Peter. The man looked up and his eyes showed recognition of Gordon, and appreciation of Gabriela. He got to his feet, shook hands with Gordon, and looked at him questioningly.

'Sorry! Peter, this is Gabriela. Gabriela, Peter. An old friend!'

'Not so old,' said the man, and he leant forward and kissed Gabriela on each cheek.

'Delighted, my dear. Charming, truly charming,' he said, and then turned to Peter.

'I see things are looking up for you, Gordon. The holiday certainly did you good.'

Gabriela blushed a little, but she smiled warmly.

'You have some polite friends,' she said to Gordon.

'I bet you're the first person who has ever said that about him!' Gordon parried. 'You wouldn't believe what most people say about the old letch!'

Peter and Gordon both laughed, and all three took a seat.

'I'm afraid there is nothing good to tell you. Despite what they said to Shelley, the police have taken the matter more seriously. They checked the close-circuit film from the night and they found the film of him leaving the bar. This is all unofficial, you realise. I shouldn't be telling you any of this.'

'I won't repeat this to anyone, apart from Shelley, and even then, only what she needs to know.'

'The footage shows him getting into a taxi, and it appears there was more than the driver in the cab. They checked the registration plates and number of the cab and there was no such taxi. The plates were stolen a week ago. The officer in charge has a strong suspicion that this was payback. Marcus Spinx has a long reach, and he is not well pleased! They are looking at this as a possible murder inquiry. I'm sorry Gordon, I don't think things are looking good.'

'Christ, Peter! What a mess. Shelley will fall apart. Have they tracked the taxi? Where did it head to?'

Gabriela said nothing, but there was a look of horror on her face.

'They are still working on that, Gordon. There's a lot of footage to go through, but they'll track it down in the end. I can't stay long, but I've time for another, though. Can I get you a drink?'

Gordon and Gabriela drained theirs, whilst Peter went down to the bar and returned.

The conversation became more ordinary: questions about the holiday, Peter's family and about how Gordon met Gabriela passed back and forth. Neither Gabriela nor Gordon mentioned any of the excitement, and it intrigued Peter how such a beautiful woman could fall for such a reprobate as Gordon.

Gabriela spun him a tale of romance, chivalry and her having a thing for lame dogs, which amused Peter.

'You haven't any friends who would be looking for another old wreck, have you?' he asked her.

She laughed, and for a few moments the mood lightened, but it was short-lived.

'I have to go. We must catch up! It was a pleasure to meet you,

Gabriela,' he said, and he looked like he meant it. 'I am sorry for Shelley, Gordon. I met Paul once or twice. He is a nice man, and they make a lovely couple. Keep in touch!'

He turned, walked to the head of the stairs, and disappeared. Gordon and Gabriela sat there, alone in the crowded bar. Their mood was sombre and Gabriela reached across the table to hold his hand.

'He seems a good friend.'

'He is, and I trust his opinion. I'm worried that Shelley's fears are well-founded.'

They finished their drinks and afterwards they left and took the short stroll back to Gordon's flat. Both were tired. It had been a long day, and they had not been prepared for the added drama.

'I'll call Shelley in the morning. The police will have got in touch with her by then. There's nothing more I can do,' Gordon said to Gabriela. 'Do you want a nightcap?'

'I don't think I do. I'm so tired.' She yawned and Gordon realised how tired he was, too.

'I'm sorry. I haven't been a great host. A good night's rest is what we need. I was going to say that things will look better in the morning, but I am not sure they will.'

Gordon kissed her and led her into the bedroom, turning off the lights behind him and shutting the door to the darkness. Together, the world was perfect, but beyond their confines, it was angry, mad, and dangerous.

NOT AGAIN

The morning arrived, and the two were awakened by the dappled sunlight through the window and the sound of traffic.

Gabriela turned to Gordon, smiled and then kissed him. Her face fell after the initial delight of being with him.

'You have to phone Shelley, Gordon. Best to do it soon.'

Gordon understood she was right, but he didn't want to destroy his ex-wife's life. They couldn't be together, but he had loved her once, and he believed she had him, at least for a short time. To warn her to expect the worst about Paul was not a task he wanted to carry out, but he believed he had to be the one.

'I'll do it as soon as I am dressed,' he said.

'I'll sort out coffee while you have a shower. She needs to know!'

'I know. It's just that I don't want to do it.'

He got to his feet and wandered to the bathroom, while Gabriela headed for the kitchen. It was a lovely morning, and the air was warm and gentle. At any other time, Gabriela would have been looking forward to exploring Gordon's hometown. These were not the circumstances she had expected, but were becoming a bit of a pattern. Things must get better, she thought to herself, but then she wouldn't complain as long as they remained together. She listened to the sound of the shower and smiled. No, she couldn't complain.

The coffee aroma filled the kitchen, and it was ready just as the man entered. He was rugged, fit, tall, and hers. A flawed diamond. But he was more than she could have ever wanted.

He picked his mobile off the counter where it had been charging. He tapped the phone and listened to the dial tone. It was ringing loud and clear, but it wasn't answered. A few seconds later, it went to voicemail. Gordon stopped the call and tried again. He repeated this several times, but the result was the same.

'I'll try again after I've had my coffee. Maybe she is still asleep. She must be having a rough time.'

'Yes, it's still early,' Gabriela said. 'She's probably sleeping in. Come have your coffee whilst it's still hot.'

Gordon sat at the kitchen table across from her and smiled.

'Thank you,' he said.

'Thank you for what?' she asked. 'The coffee?'

'No! For just being who you are.'

They sat and enjoyed each other's company for a while and the sunlit morning outside the window was dappled green by the canopy of bright leaves.

'I'll try ringing again,' said Gordon. He redialled Shelley's number and after a short time, once again he heard it go to voice mail.

'I don't like this. She should answer by now.'

He tried again. The same result.

'Let's go out for breakfast and I'll try again afterwards. If she doesn't answer, we may have to call round.'

It took a little while for them to get ready, but eventually they left the house, got into the hire car and drove the becoming familiar route to Roundhay Park and the Lakeside Cafe.

Being midweek, the carpark was busy, but not full. Women with babies and toddlers stood around, loading and unloading their charges, occupying the playground, walking the lake fringes, feeding the bird-life, or chatting with other friends. The cafe was not bursting, but there was a general hubbub of excitement with loud voices, chattering children, and the potent smell of coffee and cooking breakfasts.

The vibe was one of everyday joy. Family, friends, children, beautiful surroundings, and safety, are what give meaning to our lives. Gordon and Gabriela felt guilty enjoying this time, when Shelley was desperately worried about Paul. What made it worse was they both felt she had valid reasons for feeling so.

'I like it here, Gordon. It is beautiful.'

'It is, but there is something much more beautiful and she is sitting opposite me.'

'Oh, you smooth talker. I bet you say that to all the girls!'

'Can't say that I do. And if I have, I've never meant it like I do now.'

They both smiled, but then Gordon thought he'd better try phoning Shelley again. The mobile progressed through the same ritual of calling, later to be followed by the voice mail message.

'Damn! Where is she?'

'Leave a text message.' Gabriela suggested, and Gordon did.

Shelley, we need to talk. Give me a ring when you get this, Gordon.

'I think we had better call around at her place,' he finally said. 'It's not far.'

They walked to the car and drove back up the hill to the Soldiers' Field and then right up towards the park's main gates. Gordon turned right past the outskirts of the park, past the golf course.

'She lives in Shadwell. It is only a short distance.'

He crossed the Ring Road, and along a narrow lane, before turning right towards what was originally a small village, but now a piece of suburbia, with an affluent charm. He knew where Shelley lived, but hadn't been there for a long while. Like much of this part of his home town, nothing much had changed over the years.

Within minutes, he pulled up outside her driveway. A rustic wooden gate closed off the gravel path that curved through a long front garden and ended outside a large detached house that spoke of affluence and position. What else would you expect for two talented lawyers, he thought, but Gabriela just stared, clearly impressed.

'I'll try her phone first,' Gordon said, but when he did, the voicemail message was all that answered. 'Come on!'

He got out of the car, and Gabriela joined him. There was an iron latch and when released, the gate easily swung inwards. The two crunched their way up the path. A big detached double-garage was set to the right, but they walked up to the front door that was set back under a porch.

There was a large bell button, with faded and worn letters spelling PUSH. Gordon wondered if such an instruction was really necessary. He followed the direction and, faintly, the two could hear the sound of a deep chime.

They waited for the expected signs of the doorbell being answered, but nothing happened. Gordon pressed the bell again, and they waited, but no one answered.

Gordon backed out onto the drive and looked up at the windows. The curtains were drawn, but no lights were on, and this caused him some consternation. Shelley was a strong woman, and even with Paul's disappearance, she wouldn't allow herself any public signs of weakness. She would have got up at the usual time and been chasing both the police and him up. Shelley had work commitments and would not be in bed at almost mid-day.

'I'll just have a check around the house.'

'I'll check the other way,' Gabriela replied, and before he could say anything, she was already making her way to the left corner of the house. Gordon knew better than to object and walked to the right. The side of the house that he was checking appeared normal, and he passed the bins and headed towards the back door. There was no sound and no sign of anyone being about in the house. He slowed as he reached the far corner. Peering around the wall, he saw the back door ajar. He crept over, tense and ready to react if anyone was there. He listened again and heard footsteps, but it was Gabriela that appeared around the opposite corner. With a gesture, he signalled for her to stop, remain silent, and she did. Her face showed anxiety and mirrored his own feelings. This was not right!

He edged forward. The door had been forced. The lock was broken, and the wood splintered.

'Shit!'

He edged through and Gabriela appeared at his side. The kitchen was silent. One of the high stools near the breakfast bar lay on its side. They listened, looked around, but the house was silent and appeared empty. Gordon moved through the kitchen whilst the ticking wall clock slowed its count and seconds appeared endless.

They checked the downstairs rooms and everything was neat and provided no signs of anything unusual. The hallway held a wide flight of stairs that curved in a grand display up to the first floor. A heavy wooden banister showed the age of the house, built in a time where quality and craftsmanship were still affordable.

A thick carpet muffled any sound as they climbed, but the clock and their beating hearts seemed unnaturally loud.

Gordon slowly walked towards the front bedroom door. He assumed that would be Shelley and Paul's room. The door was open and their gravest concerns were realised. The room was a shambles. A struggle had taken place, and Shelley must have put up quite a fight. She was a fearsome woman when riled, and anyone trying to take her would have their work cut out. The bedside lamps lay on the floor, the sheets were in disarray, a vase had smashed against the wall, and there was blood on the wallpaper behind the shards of pottery.

'They've taken her!' Gabriela voiced Gordon's feelings. It appeared she had put up a struggle and made at least one of them pay. Gordon assumed there must have been at least two attackers. One wouldn't have been sufficient to overcome Shelley in full flight.

'You're right. Whoever took Paul came back to take Shelley as well.'

'What are we to do? Shouldn't we call the police?'

'We should, and we will, but we just need to have a quick check first. There may be some evidence that could help. Check downstairs, will you? But don't touch anything. If you see anything that seems unusual, call for me. I'll be up here.'

'Ok, but I'm not sure what I'm looking for.'

'Neither am I, but anything unusual.'

Gabriela headed back down the stairs, making sure she didn't touch anything. Gordon was certain someone had taken Shelley. She kept everything in its place, ordered. That was one of the reasons she had left Gordon. His life had become chaotic, spiralling out of control and she couldn't handle that. She had found the stability, order, and support in Paul. Boring, Gordon had always thought of him. Solid, unbending and dull, but those were the attributes that she wanted, and she couldn't find those in Gordon. It had worked for a while, as he was absent for months on end, but after his discharge, the opposites ceased to attract. She wanted what he didn't and couldn't offer. Gordon didn't even like himself in his self-destructive spiral.

The end proved inevitable, but her finding comfort in a colleague was an added blow to his faltering self-worth. What Gordon was certain was that the Shelley he had been married to would never have left the house in such disorder. Apart from the signs of a struggle and the broken vase, the room was as he would expect. There were two walk-in wardrobes. Paul's was arranged by colour: suits, shirts, ties, trousers, socks. Everything was in its right place. Shoes lined up under the right matching colour to the clothes above. Paul had a bigger problem than Gordon had realised. Shelley's wardrobe was an identical match: work suits, blouses, shoes, handbags, all colour and style coordinated. The two were a perfect coupling, and Gordon feared for both of them.

The rest of the upstairs showed obsessive neatness, and no photographs or other personal items. This struck Gordon as strange, but not totally unexpected.

He made his way back downstairs and found Gabriela still checking.

'There's nothing, Gordon.'

'Nothing upstairs either,' he added. 'She's been taken, and it looks like they caught her asleep. I'll phone the police.'

A few minutes later, he had finished the call and was told to wait outside the house, and not to touch anything. The two retreated through the forced door. Gabriela waited in the driveway, while Gordon moved the car that was blocking the entrance. He had just moved it a little further up the road, when he heard sirens approaching.

It was a mystery why the police always arrived with such a display, as it seemed unnecessary and attention-grabbing. Maybe the drivers just enjoyed the circus of it all, he thought.

Gabriela and Gordon almost had to jump to avoid being run over, as the first car skidded to a halt on the loose gravel. A serious looking plain-clothed officer got out of the back of the first car, with a far from happy look on his face.

He approached the waiting couple with an expression that did not bode well.

'Mr Gordon Bennet and Miss Gabriela Morales, I presume. You were the ones to call in the incident. I'm Inspector Glover. Tell me what happened.'

Gordon and Gabriela told him what they had found when they arrived.

'You haven't touched anything, or moved anything?'

'No, Inspector!'

Inspector Glover nodded to two uniformed officers, and they entered the house. They had donned blue gloves and shoe covers and disappeared inside.

'Why are you and Miss Morales here? What is the relationship between you and Shelley Jones?'

'She is my ex-wife, Inspector. I was visiting her. She was worried about her missing partner.'

'Mr Paul Montgomery?'

'Yes. She felt the police were doing little to find him. She had reported him missing, and no one was taking it seriously.'

'I wouldn't agree with that, Mr Bennet. We have procedures, and they were being followed.'

'Clearly not well enough! Now Shelley is missing, and from what we saw, kidnapped. If you had been doing your job properly, she would have been guarded, and then she wouldn't be missing too!'

The inspector's face turned grey, and he clearly wasn't used to being spoken to in such a manner.

'Gordon's right, Inspector. She was very upset when we met her. She felt sure something had happened to Paul, and that it was linked to his court case.'

Gabriela's words added to the inspector's discomfort. He remained calm and businesslike, but it cost him, as he knew she had a point.

BIRDMAN

The bars were only light-gauge, and the space narrow. He had always loved birds. Something about them, their fragility, their simple relationships, spoke to him. Happy with the basics of life in a cage, the Gouldian Finches are the most colourful and beautiful of these Australian natives. They could no longer be imported, but could be bred in England. He always felt safe with his birds and they responded to his care, happy to hop on and off his finger, and to take seed from his hand. He owned a large aviary at his home and had kept Finches since a boy.

As a grown man, he continued to care for these charming, beautiful, and happy creatures. Whilst here, he could only keep a few, but they helped to cheer him up when depressed, and they shared a bond. Patched with paint-box colours, flamboyant and truly show-offs, his finches were so different to the native birds of Leeds. Garish, maybe, but then so was he.

He hadn't expected to end up here. He hadn't believed it possible, but one bastard infiltrated his organisation, and in a rush, his house of cards came tumbling down. At least he was alone in his cell. Himself and his birds, that is. A bit of a cliché, a birdman in prison, but he didn't worry about that. He hated his loss of liberty, though. A man with influence, money and power was still afforded certain privileges. No shared room for him. That was out of the question. It took little, once he transferred out of the police cells, to Wakefield. He spoke nicely to those who decided, greased a palm, and Voila! Another request and another favour, and his birds arrived when his wife came to see him. Ariadne was a bit of an exotic bird, a little like the finches. Colourful, beautiful, from the Caribbean. He met her on a holiday in Bequia there, when she was working at the hotel. It was always nice to bring a souvenir back from your holidays, and she was it.

At first, she was a trinket, but for some reason other than his money, she seemed to like him. He, in turn, grew fond of her, to love her. She was one thing he would miss. Ariadne proved loyal, supportive, very comforting, and utterly ruthless. Like her name, she was a black spider, and her bite was fatal. She became his greatest asset and, now that he was incarcerated, she was his face in the outside world. Luck had smiled when he met her, and now that his luck had run out, she would be his right-hand woman, and he had work for her to do.

'Marcus, darling! I can't stand to see you like this. How are you managing?'

She sat down at the table across from him, the cage on the floor covered by a cloth. She reached out to his hands. Her red nails were sharp, long, and dangerous. As the two held on, a small package was slipped into Marcus's palm.

'I hate it, darling! But there are some things that I want you to arrange for me.'

He looked into her eyes and they showed a clear understanding of the implication, and with the realisation, she smiled a very unpleasant smile.

'I knew I could rely on you. I will just mention a name. Can you arrange?'

He changed the conversation, spoke about the appeal, and then he referred back to the verdict at the trial. Knowing that his meeting was probably being filmed, and he didn't want to provide anything that could be used against him, he avoided saying any name.

'Oh, before I forget. I brought the finches that you asked for. I think I got the right ones.'

Ariadne placed the cage on the table and removed the cover. In the cage were two wonderfully coloured finches. Marcus's eyes lit up with pleasure.

'Fabulous, Ari! Just what I wanted, Monty and Paul.'

He said the names with a slight emphasis, and he winked ever so slightly.

She nodded, just enough for him to realise that she understood. He kissed her passionately before she left and by that intimate contact she passed the tiny plastic bag that she held in her cheek the whole of the visit. He rested the contraband in his mouth. It nestled there until he returned to his cell. He did not remove it for a while, just in case the guards did a random check. It was only a minor discomfort. Alone with his birds, there was no need to speak. Cigarettes used to be the traditional currency in the prisons, but now it was drugs.

He smiled to himself. Ariadne was no fool. She understood and would organise the carrying out of his wishes. Being his strong arm on the outside added to his comfort. She had arrived with the small wooden cage, the two finches and a supply of seeds. She promised to look after the rest of his birds at their home, and he was sure she would. His success was based on not trusting others, even those like Ariadne, who had proven loyal so often. He still had her watched.

He stared lovingly into the cage. The two birds, so full of life, hopped from one bar to another, chattering incessantly. They, like him, were caged, but unlike them, he intended to do something about it. He opened the door and reached in, finger like a pistol, and either Paul or Monty hopped onto it. He withdrew his arm with the bird gently holding on to his finger and brought it close to his face. Bending forward, he kissed its tiny, multi-coloured head. The trusting little creature just fluffed its feathers and pecked back at the man's lips.

He reached in with his other hand and the other delightful bird hopped onto his finger. Marcus drew that one out, carefully carrying the two finches, as he sat back on his bed.

Despite his solitary life in Wakefield Jail, Marcus actually appreciated the time with Monty and Paul, as he temporarily named them. It wasn't as if he was idle. Apart from caring for his birds, there were plans to work on. He didn't intend to be in prison a day longer than necessary.

Revenge was sweet, but it was not a long-lasting savour. He wanted out, and there were others to deal with. He smiled to himself.

'You'll be back with your friends soon,' he whispered to the birds, and they twittered back their reply.

TENTATIVE STEPS

The inspector asked Gordon and Gabriela to return with him to the station. He believed that there was more to be learnt from the couple and he wanted to speak with them separately. Despite what the officers taking her initial statement had said to Shelley Jones when she reported her partner missing, Inspector Glover was concerned the moment he heard of the missing man. He hadn't been directly involved in the case, but it was high profile. Everyone had celebrated its success. The conviction of such a figure was a major achievement..

Freddy Glover was too experienced to count his chickens too soon. It was one thing getting a guilty verdict, it was quite another ensuring that any appeal failed, and there would be an appeal. People like Marcus Spinx hadn't got to where he was and held the position for so long without being a slippery eel. The man was highly intelligent, ruthless, and had tentacles across the city. Leeds was a valuable patch, and many others would we waiting to take over.

Inspector Glover was surprised how well the legal system worked on the whole. Jurors were usually safe, witnesses rarely nobbled, and the judiciary was free to carry out their lives, despite the many reasons for others to wish them harm. The problem here was that Marcus Spinx was not your common-or-garden criminal, and Glover had taken a watch and see approach.

The disappearance of the prosecutor sparked his interest, and unlike the uniformed officers' response, he was sure that foul play had occurred. He had spoken with 'higher-up' and received permission to become involved in the missing person's case, but also to watch Paul Montgomery's partner and other important people in the case. Unfortunately, he had been too late to prevent Shelley Jones from vanishing.

He was not pleased with how this had started. He was a step behind, reacting to events rather than preventing them from occurring. It was getting messy and the involvement of these two in the case muddied the waters even more.

He entered the interview room and there was the striking Spanish woman sitting at the desk.

'Miss Morales, you are not under arrest. I just want to ask you to explain why you were at Miss Jones's house, what you saw when you arrived, and your actions when you found she was missing. Would you be so kind as to tell me of your involvement?'

Gabriela looked at the policeman, and she saw certain similarities to Inspector Navarro in her home town, Calpe. He had the same world-weary look, the same shrewd expression, and she believed this was a man who could tell when you were lying. As there was no reason not to, she told him the whole story.

The inspector sat there listening, taking the odd note.

'And why are you here in Leeds, may I ask?'

Again, Gabriela told him and in a short while he had learnt all that he needed.

'Thank you, Miss Morales. I am going to speak with your boyfriend now. You can wait here, if you wish, or you can wait in reception. I am sure I won't be long with Mr Bennet. Before I go, I must warn you that there are dangerous people about and you would be very wise to allow the police to carry out all investigations. Please do not get involved, and keep a careful eye out. If anything seems suspicious, please contact me straight away. Here is my card!'

The inspector placed a card in front of Gabriela and she picked it up and followed him out. She waited in reception so that she would be there when Gordon came out.

An hour later, Gordon left the interview room, walked calmly down the corridor to reception and Gabriela was waiting for him. This was not the way that he had wanted to introduce her to his home, but he was getting used to things not turning out as he hoped. The one bright spark in all of this was the woman waiting for him. She had given him a purpose and a feeling of self-worth that he had lost. Her face lit up in delight, and he was smitten by her beauty, her warmth, and her resilience.

'You waited?' he said in mirth.

'How could I not, for my man? Oh, and there is the fact that I had no means of getting back to your house and no way to get in.'

He laughed, and the two left the police station and walked out into the warm and lovely afternoon. The mood didn't remain buoyant for long, as Shelley had been taken and was in great danger, at the very least. They drove back to Gordon's place and there was Peter, waiting for them. The police officer was standing by the steps up to the door and he had been enjoying a cigarette. He dropped the fag end and crushed it under his shoe.

'Peter, good to see you again. You've heard about Shelley,' Gordon said.

'I have, and it is a worrying development.'

'Come on up. We shouldn't discuss this on the street,' said Gordon, as he put the key in the lock and opened the door.

Within minutes, the three were enjoying strong cups of coffee and a packet of chocolate biscuits. It wasn't much to offer a guest, but it was all they had, and Peter didn't seem to mind.

'So have you any news about Shelley?' Gordon asked.

'I'm afraid not,' Peter replied, and his voice sounded nervous and hesitant, which was very unlike his usual optimism. 'I don't quite know how to say this, Gordon, but it doesn't look good. It looks as if Spinx is trying to exact revenge on those responsible for his conviction. There are probably two reasons for this. The first is simple vindictive pleasure in hurting those he believes have hurt him, and the other is to intimidate those involved in providing evidence. I suppose he hopes to get them to change testimony. It is surprising how fear can cause a memory lapse.'

'Bloody hell, Peter! What about Shelley? I can't just leave her. What can you tell me about this Marcus Spinx? I have met him, but only briefly. Doesn't he have a wife?'

'Yes, he does. Ariadne Spinx. He married her a couple of years back. She's a beauty, or at least that's what I was told.' Peter turned to Gabriela, as he said this. 'But not as beautiful as you, my dear.' Gabriela squirmed at the compliment.

Peter carried on, 'But she is more than a looker, Gordon. She has shown herself to be a smart dealer, and a big part of Spinx's firm. Those with insight say that she is as ruthless as her husband. The two of them were clever enough to keep her out of Marcus's fall. They found no evidence to incriminate her, and I'll tell you they looked hard enough.'

'So she's still in the family home?' Gabriela asked. 'Why not visit? If she's the one behind Shelley and Paul's disappearance, then we could exert a little pressure on her.'

'It's an option, but you'd be on your own,' Peter added.

'I don't suppose you have her address, do you?' Gordon asked, his mind working on their course of action.

'I'm not allowed to give you that information, Gordon. You know that. It would be a breach of privacy regulations. I had it written down on a piece of paper, but I seem to have lost it somewhere.' Peter had a twinkle in his eye and he slipped a small card under his cup.

'I wouldn't presume to give you advice, Gordon, but be careful. These are dangerous people and dangerous times. You have another to think of now.' He looked at Gabriela as he said this.

'Don't worry about us, Peter. We can handle ourselves.'

But Gabriela added, 'It's getting to be a bit of a habit! Gordon likes to make my life interesting!'

Peter laughed, and they enjoyed some small talk whilst they finished their drinks.

'I'd better be going,' said Peter, and Gordon showed him out.

Gabriela waited for Gordon to return, and when he got back, she was first to speak.

'What do you think? Shelley is in danger and we have to do something!'

Gordon sat down opposite Gabriela and he looked deeply into her eyes.

'I am not sure you should get involved in this, Gabriela,' he said. 'This is going to be very dangerous and I will have to take some risks. Maybe you should return to Calpe and I will come back to you there when this is sorted.'

'Over my dead body,' Gabriela said, and from the look on her face, she was furious. 'There is no way I'm staying out of this. I can't believe that you would ask me to. I thought you knew me better than that!'

Gordon smiled. Was there anything not to love about this woman?

'I had to ask, Gabriela. I wouldn't want to put you in danger, and I don't want you to go home. But you have to understand the risk. I intend to get Shelley back, even if that means breaking the law.'

'Well, I'm not going, so you can put that idea out of your mind. What's the plan?'

'They have taken Shelley and Paul and are threatening those involved in the case, so we are going to take the fight to them. Marcus is out of the way in prison, so we can't get to him, but we can get to his wife. Then we'll have something to bargain with!'

'How will we do that? We don't know where she is!'

'Oh, but we do!'

Gordon reached down and took the coffee cup off the table to reveal a card. He picked it up with his other hand and passed it to Gabriela. She took the card, looked at it.

'Your friend is a sly one!'

'Very true. Now we have her address. It is time to become the hunters!'

Gordon looked at the card and there was an address written, and the location was Poole Bank. He knew the place well, and it was not too far away on the road to Otley. He couldn't help smiling.

'What is it, Gordon?'

'It is just the perfect spot. Reasonably isolated. How about a trip to the Yorkshire countryside for some sightseeing? We can pick up dinner on the way!'

'I'll just get changed and be right back.'

'Put some jeans and a dark top on. Something that will offer some cover in the dark. We are working tonight!'

Gabriela disappeared into the bedroom and Gordon thought about what he needed. He rummaged through one of his drawers in his office and found the binoculars and a small rucksack. By the time he got back up to his flat, Gabriela was spruced up and ready to go.

She was wearing jeans that were accompanied by a black cardigan, silk scarf and his breath was taken away as he realised, once again, just how stunning she was, and how shabby he felt.

'Will I do?' She twirled so that he could pass an appreciative eye over her.

'Will you do? You mean will I do? Shall I get changed?'

'No, you'll do. There is something so attractive about a scruffy, dishevelled man!'

He took the hint and disappeared for a few minutes and returned a little less crumpled-looking in black jeans and a black long-sleeved shirt. He looked at her for her seal of approval.

'A work in progress, Gordon. I'll have to keep working on you! I like a challenge!' and she laughed her sparkling laugh, and he beamed in response.

'Let's go!'

He picked up the rucksack, and the two walked down to the car, and were soon on their way.

THE SPIDER

Ariadne looked at the woman bound and gagged before her. She had no compassion, no empathy, and no regrets about what she was about to do.

The woman's eyes showed fear. A fear that few experience before the final fear as they leave their lives behind. She was dressed in pyjamas, bright, comfortable, but not too heavy for the still warm weather. Her bare feet displayed toes, painted bright red, manicured, but now scratching the wooden floor as if trying to run away. Her hair was held tightly against her scalp by the gag that bound her mouth. She had stopped struggling, but her eyes darted around, desperately looking for help, but knowing none would come.

'Do you know why you are here?'

Shelley had no means of replying.

'Your man did, and so did mine! An eye for an eye, they say, but why be satisfied with just that?'

She moved in, mere inches away from the bound woman's face. Shelley could do nothing but stare at the cold, soulless eyes in front of her. They filled her vision, and she saw a terrified face reflected back, her face!

'Do you know, I have never seen someone die. I have not witnessed the moment that their lives, their hopes and dreams, end. Until now, that is!'

Those last four words contained such hate that Shelley almost vomited. She could sense the bile rise, but the gap would not allow it. Her world was crumbling around her, and she shivered uncontrollably. She felt fear, not just for herself, but for Paul. What had happened to him? Could he be gone? She couldn't bear the thought, but she was helpless. This was a new experience, as she had always been in control and prided herself on it. It was because Gordon's life had fallen apart that she could not live with him. His anguish unsettled her and wore at her confidence. He was too complicated, and she couldn't handle him. The separation enabled her to regain control, and she had found what she needed with Paul. Was Paul gone too?

The woman stroked her pale cheek with her long, black, delicate fingers, and raked her nail across the skin, almost drawing blood.

'How will you face death when the time comes? I suppose we shall have to wait and see. I'll leave you to think on that. Have no fear though, I will be back!'

The hit came so unexpectedly, hard and powerful. Shelley was caught completely unawares. The force, the pain, over so quickly as she flew into unconsciousness.

Ariadne climbed the stairs out of the cellar. She rubbed her knuckles, and she knew she had done herself some damage, but she smiled. It felt good to hurt those who had hurt her and her family. The woman below had played no part in Marcus' arrest, but that didn't matter. She just wanted to lash out and hurt people, and as her partner had already been disposed of, the prisoner would have to do until she moved on with her plan.

She composed herself. Her heart beat fiercely, her breathing rapid, and she experienced a euphoria that normally was only when she and Marcus lay together. At these times, it was often she who experienced the pain, and Marcus the one in control, but now there was no chance of that happening. Now, she was the one with the power, and she fed on the rush like an addict. She had been a willing supplicant, asking for his punishment, but now the roles were reversed she had discovered there was even more pleasure to be had hurting rather than being hurt. Ariadne was sweating with anticipation, and she looked forward to revisiting the woman in the cellar.

She glanced behind her, and almost returned, but she had work to do. 'You'll keep,' she said to herself. She straightened her clothing, took a deep breath, and entered the room to those waiting for her orders.

'Good! You're all here,' she said, as she walked through the doorway and into the next phase of her plan.

Gordon and Gabriela took a leisurely drive from his home, past Oakwood, Roundhay, to Moortown Corner and then turned right to the Ring Road. The area was settled, ageing, but had a charm and atmosphere of affluence and comfort. Gabriela stared out of the car window, taking in the sights as they drove past. It was so foreign to her, but she felt it shared something with the old town of Calpe. It was a little ragged around the edges, not pretentious, a bit like Gordon, she realised.

They soon were leaving the city and heading along a busy road and passing a few fields. They were still green, which was a surprise for Gabriela, as Spain was so dry in summer that the landscape was almost white.

There were low stone walls on both sides of the road, but large, very English-looking houses on one and fields on the other.

'We are driving into Wharfedale,' he said. 'Poole Bank is where we are heading. Marcus Spinx's house is there. It's a village and there are big farmhouses around, and some other large houses. I don't think it will be hard finding Marcus' house. We'll catch some dinner on the way. There's a good pub there. The Dyneley Arms does a good meal.'

The sun was getting lower in the sky, but it was only early evening and there were a couple of hours before sunset. In a surprisingly short time, they looked across a wide, lush valley. There was a river weaving its way across the fertile floodplain, like a wild thread of blue. Clouds were turning a soft pink as the sun was ending its sojourn.

'It is lovely, Gordon, and so green. I can't believe how near it is to the city.'

'It's God's own country, Gabriela, but unfortunately danger lurks even here. We will eat now and enjoy ourselves until it gets dark, but then we have to see if we can find Shelley. We will just check Spinx's house and see what opportunities it will give us.'

He turned right at the lights and down to the valley bottom. He had checked the map on his phone and soon they were driving down a narrow lane with six foot high stone walls on either side. The road took an s-bend and headed up the slope and before them a big stone house stood amongst spacious grounds. A long drive led to the building, and on either side were large rhododendron bushes.

Gordon pulled over onto the narrow verge on a spot where he could get an open view of the property. He took out his binoculars, the ones he had bought in Calpe a few months before.

'What are you looking for, Gordon?'

'Just checking what security there is. We don't want to wander into a welcoming party.'

He stared through the binoculars and lingered on several points for a while. As he was watching, the front door opened and six men and a woman appeared. The men were large, the sort you wouldn't want to pick a fight with. The woman stood on the steps by the doorway and spoke to the group. They nodded their understanding and got into two dark-coloured cars parked on the drive. She watched them leave. A tall, athletic, dark-skinned woman, and through the binoculars, Gordon could see that she was in her thirties and startlingly attractive. He assumed he was looking at Ariadne, Marcus Spinx's wife.

'We need to be going! Keep your head down. I don't want them to see two of us.'

Gordon pulled back onto the road and continued along the narrow lane. Gabriela lay flat with her head almost on Gordon's lap as first one dark grey car approached at speed, forcing Gordon to pull onto the side to avoid a collision. He had just got back onto the road when he had to repeat the procedure as the second flew past. Gordon saw stern faces turn to stare at the driver that dared to be on the road, hindering their passage.

The car shot past and Gordon immediately told Gabriela that she could sit up the moment the cars had gone by.

'Wow!' she said. 'They seemed to be in a hurry.'

'They were. At least we know we have the right place. I couldn't see any security cameras, but that doesn't mean there aren't any hidden away.'

'So that was Marcus Spinx's wife?'

'I assume so,' Gordon said. 'She certainly fits the description. We'll pay her a visit tonight, but first we need a drink and something to eat back at the Dyneley Arms. We should be able to find somewhere to turn around soon.'

They did, and within ten minutes, they were enjoying a drink in the pub. It wasn't too busy, but it was filling as people arrived to have dinner.

They sat together in a corner with a window looking out onto the carpark and the main Otley road.

Gabriela tasted her first warm pint of English beer and, by her expression, Gordon thought it may be her last, but he would work on it. They had ordered a meal and the fish and chips arrived after a short wait.

'So what are we going to do?' Gabriela asked.

Gordon stopped eating and hesitated.

'Are you really sure that you want to be involved?' he said. 'This is dangerous. We will be acting outside of the law and it will certainly be a problem if we are caught by the police.'

'I've already told you. I'm coming!'

'Ok. I just wanted to check. I'm glad you'll be there. There is a chance that Shelley is in the house, but if not, that woman will know where she is. I intend to make her tell me, one way or another! Whatever the situation, tonight is our best chance of finding her alive.'

'We'll get her, Gordon.'

'When it's dark, we'll approach the house and see if there are any signs she's there. I hope that woman will be there alone, but I wouldn't bet on it. We haven't anything to defend ourselves with, so we must use stealth. I hope they don't know anyone is really looking for her. If they don't expect us, then it may work. If they do, we will be walking into a trap. We'll park the car away from the house and cut across the country and approach from the rear.'

They ate without speaking, and the mood was serious. Gordon had another pint of bitter, but Gabriela decided to go with a red wine. The evening sun was setting on a bucolic landscape that was being used to hide evil actions. The two held hands as they realised it was almost time to act. Gordon went to the toilets and waited by the front door as Gabriela returned to join him. The night had fallen like a curtain and the peace of the evening was now gone.

The car park was still full, but people were leaving. Gordon drove the way to the house, but this time he took a small lane before they reached it. He had seen on his map on the phone that there was a short lane that ran to a quarry. It was shown as disused, so it would be a safe place to park the car. If anyone saw them, they would assume they were a courting couple wanting a bit of privacy.

The lane was a dirt track and rarely used, but it opened into a small but wide area before a metal gate to keep anyone out of the quarry itself. From the litter and other evidence, couples had used it for secret trysts, away from prying eyes. It pleased Gordon that this added to their cover.

He stopped the car, turned to Gabriela and kissed her passionately. No point wasting an opportunity, he thought to himself, and Gabriela clearly shared the sentiment. If anyone had been watching, then they would not have had any doubts about their motive, but in a short while, the couple quietly got out, shut the doors and headed away from the quarry towards the house.

The night was silent, and away from the city, the clear sky showed myriad stars. There was no moon and so only the faint starlight betrayed their presence. Two dark figures climbed over a stone wall and skirted along it, a wood on one side and a field on the other.

Gabriela couldn't see the house, but she trusted Gordon's sense of direction. The adventures in Calpe had proved beyond any doubt he was a skilled hunter and a ruthless enemy when his friends were in danger.

An owl hooted off to her right in the woods. Others hunted this night. She turned back and caught a glimpse of a light, and as she looked carefully, she could just make out the outline of a large house, a deeper black than the surrounding sky. Two lights were visible, one downstairs and one upstairs.

Gordon had also stopped to look. He turned to her and whispered.

'If things go wrong, get back to the car. The key is under the sun visor. Go back to my place and wait there. If I'm not back within twenty-four hours, fly back to Calpe. Promise me you will!'

'I'm not leaving you, Gordon,' she whispered. 'I'll go back to your place, but I'm not leaving you!'

The way she whispered this left him in no doubt that it would be a waste of time trying to persuade her otherwise.

'Guess that will have to do, then. We are going to check out the house. Look out for guards and cameras. We are just looking first. Stay with me until we get up to the house.'

Gabriela nodded, and the two moved further along the wall. Keeping their heads low, they moved, stooped over like old hags, so as not to show over the wall. Even in the darkest night, watching eyes sense movement, and they didn't want to give their presence away before they had even had a look.

A distant car could be heard. It was not on the road approaching their destination, but on the main Otley Road. A wispy cloud hung in the sky, dimming a few of the stars, but little more. The air was becoming chill and there were the first signs of a low mist forming. There were spectral patches gathering in the field, like souls rising to haunt the night. Gordon noted a sudden movement further in the field, but he instantly relaxed as he realised it was a late night rabbit, possibly spooked by the owl, that still called mournfully.

They reached the end of the field and the wall split in two directions. One continued to skirt the wood and the other at right angles, ran to the lane and was the boundary wall to the house's grounds. The grounds were old and thick beds of rhododendrons would provide them with excellent cover.

Gordon shimmied over the wall and down into the house's grounds. He reached out to help Gabriela, but she sprung lightly over and silently landed on her feet. They crouched down in the darkness against the wall. Gordon pointed to a large clump of the shrubs and he sprinted to the cover. Gabriela didn't hesitate and was close on his heels. They were only seconds in the open, and they had to hope that no one was watching.

The security of the shrubs gave them time to check for signs of guards. Gordon wouldn't normally have expected any, as this was Poole Bank, not an obviously dangerous area by any stretch of the imagination. However, this was Marcus Spinx's house and any notorious crime figure would ensure that they were safe at home. As the two of them stared towards the house, they both noticed a movement. Not dogs, Gordon thought. They had no means of defending themselves against dogs, but it was soon clear that the shape was too tall for any dog. The shadow passed across the front of the house in the blackness and would have been easy to miss. They waited to see what was happening, and after what seemed like an eternity, the shadow reappeared.

A bit slack, he thought. I would have had two, at a minimum. Gordon indicated for Gabriela to remain where she was. He crept around the bushes and edged closer to the corner where the shape had just passed. Gabriela watched until Gordon vanished into the void. The night became still as death and even the hooting owl had gone silent. Tension hung in the air like a noose and she worried for

Gordon. He was unarmed, and she knew he would be in danger if caught.

Silence continued and Gabriela was getting cold as the temperature dropped. Mist gathered in thicker patches between the shrubs. Was there a movement? She wasn't sure, but then a figure emerged, heading towards her. Was it Gordon? She was in a quandary whether to flee or to wait, then Gordon appeared out of the dark and smiled.

'There is a guard, but someone else has got him out of the way. He's trussed up and gagged. I don't know what's going on, but I intend to find out. Come on!' he whispered, and he took her hand and they carefully made their way up to the building, avoiding the partly lit patch under the window.

Gordon gestured for Gabriela to stay with him, and he crept down the side of the building. About ten yards along, they passed the fallen figure of the guard, unconscious and bound with his own belt. Gabriela had feared the guard was dead at first, but the figure stirred.

'Gagged with his own socks,' was whispered, and Gordon carried on.

There were no doors or low windows along this edge of the building, and they quickly reached the corner. The back of the house was very different. There was a large summerhouse of white wood and glass, with double doors opening onto a lawn. There was a denser cloud of mist gathered a little way back onto the lawn, but they could not tell the cause. They carefully crept along the wall, keeping as close as possible, as light from an upstairs window cast a silvery pool onto the lawn. At any moment, they expected to come across whoever had bound the guard.

There were a couple of steps leading up to the conservatory. The two silently and slowly approached the doors. The wooden frame was cracked and peeling, and there was a handle to the doors.

It would be a major security faux pas, but Gordon knew better than to ignore the obvious. He took hold of the handle and the door swung inwards. He paused, listened, and when he heard nothing, he gave the door a gentle push. It opened inwards just a fraction. A screw fell onto the tiled surface and Gordon realised the lock had been forced. Again, the two listened in silence, ready to act if there was a sound, but only silence welcomed them.

TURN UP FOR THE BOOKS

The inside of the conservatory was dark, but it had a few spots of light from electrical power boards, and these gave sufficient illumination for the two of them to manoeuvre through an extensive plant collection. The summer house proved larger than it had appeared in the dark, and it had a strong odour, a mixture of damp soil and something that Gordon failed to identify at first. Along one side of the room was a structure covered with a wire mesh. He ran his hands along it and he heard a flutter. He stopped, unsure, but then there was the unmistakable sound of feathers and wings beating gently, but rapidly.

A bloody birdcage! That explained the other smell, the ripe scent of bird droppings, adding to the scent of the plants. They moved towards the back of the room, pushing plant fronds and leaves aside. It's a jungle, he thought to himself, and just about as hot. Clearly, this outbuilding was heated even during the Indian summer, and it contrasted with the cool outside air. He still held Gabriela's hand, and they moved as one through this menagerie towards the main building.

Both listened for any noises, but they were met with silence. At the back of the room they found a doorway, and Gabriela reached out for the handle first. She pulled it down and pushed it gently, and it opened with a creak.

Again, there was no sound from inside the house, and this worried Gordon. This did not seem right! All his senses said this was not how it should be. One guard dispatched, and the house almost inviting them in. It made little sense! Nobody would be expecting them, so a trap didn't appear likely, but someone had already forced their way inside. He still didn't just want to walk in on whatever was going on.

Against his better judgement, he entered the house proper. A brightness from an open doorway cast a dim light and by its glow, they could see the empty corridor. They advanced past a small side table and their feet were silent on the carpet strip.

Sound came from the room, but it was a television, quietly ordinary, and they expected to find the room occupied, but as they reached the open door, they could see no one. Someone had recently been there as there a half drunk glass of white wine was on the coffee table, and a bottle in a wine cooler.

Just one wine glass, Gordon noted, so the drinker was alone. He waited for someone to walk in, but apart from the television, the house appeared empty.

They hurried through the downstairs rooms, but they found no one. In the kitchen was a big, rustic wooden table. There were three heavy chairs and one of them lay on its side. A large pair of scissors and a roll of gaffer tape were the only things on the granite kitchen surface.

'We must check upstairs. I don't like this. Be ready to run, Gabriela.'

She said nothing. Gabriel's eyes showed concern, but little fear.

They went up the large carpeted staircase to the first floor and the pair listened again for any sounds, but the house was keeping its own counsel. They separated and looked into the rooms off the landing. Each one proved empty. At the end of the landing was a large window, and they stood and stared out into the night.

'There's no one here, Gordon. The place is deserted.'

'Yes, it's quite odd, like the Marie Celeste.'

'The Marie Celeste?' Gabriela had clearly not heard the story of the deserted ship.

'I'll tell you later. Where is she?'

It dawned on him in a flash. If Shelley was here, then she would be somewhere secure, probably in a cellar.

'Downstairs. Look for a door leading into a cellar!' Gordon was already halfway back down the stairs before Gabriela had time to move.

There was no attempt at stealth now, and their footsteps sounded unusually loud in the silent house. The corridor at the foot of the steps had a doorway and when Gordon pulled it open, he saw steps leading downwards. He felt for a switch and there was a click and the staircase was brightly lit. He had to pause for a moment to become accustomed to the light, but then slowly descended into what he believed was the cellar. Gabriela was with him and the two followed the turning steps until they opened into a large underground cellar with many sections.

There was no sign of anyone being there, but in one room there was evidence that someone had been, recently. On a table were scissors and gaffer tape, a bottle of water, and some tissues. The cellar smelt of damp, but there was a distinct trace of perfume. One that Gordon recognised.

'She was here, but where is she now?' Gordon said this aloud, but Gabriela just stood, thinking.

'Why is the place deserted, Gordon? What's going on?'

'I don't know, but something is definitely not right. I think we'd better get out of here!'

They headed back up the stairs and all the time Gordon was worried that their path would be blocked and they would be trapped, but that didn't happen. The house was truly deserted.

They left the way they had entered and scooted around the outside of the building, retracing their steps. The night was still dark and the light mist was now thickening, but around the building it was clear. Gordon looked out from the conservatory door and the pool of mist hung in the air. Afterwards, he could never say what caught his attention, but something did.

'I just want to check what's out there. Come on, it won't take us a few seconds.'

He strode out onto the lawn. The lush grass was becoming dew-covered, and the air was now cold and they both shivered. The owl in the woods let out its eerie cry, and this added to the tension as they approached the bank of mist. They couldn't see much, but Gabriela realised her foot was on a hard surface. Gordon stopped.

'It's a swimming pool. Nothing to involve us here. Come on, let's get back to the car. We need some time to think. This is all very puzzling.'

They headed back and followed the edge of the building to the corner, then through the shrubs to the stone wall bordering the grounds and along to the car in the quarry.

As they reached the end of the house, Gabriela suddenly realised that something was wrong.

'Where is the guard?'

'What? Shit! You're right. He's gone. Come on, we'd better run. We need to get away from here!'

Gabriela didn't argue and the two shot heedlessly across the grass, between the rhododendron clumps to where they had entered the grounds. They reached the stone wall, panting loudly, and clambered over it in a hurried scramble.

They slowed down their pace and knew that if they were going to be waylaid, it would be at their car. Caution took over, and Gordon came to a stop at the edge of the quarry. He could make out the outline of his hire car, but nothing else.

'Stay here,' he whispered. 'I'll scout around and check if anyone is waiting for us. That guard could have got free himself, or someone freed him. Either way, we need to be away as soon as we can!'

He disappeared into the darker edges of the small clearing and worked his way to the far side. He discovered no one and no evidence anyone had been there.

After a short while, he made a decision and walked to the car. He opened the door, flipped the sun visor down and the keys fell onto the seat. He got in and put the keys in the ignition. The car came to life, and the lights came on. Gabriela ran across and dived into the passenger seat as Gordon pulled away, barely giving her time to shut the door.

Gabriela struggled with the seat belt, but managed in the end. Gordon didn't bother and drove with as much haste as was safe, back along the track and onto the road. He didn't turn right the way that they had approached, but turned left towards the house.

As they drew near, they could see the two lights still on, but nothing else. They drove rapidly past the entrance and Gabriela realised Gordon's logic. Most vehicles would drive to the house from the main road and anyone waiting for them would assume that was the way they would leave.

As it was, they saw no one as they drove away from the house. They remained silent until they got back onto the main Otley Road. They didn't realise it, but both had been holding their breath, expecting at any moment for something to happen.

'Bloody hell!' Gordon exclaimed.

'That was scary, Gordon. What's going on? Do you think Shelley was there?'

'I'm sure she was. Did you notice a trace of perfume in the cellar? That was Shelley's. It's called O! She wears it all the time. She was certainly there, but I have no idea where she is now.'

'That's not good!'

'No, it isn't, but there is nothing more we can do now. We'll go back home, but I think we need to come back first thing tomorrow and take a better look in the daylight.'

'I need a drink!' Gabriela said, and Gordon couldn't help but agree with her, but it would only be one. He wanted all his wits about him tomorrow, and he intended to be back at the house by dawn.

SUNKEN HOPES

He proved true to his word and two glasses of scotch was it. The two held each other close for the remainder of the night, and both were aware Shelley's chances weren't good. Her only hope rested with them.

It was still dark when he awoke and roused Gabriela. She smiled up at him and he realised, again, how much he loved this strong and wonderful woman. He passed her the coffee, and she took a sip, and placed it on the bedside cupboard. She stretched, her waves of dark hair falling over her shoulders. She was the most stunning woman, and he bore the responsibility of putting her in danger.

He passed over a piece of toast, spread with butter and raspberry jam. She took a bite. There was a crunch, and she smiled as crumbs fell onto the bedspread.

'Sorry,' she said. 'I'll tidy it up!'

Gordon laughed and said, 'We have five minutes and we must be off. I'll get a few things I might need.'

He left the bedroom, and went down to his office, and to an old safe covered with a tablecloth. Sitting on top was a tray with an electric kettle, a mug, and a teaspoon. He always thought it best to hide things in full view. He lifted the cloth and dialled in the combination numbers. The safe door pulled open, and he took out a flat box. He placed it on his desk and lifted something wrapped in an oiled cloth. He unwrapped the Glock pistol, put it in his jacket pocket and put the cloth and the box back in the safe, locked it and draped the tablecloth again.

Gordon walked to a bookcase that had several box-files lined up.

He found the one with B to D printed in marker-pen on the front. When he opened it, there was a small, but heavy box, which he removed. He lifted the lid and checked it was still full of bullets, pulled out the pistol, withdrew the magazine and slotted bullets into it until it was full. He then pushed it back into the handle, ensured the safety catch was still on, and put the pistol back into his jacket.

When he returned to his flat, Gabriela was ready and waiting.

It was still just before dawn when they turned off the Otley Road and headed towards Marcus Spinx's house. Apart from a couple of trucks, they had seen no other cars on the road and as they slowly drove along the lane to the quarry, an ashen grey light was breaking and the fields were still bedecked with a light mist. Rabbits were daring to venture out, looking for breakfast, and their ears and eyes were constantly darting about, searching for danger.

Gordon hadn't mentioned what he was carrying, and he hoped Gabriela needn't be aware of the pistol, but it would be folly to walk back into the grounds and the house unprepared.

They got out of the car and Gordon pulled out his binoculars and scanned the area. He had them hanging around his neck and anyone seeing them would assume the couple were out bird watching. The owl from the previous evening was now silent, tucked up in a hollow somewhere. Gordon wished he were similarly snug in his bed with Gabriela, but he had to find out what had happened to Shelley. This was personal now!

They passed the quarry, and the ground was slippery with the dew. They followed along the wall line and it was much easier than the previous time in the dark. The chorus of bird-life punctuated the air, celebrating the survival of the night and the coming new day. Gordon kept stopping to check the area and for signs that anyone was in and about the house. He could see nothing, and apart from a few cattle in a nearby field, the birds and the rabbits, the area was clear.

Gabriela said little, but she looked pensive. She spoke for the first time when they reached the corner wall of the house's grounds.

'What are you expecting to find, Gordon?'

He looked at her and said,

'I am not sure, but anything that might help us discover what has happened to Shelley.'

'It might not be good.'

The look on the young woman's face made clear what she meant.

'I know, Gabriela. Shelley had been there, I'm sure of it. I recognised her perfume. I fear what has happened. The chances of us finding her are not good, but I have to do it. If anything has happened to her, I will make them pay. Neither Ariadne nor Marcus Spinx will be safe if they've harmed her.'

He raised the binoculars a final time and saw no sign of life.

'Come on,' he said. 'Let's see what we can discover!'

The two climbed over the stone wall and wandered, keeping out of direct sight of anyone in the house. They reached the point behind the clump of rhododendron bushes where they had hidden the night before. It appeared deserted. No car in the drive, no guard, no sounds and more concerning, they could see the lights still glowing in the bedroom window and downstairs in the lounge.

There appeared no point in caution, but they ran across the open ground to the corner of the house where the guard had been. They then skirted along the outside to the large summer house.

'Well, we are here to find out, so let's find out!' Gabriela led the way and they saw that the door to the conservatory still lay open, just as they had left it. Gordon entered. The air was cooler, but the smell was the same. The large aviary bustled with noisy, twittering, brightly coloured birds.

'At least they look pleased to see us,' said Gabriela.

'Be careful not to touch anything. If we have to call the police, they don't want our fingerprints confusing the scene.'

They searched through the house. Still deserted, there was nothing to show that anyone had been there since the night before. Gordon was becoming frustrated. The cellar still held traces of Shelley's scent, but that was fading.

Eventually he said, 'It's no use. We may as well go. We had better contact the police, but that can wait until we get home.'

They left through the conservatory and as they looked out onto the gardens, it was clear what the mist had hidden. About twenty yards away was a rectangular swimming pool. It was large, there was a low springboard at the far side and there was a wide border of paving. There was a table, but no chairs set to the side, and Gordon thought it was a sign of extravagance, as there would be few days when it would be warm enough to use. Not like the ones in Calpe, he thought. The feeling he had experienced the night before returned. There was something sinister that he couldn't explain, but it worried him and he couldn't shake it.

Gabriela was walking back around the house when he stopped.

'What is it? What's wrong?'

'I don't know! I want a look at the pool. Wait for me.'

'No, I'll come with you!'

Gordon walked purposefully, with Gabriela following. The sun burst through as they reached the poolside, and it lit the water. Both stared down into it.

It took a moment to realise what they were looking at. Four chairs were arranged at the bottom of the pool and a bound figure sat in each one. They were motionless, mouths open in a silent scream and obviously long dead. Two heads of long hair swayed gently in the water, and were the only movement. They recognised the black woman, Ariadne, and the other was Shelley!

They stared in horror at the tableau below them. It was like a grotesque dinner party of the dead.

'Oh, Gordon!'

There was nothing they could do. The seated figures were beyond their help. They had been in the water all night, and the thought was chilling. They held on to each other and tried not to imagine the victims being dropped into the water, knowing that they were doomed.

Gordon telephoned the police, and they instructed him to remain at the house and not to touch anything.

He led Gabriela away from the pool, back to the front of the house, where he realised he had the revolver. Unsure what to do, he left it inside his jacket and hoped the police didn't search him. He didn't think they would. It would be folly to call the police to a crime he had committed.

When he thought about Shelley, his guts twisted. They were divorced and their differences were major, but she and her partner did not deserve such a fate. He held on to Gabriela and swore once again he would let nothing bad to happen to her.

The pressing question nagged at him. Who was responsible? It certainly made little sense that Marcus Spinx would have authorised it. Gordon didn't doubt he would have wanted Shelley dead as payback for his imprisonment. But his own wife, Ariadne? It didn't seem right. No, someone else was behind this, but who and why?

'Who would do this, Gordon? Poor Shelley. Oh, God! It's too horrible!'

Gordon could say nothing. She was right. He had seen some terrible ways to die, been the cause of some, but this cold, slow execution was the stuff of nightmares. The victims would join with his others and visit him at night in his asleep.

It took a very long time before sirens heralded the approach of the police. The sound grew louder and three cars came hurrying up the driveway and pulled up to a halt. Gabriela and Gordon separated and stood waiting, as the police got out of the squad cars and a familiar figure strolled over to them. Inspector Glover raised an eyebrow as he saw who the two waiting were.

The tall, thin figure was dressed in a long leather trench coat and carried himself with an air of annoyance as he walked towards them.

'Miss Morales, Mr Bennet, it appears that you have a rather unpleasant knack of being the harbingers of bad news. Bodies have been reported. Would you care to show me?'

He phrased this as a question, but the implication was much more of an order. Without waiting for a reply, he turned to the uniformed officers.

'Stay here! I'll just see what we have. Forensics are on their way, so just make sure that no one comes wandering about. It that too difficult for you?'

The sergeant he addressed looked suitably chastened, and Gordon was sure that he would not want to be the cause of Inspector Glover's displeasure.

Turning back, he said, 'Go on then, take me to them!'

Far up of the valley side, a pair of binoculars were tracing the movements at the property. The watcher had been instructed to keep a lookout. He had been there the night before, part of the cleanup. It should have been straightforward, but two people turning up at the house was unexpected and the killers were almost caught in the act. It wouldn't have really mattered and two more bodies would have joined the others in the pool, but he waited a while until the couple left, then finished off and followed suit. He was ordered to remain, to watch what happened.

It had not been a pleasant night, cold and damp, but he was used to a bit of discomfort. Military training had its uses, and even though he no longer served his country, his new masters valued his skills.

He had watched the house and wasn't entirely surprised when he saw the same car that had been at the quarry arriving just before dawn. He took photographs using a long lens, as the couple found the pool and its occupants. There wasn't any more he could do. He'd been instructed to observe and photograph anyone coming to the property, nothing more. With the arrival of the police, it was time for him to make his getaway. Tired and cold, he wanted a hot bath more than anything. Leaving nothing to show he had been there, he left. He knew the police would start searching, and he took the opportunity to return home.

Gordon, Gabriela and Inspector Glover walked around to the back of the house and, as they approached the summerhouse, they stopped.

'Someone has forced the doors, Inspector. The bodies are in the pool. You won't mind if we don't accompany you.'

The police officer walked towards the pool. Gordon and Gabriela retreated to the front of the house. It took longer for the inspector to return than they expected. When he finally did, he carried that world-weary, hangdog expression. His face showed only a stoic resignation.

'I can see why you didn't want to accompany me, Mr Bennet. You know who they are?'

'I know the two women. One is my ex-wife, Shelley Jones, and the other I believe is Ariadne Spinx, Marcus Spinx's wife. This is their house.'

'I am sorry for that, Mr Bennet and I offer my condolences, but I have to ask, why you are here, and what happened?'

Before Gordon could answer, a van pulled up. The forensics team had arrived.

'Give me a moment!' the inspector said, and he walked off to organise the crime-scene. He was busy for a while issuing orders to the uniformed officers and directing the forensics team.

He returned with two men in uniform.

'The house is empty?'

'Yes, the house is empty,' Gordon replied. 'We have been in, but we tried not to disturb or touch anything.'

'Very wise, Mr Bennet. This is a murder scene!' he said to the two men. 'Check the grounds, seal off the house until forensics can work on it, and have someone at the gate. No one is to enter! No one!'

The officers nodded, turned, and hurried away. The inspector stared around, taking in the scene.

'How did you get here? If I may ask.'

'We came by car,' said Gabriela, speaking for the first time. She pointed back through the shrubs to the corner of the wall.

'We came that way. We left the car near a quarry,' Gordon added, and the policeman followed their gaze.

He turned, walked back to a police van that had arrived, and spoke to the men inside. He gestured to the wall and the quarry beyond. The two men walked to the back of the van, opened the door, and took out two large police tracker dogs. They set out in the direction that Gabriela and Gordon had arrived from.

Gordon and Gabriela were getting a little tired of standing around, but they had to wait. The inspector returned, and he addressed them.

'I will ask you and Miss Morales to go with one of my officers to the station, Mr Bennet. You are not under arrest, but are helping us with our inquiries. Do you understand?'

Gordon nodded, and Gabriela followed suit.

'Thank you. We will get a full statement from the two of you. You are getting used to the process by now. I am very sorry about your ex-wife. I really do mean that. No one deserves what happened here, particularly when an innocent party. A victim of being in the wrong place at the wrong time. I will speak with you shortly.'

A uniformed policeman arrived, and he was instructed to take the couple back to the station. Gordon and Gabriela followed along and got into the back seat of a police car. They waited whilst the inspector spoke to the driver and then he got into the driver's seat and they started the journey back into Leeds.

By the time they had arrived back in Leeds, both Gabriela and Gordon were feeling quite despondent. What they had witnessed was truly horrific and Gordon, in particular, felt responsible, both for Shelley's death and Gabriela's distress.

Gabriela couldn't get the image of the four seated at the bottom of the pool out of her head. She kept replaying the imaginary scene of how Shelley would have felt as she was dropped into the water, bound to the chair, helpless and friendless. She had only briefly met

Gordon's ex-wife, but she had sympathised with her.

Gordon held her hand all the time they were in the back of the car. It was all the support he could give. He had promised her a lovely holiday, a break from all the terror that she had endured in her hometown of Calpe. Any hope of that had vanished almost from the moment they arrived in the country. He began to feel that Inspector Navarro was right. Trouble seemed to follow him!

He knew better than to worry about things he couldn't change, but he wanted to make whoever was responsible pay!

The police car pulled into the police station, to the typical setup. The car park was in a compound and they got out and were taken through into the station.

'You will be interviewed separately, so please wait in here,' he said to Gabriela.

Before Gordon could object, Gabriela put her hand on his arm.

'It's OK, Gordon. I will see you afterwards.'

She was right, but angry and upset, he wanted to lash out at something, someone, but he realised that this was neither the time nor the place. He left Gabriela and was taken into an interview room.

The previous interviews had been clinical and, as Paul was unknown to Gabriela, fairly unemotional. This time, Gabriela had met Shelley, taken a liking to Gordon's ex-wife and understood her worry about her missing partner. No one deserved the fate of the four in the pool. She could only imagine the horror of Shelley's last minutes. The police woman took her statement in a very businesslike manner, and that made the whole thing more terrible to bear. At one point, Gabriela broke down, sobbing, and this did jolt the interviewer into offering some sympathy. She provided a cup of tea and a box of tissues. When Gabriela had composed herself, she continued with her account. She explained why she and Gordon had visited the house the previous night and returned the next morning. She described all the events and finally the discovery of the bodies in the pool. The police woman presented Gabriela with a copy of the statement to read and sign.

Gabriela took her time to check the accuracy of her account and to make sure that she had missed nothing. When she was satisfied that it was as accurate as it could be, she signed. The officer took the papers and left her alone with her nightmare. Gabriela knew this was a nightmare for Gordon too. She hoped she had done the right thing, but she felt that honesty was the best way. She was sure Gordon's account would match hers.

The thought of Gordon upset her again. She loved the brusque, beautiful man. She knew his past and how it scarred him, but she could see the child that had been so hopeful for the future. The man who had had his dreams stolen, but come through it all, with his decency and honesty intact. She knew he had wanted to impress her, to show her the city and district that had shaped him. All they had wanted was to be together after all that had happened in Spain. She wondered if it was too much to ask. It appeared it was. Maybe Inspector Navarro was right. Trouble followed them.

She waited, alone and miserable, and it seemed an eternity, but eventually the door opened and in walked Inspector Glover.

'Miss Morales, I am sorry to have kept you waiting. I have read your statement, and it tells the same account as Mr Bennet's. What you witnessed is not something anyone should have to. Unfortunately, it is not uncommon in the life of a police officer. I have spoken with Mr Bennet and told him the same thing. I believe you both may be in danger. My advice would be for you both to leave and return to Spain. I can't make you leave, but for your own safety, I think it would be wise. Mr Bennet might need some persuasion from you. He is a stubborn man, and I know his background. He is a magnet for trouble, so maybe you should reconsider your relationship. Whatever, we will need to know where you are. You will be required again, so if you leave, we will need details.'

'You may be right, Inspector, but I don't think Gordon will leave. This is his home town! He won't be driven away.'

'You are probably right, but I have also told him to leave this investigation to the police. We will investigate and catch whoever is responsible. I will not have Mr Gordon Bennet, or anyone, behaving like vigilantes! Do I make myself clear?'

'Very clear, Inspector. I will let Gordon know.'

'I have already told him, in no uncertain manner. Keep out, Miss Morales! And keep your boyfriend out of police business! I won't hesitate to arrest either of you if you don't! You are free to leave. He is waiting for you. Good day, Miss Morales.'

QUARRY

Gordon and Gabriela left the police station, and their hire car awaited them in the car park. Inspector Glover organised for it to be brought to the station. A quick forensic check revealed there was nothing of any importance inside the car and so they could take it.

Gordon breathed a sigh of relief that they didn't search him, and despite the pistol pressing into the back of his chair during the long interview and statement taking, it remained undiscovered. That relief was short-lived, though. Unbeknown to them, they were being watched from a distance.

The silence in the car on the way back was deafening. The events of the last twenty-four hours worried them both, and dark and horrid visions kept drifting back. Gabriela reached across and rubbed Gordon's shoulder.

'I'm sorry about Shelley, Gordon. It is a shit thing to happen to anyone, but worse when it is someone you once loved.'

'It just seems like a nightmare. We came so close last night. If only we had checked what was on the lawn when we saw the pool of mist. Maybe we could have saved her. Saved the others.'

'It was probably too late. Maybe the guard could have been saved, but the others would have been in the water longer. We saw no sign of anyone when we arrived, but they might have been out in the mist and we just didn't see them.'

'I want to make the bastards pay! But who are they? Why did they do it? It just doesn't make sense. It can't be Marcus Spinx. Why would he kill his own wife? No, there is someone else behind this and we need to track them down.'

'We will, Gordon. If anyone can, you can!' and she sat back in the seat and stared out of the window, not really seeing anything, but was lost in her thoughts. She had meant it. If anyone could bring the killers to justice, it was Gordon. And she knew that his justice would be terrible!

They continued on their way back and neither said more. Gabriela just looked wistfully out onto the city streets and Gordon wondered what she was thinking and what he could do to make it right. He knew, deep inside, that nothing would ever erase what they had seen. There was nothing he could do, apart from finding who was responsible.

Gordon was driving on autopilot. As he approached Moortown corner, he pulled up at the traffic lights and was about to turn left towards his home. He saw a car behind him, but he paid it no mind. In other circumstances, he would have been on alert, but Shelley's death was a deep and personal hurt and he wasn't as focused as usual. The traffic lights changed, and he moved, turning to the left. She had to try driving on this side when the drama was over, Gabriela thought.

The car behind fell back a little, but followed the route and the driver made a mental note of where they were heading. He knew his orders. Keep it simple, he thought. The car he followed was staying at the speed limit, and unless it turned off suddenly, it would be easy to keep on its trail. This was an unfamiliar area of Leeds. The houses were affluent, and very different to the area where he lived. His home was poor, and it irked him that some people held money, power and influence, something he had never possessed, but he was working on it. This new job promised substantial rewards for work well done. Tailing someone was straightforward, and he hoped it would lead to even better things.

The cars passed the entrance to a park, and well-tended flowerbeds. On the opposite side was a sunken area with tennis courts. His kind didn't play tennis. If they were lucky, they could watch it on the television. Tennis was for snobs!

The road crossed a vast expanse of sports fields and he saw a strange rocket shaped tower in front, but as they got nearer, he recognised it as a clock tower. The tailing driver watched the car in front cross the junction and then take a sharp right along a narrow laneway. He carried on and parked on another side road, and then got out, and retraced his steps to the narrow road Gordon and

Gabriela had driven into. It was tree-lined, full of cars parked along either side, partially blocking the pavements, and allowing only room for a single car to drive along. Further on, he recognised Gordon's car parked near the end of the lane.

He strolled nonchalantly down the street, as if he was a relaxed walker on his way to the wood at the end. An elderly man shuffled his way towards him, and he stood to the side to allow the man to pass.

'Good afternoon,' he said, and the elderly gentleman smiled back.

'Good afternoon,' he replied, and carried on his way.

The man tailing Gordon and Gabriela carried on walking, but he stopped next to the parked car. He knelt down as if tying his shoelaces and slipped an object under the wheel arch at the driver's side of the car. There was a click as the magnet took hold and held the small box tight to the metal.

He got back on his feet, trying to figure out which house Gordon and Gabriela had entered. After a second or two, he continued his walk to the end of the road. He reached the junction, turned right down the steeply sloping cobbled road and then back onto the parade of shops.

The wood on the left-hand side was a lush, dark green. The leaves of the oak trees had lost their spring vibrancy and showed early signs of their autumnal change. My life's changing too, and for the better, he thought. Another successful mission! He hoped his new boss would be very pleased with his work.

Looping back across the front of the shops, he turned to find where he had left his car.

He got into the driver's seat, took out his mobile, and made a call.

'Hello? It's Bryan. Everything has gone as planned. I've left the tracker as you instructed.'

There was a brief response on the other end, and then the phone went dead. Bryan smiled to himself. His new career was starting really well.

Gordon and Gabriela needed a stiff drink and something to eat. They had missed breakfast, and it was now late in the afternoon. Gordon got busy cooking a quick meal, whilst Gabriela took a shower and changed. He took this opportunity to put the pistol and ammunition back in the safe. Gabriela knew nothing about it and he wanted it to stay that way, at least for the time being.

He had faced danger many times. Comrades had died in battle, but this was different. This was truly personal. When Gabriela's life had been in danger in Calpe, he had felt the same anger and he swore he wouldn't allow it to happen again. He knew he couldn't guarantee this, but he would die to make it so. Shelley had asked for his help and he had failed her. She had died and Paul was probably dead.

There was nothing he could do to hide from the pain and guilt he felt. It ate into him like a cancer. It wasn't just her death, but the terrible manner. Gordon was not used to failure, at least, not where those he cared about were concerned.

When Gabriela appeared showered and changed, Gordon went to spruce himself up, but he was lacking any enthusiasm. He wondered who could be behind the killings. Why would someone kill Shelley, the guards, and Marcus' wife Ariadne? It just made little sense. Anger didn't help. Gordon had no leads, and he didn't think the police had any either.

'Come on!' he said to Gabriela. 'There's no point sitting here miserable. Let me take you for a ride to see some more of Leeds. It'll help keep our minds off what's happened!'

Gabriela didn't object, and the two went out to the car. The late afternoon was still stunning, and the trees that lined the street dappled the light. They drove down to the main road. The two said little as they drove along and, after a short while, the road merged with a major road heading up a long hill.

'We are heading towards a place called Wetherby,' said Gordon. 'There's somewhere I want to show you. I used to visit with my parents when I was a child. It's very pretty.'

'That sounds nice, Gordon. We need some cheering up.'

Soon, Gordon turned right onto a dirt track and a small area to park cars. He stopped the car, and they got out and started the trek up the narrow lane lined with brambles to a disused railway line.

No one else seemed to be around. The air was loud, full of bees buzzing, insects chittering, and birds singing. Gordon held Gabriela's hand, and they smiled for the first time that day. They walked onto the old railway line and down the banking on the trail that led into a wood, dense with trees and with an under-layer of bushes. A small stream ran alongside the trail and after a short walk, the track reached a stile. As they climbed over, the wood opened onto a recently harvested field that showed little but the rough male stubble of cut wheat. On their right, the stream broadened out into an area that had once been a small mill dam but had become swampy, with only a few pools of clear water edged with thick beds of bulrushes. The old sluice-gate lay broken, but the machinery still stood, cloaked by dense vegetation. There was the powerful scent of Himalayan Balsam, and Gordon found some ripe seed heads and showed Gabriela how they sprung apart when touched, throwing their seeds wide. She loved the surprise as the spring-like pods burst, but her joy was tempered when Gordon explained how they had been introduced and become an endemic weed.

The two became lost in the beauty and tranquillity and for a while, they almost forgot the tragedy of the past days.

The walk entered a new woodland and on their left a beare of hazel trees. Gordon explained the Anglo-Saxon name and the gentle wood was beautiful and delicate. They continued on and emerged into a grassy area that sloped upwards to a small craggy outcrop.

'This is Hetchell Woods,' he told her. 'I came here with my parents.'

They scrambled up to the base of the crags and gazed at the overhang. The air was cooler here in the gritstone's shade and Gordon climbed up a few feet onto a ledge under the overhang. It was well-worn, with easy footholds, and Gabriela needed no help to clamber up and sit next to him on the cold, rough stone. They wrapped their arms around each other and kissed a short but passionate kiss. When they separated, they smiled and knew, despite all that had happened, there was beauty and love still in the world.

'Can we climb to the top?' she asked.

'We'd better take the trail. I nearly lost a friend of mine climbing these rocks when I was a teenager.'

She didn't argue, but nimbly slipped back to the ground and Gordon joined her. They moved to the edge of the rock-face and scrambled up the steep track to the top. They walked to the edge, and the land opened up before them. The sun was lower in the sky, and the light less strong, but the view was staggering, peaceful, an example of all that made Yorkshire a green and pleasant land. Birds flew, lost in their own world, oblivious to the machinations of the humans that dwelt below them, singing to the world in a language that only they knew.

There was nothing the two could feel but exhilarated as they stood close to the edge of the rock and the valley opened out. Gabriela gazed back along the trail they had followed, and it looked tiny below them. She could see the railway line and she traced it back to where they had left the car. She saw their car in the car park, but in miniature. There was another car parked nearby. Two tiny stick figures got out of the other car and she watched them approach theirs. This struck her as unusual behaviour, and she nudged Gordon gently.

'Look! Look back at the car. There are two people near it. What are they doing?'

Gordon followed her gaze to where she pointed, and he saw what she meant. The two tiny figures were walking around their car.

'I'm not sure,' he said. 'But I don't like the look of it. I hope they're not going to break in!'

'It doesn't look like it. They're bending down. What are they doing now? Are they putting something there?' Gabriela's voice was now concerned.

'We need to get back and find out what they are up to! Come on!'

Their peaceful afternoon was spoilt, and they hurried down to the base of the rocks and headed back along the route they had strolled along earlier. They hurried and soon they left the small wood and crossed the railway line. Gordon put his finger to Gabriela's lips to indicate silence, and the two edged to the top of the embankment. They moved behind a hedge to where they could look down to the carpark, unseen. Their car was alone. The other had gone.

'Come on, they've left,' Gordon said. They carefully walked down to the car.

'Am I being, how do you say it, paranoid, Gordon?'

'That is how you say it, and no, you are not. After all that's happened, you can't be too careful. Don't touch it. We need to check what's happened.'

Tyre tracks in the earth showed where the other car had been. Gordon bent down and checked under the rear wheel-arch. There was nothing, but when he checked the driver's side, he found a small black box stuck to the top of the wheel arch. Gordon had seen several similar devices in his work with the military. He whistled and stepped back.

'Do not touch the car. Just look above the front wheel.'

Gabriela did. She saw the package, got back on her feet and rejoined Gordon.

'Is that what I think it is?' she said, as they backed away from the car.

'It sure looks like it. I've seen IEDs before and that looks like one.'

'What are we to do?'

'We're going to do nothing. Any slight move could trigger it. We need to call the police and we need to keep away from it and stop anyone else getting close.'

Gordon and Gabriela walked down to the edge of the road and Gordon took out his mobile and called 999. After a couple of conversations, they finally put him through to the police, and he asked to speak with Inspector Glover. When he gave his name, the officer on the other end appeared to recognise it and a few moments later, a new voice spoke. Inspector Glover's tone was world weary.

'What can I do for you, Mr Bennet? Have you some more bodies for me?'

'Not on this occasion, Inspector, but you nearly had two more.'

Gordon explained the situation and the inspector's tone altered dramatically.

'Stay where you are, Mr Bennet. Do not go near your car and don't allow anyone else near it. Where are you exactly?'

Gordon gave their position and the inspector spoke again.

'The usual drill, Mr Bennet. Touch nothing and wait where you are!'

Gordon didn't argue and the phone call ended and Gordon and Gabriela were back in the all too familiar scene of waiting for the police to arrive.

NEWSTIME

There was a knocking on the door, and Marcus stopped stroking the bird and looked up. He hated interruptions. Some found solitude hard, but to him, it was a blessing. With his birds, his books and visitors, he had settled into a routine. He had money, and that meant power, and he was shrewd enough to use it sparingly, but effectively.

'Come in,' he called.

The cell door opened, and the familiar face of Franco, the warder, appeared.

'I hope that I'm not interrupting you,' he said, which seemed a strange way for a guard to behave.

'You are ok, Franco. What is it you want?'

'I want nothing, Mr Spinx, Sir! I, I, I don't know how to say this. I am sorry, Mr Spinx.'

'Spit it out, man! Spit it out. What are you trying to say?'

'Maybe you need to watch the news on the television, Mr Spinx. It is terrible news, Mr Spinx. Terrible news!'

'Stay here,' Marcus told the guard.

He walked over to his large flat-screen television, picked up the remote from the cupboard, and pressed the button. All the time, the bird balanced on his other finger.

The television came to life, and he selected the local news channel, and his life changed forever!

The headlines eventually came on and the reporter was standing outside a place he knew very well. It was his house.

'This morning, a terrible crime was discovered in the house behind me. The owner is Marcus Spinx, a Leeds identity. He was recently found guilty of major crimes and is in remand awaiting sentencing in Armley jail. Visitors to the house this morning discovered the bodies of four people, two men and two women, in the swimming pool. Police are treating this as a murder case. The bodies are yet to be formally identified, but one of them is believed to be Ariadne Spinx, the wife of Marcus Spinx, and the other is a well-known lawyer, Shelley Jones, the partner of criminal prosecutor, Paul Montgomery. Mr Montgomery himself was reported missing by Miss Jones just a few days ago. The police are not releasing any further details, but say they are pursuing all lines of inquiry to solve the case. This is Simone Jolly, reporting from Poole Bank.'

Marcus froze. Ice held him tight, and its grip was unyielding. Ariadne was dead! She was his link! His connection! His arm outside these walls, and his love! After the shock came anger and it burnt furiously! The guard saw the impact, and he stepped back, afraid for his own safety. Marcus stood motionless and Franco waited for him to say, to do something. Eventually, Marcus looked down at his hand. In his grip was the lifeless bird. It was gone, crushed, and the realisation of what he had done allowed Marcus to weep. He never cried for a human life. He hadn't cried for his parents or when he killed his first wife and he couldn't even cry for Ariadne, and he truly loved her. The bird's lifeless body broke his heart, and he swore he would find out who had done this to him and he would exact his revenge. They would pay! Oh yes, they would pay!

After delivering the news and seeing Marcus Spinx's reaction, Franco decided it was a good time to beat a hasty retreat. He backed out of the cell and locked it behind him. He saw the dead bird in the prisoner's hands and thought it might be a shrewd move to buy a replacement. His relationship with the wealthy inmate was proving profitable and a bit of an investment might prove well worth his while.

Franco's replacement finch was indeed a smart move, and Marcus seemed touched by the guard's thoughtfulness. He was clearly depressed. The visit from the police, the formal identification of Ariadne, and the subsequent inquiry proved a distraction, but not a cure. Marcus Spinx used the contact and the chance to get out of the prison to discuss the situation with his lawyers and start the appeal process. It also provided him with the opportunity to get messages to trusted friends and colleagues. He knew someone would know who murdered his wife, and he had sufficient money to tempt anyone. It didn't make him feel better, but it gave a purpose. He would find out who it was, and then he would plot his revenge.

Messages came to him through the lawyers and through the guard. Franco would do anything for money, and Marcus reeled him in. His requests, at first, were only for certain items to be delivered, messages, perks, items he could use to maintain his influence on the inside. Franco was delighted to help, and bit by bit, he fell under the prisoner's control. Marcus smiled to himself. Greed was the ultimate shackle, and Franco was nothing if not greedy.

CASCADE

The killing of Shelley had been terrible and was cause enough for Gordon to seek out whoever was behind it and bring them to justice, but an attempt on his and Gabriela's lives was the final straw. Any chance that he could walk away and leave it to the police had gone. However, Inspector Glover saw things differently.

'Now listen here, Mr Bennet and Miss Morales. You must leave this to the proper authorities. I do not want you involved any further. Is that clear?'

His tone suggested that he didn't want, nor expect, any argument, but he didn't know either of the two sitting before him.

'It is very clear, Inspector, but someone is out to kill us, and we won't sit back and let it happen!'

Gordon's voice remained calm, frighteningly calm after the narrow miss. He had been shocked and devastated by Shelley's murder, but now he felt angry, more than angry.

'Can you provide us with twenty-four-hour protection, Inspector? Because if not, you can't expect us to sit and wait for whoever it is to have another go!'

The look on the police officer's face showed that his budget wouldn't stretch that far, and he had to accept that there was nothing he could do.

The device on the car had eventually been disarmed and forensics had towed the vehicle away for further investigation. A replacement hire car had been provided by the rental company, at the department's expense. Statements were taken, theories put forward, but no leads were forthcoming. Obviously, someone wanted to silence Ariadne Spinx, and be a warning to her husband. The question was, why? What was going on? Was Shelley just collateral damage?

All three thought the same, and not one of them had any real insight. The inspector intended to pay Marcus Spinx a visit, and see if he could provide any insight, but he expected little cooperation.

'I have given you my advice. It is up to you whether you take it! I can do no more, but be very careful. They have tried once and will almost certainly try again! The trigger device on that bomb was a complex movement sensor. If you had opened the door, it was sensitive enough to have set the explosive off. Whoever planted it was very professional. You were lucky this time. You probably won't be again. The best thing you could do would be to take Miss Morales back to Spain. It is probable that they wouldn't follow you there.'

'Sorry, Inspector, but we won't be doing that.'

Gordon looked at Gabriela, and she nodded her agreement.

'We don't take kindly to being threatened, and we want whoever killed Shelley and Paul brought to justice,' said Gordon.

'We know the risks, Inspector!' Gabriela added.

'I'm not sure that you do, Miss Morales! I'm not sure that you do. Take care how you go. You are aware of my feelings. It would be wise if you listened to them.'

The inspector got to his feet and opened the office door to allow the pair to leave. He gave them the key for the new hire car and told them where it was parked.

Gabriela and Gordon were pleased to get out of the police station and the fresh air was a welcome relief. It was late into the evening and the darkness had settled over the city. They walked to the carpark and a few presses of the button on the key got a response from a white car below the car park light.

'Do we need to check it?' Gabriela asked.

'It will be fine. They wouldn't dare do anything here, but I will have a look.'

Using the light from his mobile, Gordon gave the car a check underneath and when he found nothing, he opened the door for Gabriela and then got into the driver's seat. He took a moment to adjust the seat, the mirrors and then they drove off back towards his home.

Gordon noticed Gabriela was shaking, and he reached over and gave her hand a squeeze.

'Come on, Gabriela. You're fine.'

'We were so close, Gordon. If I hadn't seen them, then we would be dead.'

'That's true, but you did see them, and we are fine. They didn't get us and now we will be prepared. Do you want me to take you back to Calpe? I will do if you want!'

'No, Gordon. I'm terrified, but we can't run away. You, we, owe it to Shelley to find out who is responsible. Take me to your home, hold me in you arms and I'll feel safe. I'll get over it.'

Gordon smiled. How could he not love this woman? She was strong, resilient, and she loved him. Wherever she went, he wanted to be at her side. Together, they would find who was responsible and, by God, he would make them pay!

The rest of the drive home became a bit of a blur. Soon they approached the clock tower and turned into the familiar street and Gordon found a space to park, a bit further from the house than usual. They got to the doorway, both emotionally drained from the day. The key turned, and they entered onto the safe and familiar staircase up to Gordon's private rooms. Lying on the doormat, they saw a large envelope. There was no stamp and no writing as Gordon picked it up.

He shut the door behind him and together they walked the steps up to his kitchen. Both felt a sense of foreboding, but neither said anything at first. Gordon went to his drink cupboard and filled two glasses of wine and placed them on the table. The two sat facing each other. The envelope was on the table between them. Gordon picked it up.

'Why do I feel that this isn't good news?'

He tried to smile, but it was forced, and Gabriela couldn't look away.

'Just hurry and open it!' she said. 'I can't stand the tension!'

His thumb slid under the flap and forced the glue to give. There was a slight tearing at one edge, but Gordon opened the flap and pulled out a folded piece of paper. He opened it, waited a moment as if frozen in time and then put it down on the table so that Gabriela could see its content.

She looked down at it, and there were just two words, 'Miroslav Bilyk'. The rest of the paper was blank.

'Who is Miroslav Bilyk?' Gabriela's voice sounded surprised. She wasn't sure what she expected in the envelope, but the name must be important, she felt.

'I have no idea! I've never heard it before. It means nothing to me, but someone wants us to know it. I will contact Peter. He might know who Miroslav Bilyk is and maybe what his significance is.'

Gabriela yawned and Gordon realised how much of a strain the day had had on them. They had been up at dawn, discovered the murders and nearly been added to the list.

'It will wait until tomorrow. Come on, bed!'

Gabriela didn't argue and was too tired even to shower. The couple fell into bed after removing their clothes and, within seconds, were asleep. Unfortunately, they did not experience peaceful slumber. Their subconscious minds kept reliving the horror of the day.

Just before dawn, Gabriela awoke to find Gordon standing at the window, staring out to the street below. She got out of bed silently and her bare feet made no sound on the linoleum-covered floor. Standing behind Gordon, she rested her chin on his shoulder. She wrapped her arms around his waist and enjoyed his solid presence.

Gabriela looked over his shoulder and saw what he was looking at. She had thought he was just lost in reverie, but she noticed a movement. A cat was moving slowly, prowling along the top of the garden wall. The street light illuminated the scene and as she watched, the cat jumped down onto something on the pavement. There was a flurry of motion and then the cat jumped back onto the wall with something in its mouth. As it re-entered the light, she recognised the remains of an enormous rat, hanging like a dark moustache.

'It's a dangerous world out there,' Gordon said, without turning. 'There are hunters and hunted, and I think it's time we became the hunters.'

Gabriela gave him a hug and breathed in his smell. He was her everything, and as he had done in Calpe, she knew he would not rest until he had caught Shelley's killers.

'You're right. The name must be important. Maybe Peter will know something. You can call him, but not at this time in the morning. I need a shower and then back to bed until a reasonable time to get up on holiday.'

'Not much of a holiday!'

'Have a shower with me and I'll make it a better one!'

She let go of him, laughed and slapped his back, took hold of his hand and led him into the bathroom.

Several hours later, Gordon was on the telephone. The voice on the other end was Peter's and after quite a long talk, he put his phone away and turned to Gabriela.

'He's coming round later this afternoon. He has heard the name Miroslav Bilyk, but wants to do some backgrounding and doesn't want to talk on the phone. So we have a bit of time to fill. How about lunch?'

Gordon had little in the house, so that meant going out.

'Where are we going?'

'I thought we'd try the city,' Gordon said, as he opened the door, and two of them grabbed a light jacket and made their way down to street level. Gordon was confused for a moment as he couldn't see his car parked on the street, but then realised he was looking for the hire car that had been left at the police station. The new one was a different colour, and he recognised it further down the street.

'We'd better check it, Gordon. You can't be too careful.'

'Yes, they will still want us dead. They will be looking at new ways, though, as they'll expect us to check the car every time. Anyway, I'll check it!'

Gabriela looked up and down the street. There was no one about. The street had a tranquil atmosphere created by the ageing buildings, established trees, and peace. She could see why Gordon liked it here, she liked it here too. It still had the old village atmosphere within a bustling city. She saw nothing to cause her any alarm, but she knew they were in danger and someone in this city wanted them dead.

Satisfied the car was safe, Gordon unlocked the doors and held the passenger door open for Gabriela.

'Gracias, señor amable,' she said in mocking tones, but smiled and kissed him on the cheek as she got into the car.

Gordon was still smiling as he shut his door, fastened his seatbelt, and turned the ignition. The car was still full of fuel and so he could drive straight into the city.

It was not rush hour, and the roads were relatively quiet. He had decided to park near the old Quarry Hill flat site and walk into the city. He wanted to show Gabriela the old market and then eat in the spanking new and suave shopping centre.

They wandered up the rise towards the market, and the streets were busy with people going about their day-to-day business, not aware of the drama that was occurring in their city. Clouds had gathered and there was a chill in the air that had not been present in the first few days of their holiday. Gordon hoped that this was only a temporary change and that it wasn't a portent for the days ahead. Gabriela pulled him closer and welcomed his body heat as they picked up the pace to get indoors.

They soon reached the top of the hill and Gabriela looked up at the magnificent old building with its ornate marble and stone frontage. But it was too chilly to linger and Gordon pressed his way through the crowded entrance and the pair found themselves in a new world.

Despite the crowds, there was a muffled effect that, mixed with a melange of aromas, was almost overpowering. They moved down a surprisingly steep, but narrow walkway edged with shop fronts that were so close it was almost possible to touch each side by just stretching out the arms. Despite the almost claustrophobic atmosphere, the place had a welcoming, homely feeling that was womb-like and safe. Gabriela's face lit up as she stared at the range of stalls and businesses selling an array of goods. Butchers, bakers, fabrics, clothing, barbers' shops, tobacconists, fruit stalls and fish dealers, sat cheek to jowl in the vast undercover area. The roof was a dizzying lattice of wooden and iron arches, created by an eccentric engineer.

'Wow!' she said. 'This is, how do you say it? Really something!'

Gordon laughed at her joy, and for a few moments they were back on holiday, enjoying each other's company. Alas, Gordon recognised the transient pleasure for what it was, just a temporary respite from the madness that they had become involved in since they arrived in the city. Even so, he enjoyed being with Gabriela as she explored the market, bought some jewellery items from a stall and then a jacket. Clearly, she wanted to be ready for the colder weather outside.

The crowds milled around and occasionally someone would bump into him, but Gordon felt they were pretty safe in such a busy area. That was until he noticed someone who appeared to be following them. This wouldn't have been unusual as there were only limited routes through the market, but out of the corner of his eye, Gordon noted that the man kept a distance between them, even when Gabriela was standing for a long time checking some silver bracelets. To make matters worse, the man made no attempt to buy anything and his eyes focused on Gordon and Gabriela. Once Gordon became aware, he found he couldn't fail to notice the man's clumsy attempt to trail them. He waited until Gabriela began choosing jackets, which meant her trying them on in a small changing room. She was completely involved in finding the right one and just the right fit, and failed to see Gordon slip away into the crowd.

As an ex-military officer, Gordon had little difficulty in vanishing and reappearing immediately behind the watching man. The man's face had become concerned, as both his targets had disappeared like mist on a sunny dawn.

Bryan was not happy. It had been fairly easy, previously, to follow his orders. He had tailed the car, found where the man and girl lived, and fed the information back. He thought his mission was over after he fitted the tracking device, but no. A call late last night instructed him to continue to tail the two. He had been told about the new car and to check which one they were using. His orders told him to keep them in sight at all times, and to inform his contact when they started back to their home. The job was straightforward, but the way the caller spoke made him nervous. The tone of voice made it clear this was a job he was not to fail at, but the good thing was, a sizeable payment had been transferred into his bank account. Money always made Bryan happy, and this was more than a week's wages, but still it couldn't stop the itch of anxiety playing in his head.

He had been in place since first light to ensure he didn't miss them leaving the house. Thankfully, he hadn't left, and mid-morning they appeared and got into a car further down the road. There was no problem tailing them into the city. Bryan knew it well and realised where they were going to park and he found a space nearby and ran back to see them walking towards the market. He had had to hurry to catch them up, and he followed along behind. They didn't seem in a hurry and took their time, just like any young couple. He was envious of the man. The woman was a stunner, and he knew what he would like to do if he got the opportunity. Fat chance! he thought.

He followed them up to the indoor market, and then inside. He only had to keep them in his sight, make a note of what they did, and anyone they spoke to. It had been easy so far, and with luck, it would continue to be.

He watched as the girl tried on clothes, and her partner stood around looking a little distracted. Bryan was ten yards away, keeping them in his sight, but the girl went into the shop with a few jackets to try them on. His eyes followed her, watching her curves and her movement, but when he looked back at the man, he had gone!

Bryan panicked! Where had he gone? Shit! he thought to himself, but before he could do anything, a hand took hold of the back of his neck. A warm breath followed, and then a quiet, but unnerving, voice whispered.

'I don't want to do it here, but I will break your neck in an instant, if you don't do as I say!'

The tone of the voice left him in little doubt it was not an idle threat.

'Who sent you?'

The throng of people took no notice of the two men talking, and no one noticed the pincer-like grip the man in front was held by.

'I don't know!' the held man stammered.

Gordon was almost prepared to accept this was the case, but almost wasn't sufficient, and his grip did more than just hold the man where he was. The victim's face turned a little red, and Gordon knew the nerves were inflicting considerable pain, and he upped the pressure.

There was a panic in the man's voice as he said,

'I'm telling the... I don't know! I don't know! He phones me. I just get a call!'

Gordon didn't release the man, nor decrease the pressure, but he used his spare hands to search the man's clothing for a mobile phone. It took a moment or two fumbling, but he reached into the jacket pocket and pulled out the phone. Without looking at it, he pocketed it and spoke again.

'I will take your phone. Just a little keepsake. You're not very good at this job, are you? I guess this is your own phone.'

From the way the man reacted, he knew he was right.

'That's good then. It will have all your contact details. I'm going to let you walk away in a moment, and I suggest you get far away from me. I am busy shopping and I don't want you hanging around.'

Gordon looked about, and still no one noticed anything out of the ordinary. People pushed by, busy doing their everyday things. He released his grip, and the man sagged with relief.

'What time do you have to report back? You'd better tell the truth, or it will be the worse for you.'

The man squirmed, confused. He was unsure what to do. He turned to face his opponent. It had all been going so well.

'I have to call at 8.00 tonight. They expect me to report on your day and who you've spoken to.'

His voice was husky, and he struggled to catch his breath. He was scared, no, terrified. He had read about the bodies in the swimming pool. It had been on the news, and he suspected who was behind it.

'Well, we wouldn't want to keep them waiting, would we? You know where I live?'

This was more of a statement than a question, and the man nodded.

'Well, be at my door at 7.15 tonight. If you play your cards right, you might get to make that call! If you don't show up, you had better be running away from here as fast as you can, because your boss will be after you and so will I! Believe me, you and those you care for won't want either of us catching you! Do you understand?'

This time, the man in front of him mumbled.

'Yes! Yes! I'll be there seven fifteen.'

'Don't be late. If things go ok, I'll give you your phone back and no one need be any the wiser. These are nasty men you work for. Very nasty men! Now go!'

Bryan didn't need telling twice, and the now crestfallen man hurried off, rubbing his neck and trying to put as much distance between himself and the man he had been tailing.

Gordon watched him scuttle away before he walked back to the stall, as Gabriela appeared to find him waiting where she had left him.

'I hope it hasn't been too boring, Gordon. I think the jacket was worth the wait.'

She kissed him on the cheek and held a carrier bag in her left hand.

'No, I'm sure it's worth waiting for. Can I see it?'

'Not until we get back to your place. Did you say something about eating? ¡Tengo mucha hambre!'

She laughed, and Gordon did too, and he led her out of the

market to find a place for lunch.

Later that afternoon, they returned to Gordon's place. There was a brief telephone conversation, and within ten minutes, there was a knock on the downstairs door. It was Peter, and he smiled at Gabriela as he walked into the kitchen.

'Lovely to see you again,' he said. 'Are you sure you want to be with him?' He gestured to Gordon. 'I am sure I would be a much better choice!'

'Oh, let me see,' she said, as she looked at both men, scanning them up and down. 'Sorry, but I think I'll stay with the one I have!'

She laughed, and the two men joined her.

'Drink, Peter?' Gordon asked.

'I thought you'd never offer.'

Gordon went into the kitchen and returned with three large drinks. He placed them on the table where the others were waiting. Peter lifted the glass.

'Cheers,' he said, and all three took a long drink.

'Did you find anything out about the name I gave you? Who is Miroslav Bilyk?'

Peter looked at both Gordon and Gabriela, paused, and then spoke.

'I had already heard the name, and he is well known in the city. He is the leader of the council, an honest, upright member of the community. Or at least that is his public face! Comes from the Baltics, originally, but no one is quite sure of his background. Came into the country during the troubles in the early nineties, and was wealthy enough to set up a range of businesses. He started by opening his first club, New Times, and it became quite a place to be seen. From the very start, there was chatter. There was talk of the usual club activities, prostitution, dealing and violence, but the police couldn't find anything that would stand up in court. Miroslav Bilyk is a shrewd and ruthless businessman, and there was no one prepared to give evidence against him. A few years back, there was a case brought, and the police were hopeful about getting a prosecution, but the principal witness was found bound and gagged at the bottom of the River Aire, and the case was dropped.'

'That sounds familiar! Maybe he's moved on to pools now,' Gordon noted.

'There's more,' Peter added. 'He grew his businesses and moved into building supplies, concrete mainly, and again, more rumblings. Competitors seemed to be accident prone, but no one could find anything linking Miroslav to any of it. He appeared to be squeaky clean, but...'

'There's always a but!' Gordon added and Gabriela sat, mesmerised by the tale.

Peter took a break and had another gulp of his drink, and his Adam's apple bobbed as he swallowed.

'Chance of another?'

Gabriela got to her feet this time, shot into the kitchen and returned with the whisky bottle. She topped up the three glasses and Peter took another drink and continued,

'But we know he isn't! He's as dirty as they come, but proving it is tricky. Anyway, he has had political aspirations, got onto council and is now the leader. He has some powerful friends, and some powerful enemies. I have to tell you Gordon, he is a dangerous man. He is ruthless and cunning. Do not underestimate him. If he is involved in Shelley's murder, you need to understand who and what you're up against. Why do you suspect him?'

Gordon and Gabriela explained all that had happened, the discovery of the device planted under their car, the envelope that had been posted through the letterbox with only the name Miroslav Bilyk. Gordon said nothing about the incident in the market, as he hadn't told Gabriela.

'This is dangerous stuff, Gordon. You have Gabriela to look after. Why don't you leave it to the force?'

'Can't do that, Peter. This is personal. What's more, Gabriela is the one to keep me safe. Only a fool would underestimate her!'

'I believe it. I am sorry, Gabriela. I didn't mean to offend you!'

'Don't worry, Peter. We both understand what we are involved in. This isn't the first time.'

Gabriela smiled and added,

'We didn't look for trouble. It came knocking on our door, but we won't run away. We have to find out what happened to Shelley and her partner, and who is responsible, but now we have a name.'

BETWEEN A ROCK AND A HARD PLACE

The rest of the discussion was short, as Peter had to return to work, and he had already stayed longer than he had intended. When he left, he repeated his warning, and Gordon and Gabriela assured him they would be careful. The two returned to the kitchen and Gordon busied himself preparing a meal. Gabriela strolled into the bedroom and reappeared wearing the new jacket she had bought in the market.

'You like?' she asked.

'I do! Well worth the wait!'

He checked what food he had in, and then the two walked to the shops to get a few more things that would be needed.

As they went down to the main street, Gordon took the opportunity to tell Gabriela what had happened whilst she had been trying on the jackets. Her faced dropped.

'I had no idea. I didn't see anyone,' she said.

'I didn't either until I was waiting, but he had been following us since we left the house in the morning.'

'And he's coming to the house this evening?' Gabriela's voice showed that she was not altogether comfortable with the idea, but she didn't say so.

'He will be here at 7.15. I have his phone and he will get a phone call at 8.00 from his handler. He wants a report on our movements today. I want to be there when he answers the call and I want him to arrange a rendezvous for tonight. This is our chance to get closer to whoever is behind this.'

'Will he do as you ask? Can you trust him?' Gabriela asked, as they walked into the small supermarket.

'Trust him? No! I wouldn't trust him an inch, but he knows what I will do to him if he doesn't, and he knows what his masters will do if they find out he has failed them. Fear will make sure he turns up, and I hope fear of me will ensure he does what I tell him. After that he had better run, and keep on running. But if things turn out as I hope, he may stand a chance.'

Gordon spoke to the butcher behind the counter.

'A pound of beef sausages, please.'

The man responded and handed over the wrapped sausages. Gordon added them to his basket and headed for the remaining things he needed. He picked up three bottles of wine and walked over to the checkout.

'So what are you cooking?' Gabriela asked.

'A bit of a surprise. A local speciality, toad-in-the-hole!'

Gabriela's face was a picture of confusion and Gordon couldn't help but laugh.

'Come on. We've time for a meal and a rest before our meeting. We may have a busy night ahead of us.'

Later that afternoon, the two enjoyed a meal that surprised and delighted Gabriela. Gordon explained that the batter mixture the sausages were in was Yorkshire pudding and together with the sausages the meal was called toad-in-the-hole. They laughed a little, enjoyed each other's company and for a short while forgot about the horror of the last few days. They washed up, dried the dishes and were putting them away when there was a knock on the door. Gordon glanced at the wall clock and it was 7 pm.

'Looks like our guest is early,' Gabriela said.

'Probably, but I need to get something. I'll let him in. You wait here, but when you hear me let him in, come down to the office.'

Gordon shot down the stairs and made a detour into his office. He got his pistol, checked that the magazine was full, and slipped it into the back of his trousers. He continued down to the front door and called out,

'So you came after all?'

'You knew I would. You gave me no choice!'

The voice was recognisable, and the tone despondent.

Gordon opened the door and the man he had waylaid at the market stood facing him.

'You'd better come in. We have matters to sort out.'

'They'll kill me!' he said, as he crossed the threshold and sealed his fate.

'Follow me!'

Gordon led the way up the stairs and turned into the office. He indicated a chair to his visitor, and the man sat down. Gordon sat behind his wooden desk in his swivel chair.

Gabriela walked in and looked at the man with a far from welcoming expression.

'Why were you following us?' she said. 'I could kill you!'

The look on her face made clear she wasn't joking, and the man looked suitably worried.

Gordon stopped her before she could carry on lambasting the visitor.

'Gabriela, please,' he calmed her and carried on. 'Time is short. There is a lot to do, and you can kill him afterwards if he doesn't do as we want.'

The man's face turned ashen as he got a clear impression that Gordon wasn't joking.

'I am going to give your phone back to you later. When we get the call at eight, you are going to answer it. You will tell the caller you tailed us all day, that we went into Leeds and visited the market. You will say you need to speak with them privately. That you are worried the call could be being listened to. Say you have something important to tell them. Have you met with them before?'

The man looked as if he was about to be sick, but he nodded his head.

'Good! Well, you are going to organise a meeting with them tonight.'

'Where did you meet before?'

The man told him.

'That would be fine. Arrange to meet there again. Whatever time suits them is ok. I will be sitting opposite you and if you give any sign something is wrong, I will kill you!'

Gordon pulled out the pistol from behind his back. The man turned an even deeper grey, and he sagged in the chair. Gordon got to his feet and passed the pistol to Gabriela.

'Keep it pointing at him. I need to check that he isn't armed or wired. If he does anything, shoot, but make sure you miss me!'

The seated man froze solid and stiff. Terror filled his eyes. This was no professional, Gordon realised, which suited his needs. He needed him to comply. If he knew the danger wasn't from Gordon and Gabriela, but the people he worked for, he wouldn't do as he was told.

Gabriela held the gun steady as if she knew what she was doing. In truth, she had never held a gun before, and never pointed one at anyone intending to fire. It was all she could do the keep her hand from shaking. Her target stared at the end of the pistol barrel trained at his head.

Gordon checked him and then walked back to Gabriela, smiled knowingly, and took the pistol from her clenched grip.

'Good, you are playing by the rules. Keep it up and you might get through this unscathed!'

Gordon's voice reassured the man and Gabriela. The thought of firing at another person was not something she had imagined she would ever do.

The moment the pistol was taken from her, she felt a great weight lift and she almost danced for joy.

'Gabriela, can you get our friend here a drink? I think he needs to calm his nerves.'

She left the room and Gordon leaned in to the stranger sitting in the chair so that his face was mere inches from him.

'Now, I need you to listen to exactly what I am telling you. The smallest deviations from my instructions and it will not be good for you. Do you truly understand?'

He nodded, and Gordon patted him on his head.

'Make sure you do!'

Gabriela appeared with a whisky for the man, one for Gordon and for herself.

'I thought we all might need a drink.'

The man in the chair took the glass she offered him and downed it in a swift gulp.

'There's five minutes. You know what to do?'

Again, the stranger nodded.

Gordon sipped his drink, but Gabriela followed the lead of the stranger and downed hers in one go.

'What's your name?' Gordon asked.

'It's Bryan.'

'Well, Bryan, I hope you are good at putting on an act. Your life might depend on it!'

The call came at the arranged time and Bryan was shaking when he answered it. The conversation was businesslike, and he kept calm enough to recount Gordon and Gabriela's movements during the day. There was a moment of tension when the man asked for the meeting. There was questioning of the need, but the voice on the other end eventually seemed satisfied and a time and place was confirmed.

The two listening couldn't hear clearly, but they picked up sufficient to be satisfied that Bryan hadn't said or done anything that would raise any suspicion.

Bryan looked up at them, and worry was etched on his face.

'Now tell me the arrangements, Bryan. Miss nothing out!'

Gordon took the mobile from him and the two listened as Bryan explained where the meeting was to take place and when. After Bryan had finished, Gordon said quietly,

'You have done a good job, Bryan. I can tell you that you no longer need to worry about me, but unfortunately, I can't say the same about your friend on the phone. He and his bosses will become very, very angry if, and when, they learn of your part. I can't make you do anything now, but my advice would be to get as far away as possible from Leeds. There are three hours before the meeting, so I would use them! Get your things and leave as soon as possible. You may not know who you've been mixing with, but believe me, they would kill you as soon as look at you. Be warned, if I ever see you again in Leeds, you will have to deal with me, and you wouldn't like that, either. I quite like you, Bryan, so get going and good luck!'

Bryan leapt out of the chair as if he had been stung. He had the look of a trapped animal and Gabriela couldn't help feeling sorry for him.

Gordon escorted him down the stairs and out into the evening.

'Believe me! Don't come back to Leeds. For your own good, disappear!'

Gordon left him, went back inside and shut the door, locking it. He walked up the stairs, deep in thought. Gabriela had moved back into the kitchen on the next level.

'Well?' she asked as he came in.

'Well, we are going to the meeting tonight. Eleven-thirty, and I hope we come as a surprise for Bryan's handler. If not, we are in deep trouble!'

RENDEZVOUS

The night was dark, the air still, and a touch of frost was falling when they arrived. The two had prepared for the meeting as best they could. Gabriela dropped Gordon off near the rendezvous site half an hour early and, dressed in black, he disappeared into the bushes where he could wait.

Gabriela drove past the site and continued on. She found the experience of driving on the left-hand side of the road challenging, and luckily, there were few cars in the area. In particular, she struggled with the gear stick in her left hand and needed to keep reminding herself where she should be. Gabriela had to play a leading role, and she hoped she was up to it.

Gordon waited in the bushes near to the tennis courts. At this time, the buses had stopped running, and apart from a few late night drinkers leaving the pub up the road, the area was eerily quiet. His loaded pistol was stashed in the back of his trousers. He knew this was a life and death meeting, and he hoped that Gabriela and he would come out of it unscathed. Crouching low, his face blackened, he waited, and the image of his recent time on the great rock at Calpe came to mind. He'd managed to get out of that dangerous situation and he only hoped that he and Gabriela would be as fortunate this time.

The leaves were turning, and some trees had shed their foliage in preparation for the approaching winter months. Fortunately, they were still soft and they would not make his movement audible, but he knew the benefit of remaining like a statue. Human eyes are particularly attuned to movement, even in darkness. A sound of

90

flapping wings broke the quiet as a bird flew from one tree to another, followed by a hoot. Gordon smiled. Is that the same bloody owl? He didn't believe in omens, but even so, he hoped it was a lucky sign.

Remaining motionless made Gordon uncomfortable. Crouched low, his muscles tightened, but he worked through the pain. He didn't expect the man they were meeting would be an amateur like Bryan. They would have a more difficult time subduing this one, he expected. He couldn't think why they would use such an inexperienced man to tail him, but maybe they just saw him as expendable. Gordon hoped Bryan had taken his advice and by now was a long way from Leeds.

He thought about Gabriela, and the danger he was putting her in. She had to drive to the rendezvous and meet Bryan's contact. Dressed in black, and in the dark, he hoped they wouldn't recognise she wasn't Bryan, until the last minute. There was always the danger that they would shoot and just be rid of him, but hopefully, they would want to get his information first. Gordon had to play his part. He wanted to speak with the next up the chain. He wanted more information on the instigator of all this. The name Miroslav Bilyk had been given to him, but why would he want to get rid of Ariadne, Shelley and the guards? Marcus Spinx was in jail and no threat, so why kill his wife?

The hoot of the owl broke his reverie, followed by the sound of a car approaching. On the other side of the tennis courts was the main road, a small lay-by for buses and the main park gates. Tall trees lined the road, and the flagged pavement was uneven, lifted in parts by the roots of the great trees. Lights approached from the direction of his old school. Gordon kept his face down so the lights didn't catch his eyes and give his presence away.

The car pulled to the side of the road almost adjacent to the bushes that sheltered Gordon, and the engine and the lights were cut. Everything went back to its eerie silence. Gordon couldn't help but hope that the car didn't contain a courting couple, oblivious to the arranged meeting. He didn't want the arrangement muddied.

The car remained unmoving, silent and in darkness. It was twenty-past eleven. By arriving early, they got to check the lie of the land. A sensible precaution, and he felt whoever was in the car would be surveying the area, checking for anything unusual, not that they had reason to suspect Bryan. He was simple cannon-fodder, a foot soldier who served his master without having any knowledge of what was going on, and they liked it that way.

Gordon kept watching, immobile and getting more uncomfortable by the minute. He couldn't check his watch as the light from it would be a giveaway that he was there. Just when he wondered if Gabriela would arrive, there was the sound of a car approaching from the opposite direction. The new vehicle came to a stop opposite the parked car, but ten yards back and after a second or two, the lights were turned off and on in quick succession.

Gordon was so close he could almost reach across and touch the first car, but he didn't move. He felt pride that Gabriela had kept her nerve, driven the car on the opposite side than she was used to, and remembered the signal.

The other car flashed its headlights and matched the signal that Bryan had explained. There was a brief pause and Gabriela's driver door opened and a figure in black got out. Gordon barely recognised her silhouette as she stood in the road. Another figure got out of the other car, mere inches away from where Gordon hid.

A voice called out.

'What was so important we had to meet? What have you got to say?'

The voice that answered was not Bryan's nor Gabriela's.

'Do anything and you are a dead man!'

Gordon whispered this into the man's ear. He held the pistol to the stranger's head, leaving him in no doubt what it was. In response, the man raised his arms.

'Now, let's get back into your car. Get in the driver's seat. I will be behind you. Any thought of escaping will mean I blow the back of your head off! Do I make myself clear?' he whispered.

The man nodded.

'Let's go.'

As the man got in, Gordon opened the rear door and followed suit.

Both doors shut, and the driver sat, frozen in place.

'Do you have a gun?'

'It's in my jacket pocket.'

Gordon leaned forward and reached over and, whilst holding the gun to the man's head, he removed the pistol. The front passenger door opened and Gabriela got in and sat next to the driver. She left the door slightly ajar and the interior light stayed on.

'Did I do it right?' she said to Gordon.

'You were perfect,' he replied.

He prodded the back of the man's head.

'Who are you?'

'Fuck off!' came the curt reply.

Gordon responded with a heavy blow with the pistol, throwing the man forward, his head striking the steering wheel.

The man sat stunned. He would have a nasty cut, but Gordon had no sympathy.

'I only ask questions once, and I won't hesitate to use force!'

'I'd start talking if I were you. You won't like him if he gets mad!' Gabriela added.

The man turned to her, and she saw him for the first time in the dim light. He appeared about mid-thirties, harsh looking, with Slav features. His nose was prominent and bent in the middle. His cheeks were sunken, and there was the look of an addict about him.

'I don't like him and I don't like you!'

The blow was stronger than before and this time the man slumped, unmoving, head pressed against the steering wheel.

'Don't ever speak to a lady like that!' Gordon said to the unconscious man.

Gordon got out of the car and went to Gabriela's side.

'We can't stay here. We need to go somewhere quiet so I can get some answers from him. Can you follow me in our car? The roads will be quiet, but we will be going quite a long way.'

'Yes,' she replied. 'Is he alright?'

Gordon looked at the man slumped at the wheel. He was breathing.

'Sure. He'll have a hell of a headache when he wakes up, though.'

Gordon dragged him out and into the rear seat. Gabriela was relieved to see his chest rise and fall. Cable ties appeared in Gordon's hand and he fastened the wrists of the man behind his back. He sat him up and fastened the seat belt, holding him in place.

Gabriela's eyes flitted around, checking that no one was seeing what was going on. Luckily, the street was deserted, but the owl called another mournful tone.

Gordon rummaged through his clothing and found the car keys, a mobile phone and a wallet. There was also a loaded magazine in his jacket pocket, and Gordon took it. He leaned in to Gabriela and kissed her.

'You have been brilliant, as always! Follow me!'

Gabriela walked back to her car, started the engine and waited for Gordon. The car she was to follow did a three-point turn and then headed along the road, passing alongside the sports grounds.

When they reached the clock tower, they headed back up the main road the way they had come, along a route Gabriela recognised and then out of the suburbs toward Pool Bank. Gabriela felt more comfortable driving when she had to follow another car. It made keeping on the correct side of the road easier. They passed familiar landscapes until the Dyneley Arms and then headed into unfamiliar areas. Gabriela was wondering what Gordon's plan involved. She knew he intended to capture the man who was Bryan's contact, but he had been hazy about what he intended to do next.

The route led them down a steep incline, and as there were few streetlights, she couldn't see much of the countryside they were now driving through. They carried on for about half an hour and passed through a couple of small settlements before they entered a larger town. Gordon took a left turn and headed along streets that were lined with sizeable houses. The road narrowed, and they headed up a very steep incline and left the houses behind as they climbed up the steep valley side. On her left, the valley was dotted with pinpricks of light, like stars in a clear sky, but above, the night was cloudy and the moon and stars were hidden.

Driving at a slow pace, they approached a large building, took a right and parked on the rough ground. Gabriela parked next to Gordon and got out. The night felt colder, the wind brisker, and the moon suddenly appeared from behind ribbons of clouds. It was quite startling, and she saw the silhouette of a fortress-like structure against the sky.

'The Cow and Calf,' Gordon said, as if she should have heard of it. 'A famous landmark here. It's a cliff left after an ancient landslip. A fabulous beauty spot. Fortunately, there's no one around but us.'

'What are we doing?' she asked, but Gordon didn't reply as he busied himself getting the now conscious man out of the passenger seat.

'We're going for a little walk,' he said. 'I think you'll enjoy the view and then you're going to tell me what I need to know.'

The man said nothing, and Gabriela wondered what Gordon had planned. She had seen what had happened to Shelley and the others, and she wanted those responsible to be brought to justice.

The three made their way up the rough track. They struggled a bit on the difficult trail in the dark. The rough ground conspired to trip weary feet, and the man stumbled several times. Gordon prevented him falling by gripping his arm. The moonlight made the climb possible, but it kept disappearing behind the clouds, forcing them to stop at intervals.

Eventually, they reached the base of the crag, and the three took deep gulps of air. The moon reappeared and the valley could be seen spread out before them in grey-scale. The lights of the town sparkled, and the roads were intermittent rivers of light. Above them, the black, forbidding rock appeared, a gothic setting for an act of tragedy, and Gabriela shivered, but not from the cold air.

They stood near an opening that was dark, silent, and sheltered from the wind.

'Up we go!' Gordon urged, and the unwilling man struggled upward on a narrower and steeper trail, his arms still bound behind his back. Gordon realised this was now an impossibility. He pulled out a penknife, flicked the blade out. The steel caught the moonlight and shone with a mercurial lustre. Gabriela caught her breath. The man's face turned even paler in the moonlight, if that was possible, and he gasped.

'Don't try to run! You are dead if you do!'

Gordon's tone was far colder than the night air. He cut the ties and released the man's hands. He rubbed them to get the feeling back, and then felt his head, checking the damage. The man didn't have time for much before a pistol jabbed into his ribs got him moving again. They reached the top of the cliff and Gabriela struggled along behind. By the time she reached them, Gordon was standing behind the man at the edge of a drop into the quarry.

The wind was quite blustery, and the man looked into Gordon's eyes and saw something that clearly frightened him.

'Now, the last time I asked you, you tried to be clever. Believe me, I'm not joking, so don't try it again. If you answer my questions, I will let you go. Do you understand?'

Gordon's voice had a frosty edge, much like the wind that was gusting around them. The moon reappeared and Gabriela saw how close the man was to the edge. She had a flashback to Calpe, where she was held on the sea cliff edge, and she froze in fear.

The man nodded.

'Who do you work for?'

'If I tell you, I am a dead man!'

The voice was calm and had a sincerity that Gordon believed.

'If you don't tell me, then you are a dead man, anyway!'

'There are ways to die. Some are preferable to others. I won't tell you.'

Gordon paused and thought about the situation, and then he tried another tack.

'Does the name Miroslav Bilyk mean anything to you?'

For a fleeting moment, there was a look of shocked surprise, and Gordon knew the answer.

'Thank you! That answers that question. Did he kill Shelley Jones?'

On this occasion, a puzzled look crossed the man's face.

'Ok. Did he kill Ariadne Spinx?'

The man could not hide his response, and again it was clear the name was familiar.

'You're going to do something for me! You are going to make a phone call to Mr Bilyk. Call him now!'

The man looked scared at this.

'Can I have a cigarette? I need to calm my nerves.'

Gordon nodded, and the man pulled out a packet and lighter. Gordon took them off him. He passed the man a cigarette and used his lighter. There was a sudden flare as the gas ignited and Matija leaned forward and drew in a deep drag, lighting the end of the cigarette. He pulled the smoke into his lungs and blew it out with a deep force.

Gordon pulled out the mobile he had taken earlier. He passed it over and the man's hands shook with fear as he took it.

'You have the number, I'm sure, so don't mess with me!'

'I can't do it! He will kill me!'

The man's voice spoke the truth, and Gordon recognised it.

'Well, if you don't, I will kill you. Make the call and I will let you go. You will have a brief opportunity to get away. You will have a chance. If you don't, you will die now.'

Gabriela knew this was the pivotal moment, a knife-edge, and the man could go either way. His face in the light revealed him weighing his options. There wasn't a good choice, but the need to survive won out.

He punched a series of numbers into the phone and then paused.

'Tell him where you are, who you are with, what happened and that I want to speak to him!'

Gordon's voice held nothing back. Anger and passion convinced the man, and he tapped the call button.

A voice came on the phone.

'Yes?'

'It's me, Matija. I need to tell you something.'

Matija spoke to the man on the phone and told him what had happened, where he was, and that Gordon wanted to speak with him.

A series of expletives were clearly audible, and the intent was obvious. He passed the mobile back to Gordon.

'Mr Bilyk, I have your man here. Yes, he is well, at the moment, standing on the very edge of a cliff. He took a bit of persuading, but he told me. You murdered my ex-wife, Mr Bilyk. That was a mistake! A big mistake! I am coming for you, and I will kill you! I just thought I should let you know. He has told me many things about you and your business. I am coming! You won't know where or when, but I am coming! Good night, Mr Bilyk. I'll pass you back. See you soon!'

Gordon didn't wait for an answer, but passed the mobile back. Matija shook and his voice was desperate.

'Yes?'

'Можеш да бежиш, али не можеш да се сакријеш! Имам твоју породицу и они ће умрети ако се не убијеш!'

The voice was loud enough to understand the anger, if not the meaning of the Serbian, but Matija just stood horrified. Without warning, he stepped back into thin air and plummeted down to the rock-strewn quarry below.

There was a dull thump, but the darkness obscured the man's death. Gabriela cried out, and Gordon was stunned. Matija had chosen the quick death rather than the one Bilyk would have delivered. Gordon turned to Gabriela and held her in his arms. The moment was brief, but necessary for them both.

'I'm sorry, Gabriela. I would have let him go!'

'I know, but something made him. What did the man say?'

'I can't speak Serbian, but I don't think he was giving him a choice. Come on. I need to get the phone back.'

The clamber down was easier, but neither wanted to enter the quarry. Gabriela remained at the entrance whilst Gordon went in. He found the body spread-eagled and broken. The light from the moon revealed the dead man. His skull had struck a boulder and was crushed. The mobile took some finding, but it was intact and Gordon took it and returned to Gabriela. He needed the information on the phone, but more importantly, he didn't want the police finding his DNA on it. It would take more than the truth to get him out of that situation.

The two hurried back to where they'd left the cars. Gordon got in the hire car and moved it away from the other. Gabriela waited in the passenger seat whilst Gordon got back out, and went back to Matija's car. Fumbling in the glove box, he pulled out some papers and stuffed them into the petrol filler. Gordon struck the lighter, held the flame against the paper and hurried back to Gabriela. There was a sudden whoosh. The petrol ignited and an ear-shattering explosion followed and the car burst into flames.

COGS TURN

Marcus Spinx was beside himself with anger and despair. He felt impotent, and that was a feeling he had rarely felt before, but he had made some progress. He had sworn that he would find out who had killed Ariadne and have his revenge, and he had at least succeeded in part. In his cell, he worried he would go out of his mind, and without his birds, he possibly would have.

It was not as if he had been left alone. The murder of his wife meant that he had spent hours being interviewed by the police. Did he have anyone who wished him harm? He almost laughed at that one. Had he received any threats? Yes, he had been threatened many times, but he always ensured any threat was removed. There was even some questioning whether he had fallen out with his wife, but that was only half-hearted, as it was clear how Ariadne's death had affected him. He had actually helped the police for the first time in his life. He wanted them to find who was responsible, and then he would ensure that they suffered in jail before he finally arranged their demise.

His lawyer had been a regular visitor, particularly as he was lodging an appeal against his conviction. He had a good relationship with her. She was thorough, professional and, above all, his to control. She had assisted his trial lawyer, who had been such a disappointment, but Cherry Jung had shown she had the one thing that he needed, a total lack of morals. He liked her. She had only one aim, and that was to improve her wealth and power. She made a good living, but she wanted more, and he could give her more. Money talked, and she listened and learnt well. He had sounded her out, and she carried through his instructions to the letter. He had tested her, and she hadn't let him down yet. Now he had need of her. She had to get him out, but whilst she was doing that, he wanted her to carry out his wishes on the outside of the prison. Before, Ariadne had been his rock, his reliable lieutenant, but Cherry, beautiful Asian flower, might be the next best thing. Time would tell.

They led him down the corridor into the private room for legal consultations. Cherry was sitting at the table, her briefcase at her side. There was a folder on the table next to her, and she was busy writing when Marcus entered. She looked up at him and smiled. Her almond brown eyes stared at him with predatory intent, and her smile matched to create the impression of a predatory beast. The smart, fashionable suit she wore was tight in the right places, and she knew it. Her makeup was immaculately applied and not a hair on her head was out of place. At a guess, he would put her approaching thirty, and she had come a long way professionally. Defence lawyer work was not for the faint-hearted, but she was clearly thriving.

'Good afternoon, my dear. I hope that you have some good news for me! All I seem to have had recently has been dreadful.'

Marcus' demeanour surprised his lawyer. In his situation, she wouldn't have been so calm. She couldn't help being impressed by her client. Though considerably older than she was, there was something attractive about his calm, his presence and, of course, his money. She liked money, and it appeared he had a lot. Her firm was expensive, but value for money, for those who could afford their services.

'Mr Spinx, it is good to see you. Yes, I believe I may have some better news for you. My condolences on the death of your wife. I can't imagine the shock and grief it must have caused you. A terribly strange and confronting matter.'

'I can't express my grief, Miss Jung. Ariadne was my world. I trusted her implicitly! Now she's gone and I have no one on my side.'

'I can assure you that you do, Mr Spinx. I am on your side!'

'You are very kind, Miss Jung.' Marcus smiled as he said this and Cherry Jung beamed in response.

She spent the rest of the meeting giving her client an account of the progress of the appeal. She explained how the missing prosecutor, and the death of his wife, had thrown the case into turmoil. The police had failed to make any obvious case, and she was going to apply for bail on compassionate grounds. The police would oppose it, but it was worth a try, in the circumstances.

'I will need you to make a convincing broken and grieving widower, Mr Spinx. I am sure you can do that.'

'Believe me, Miss Jung, it will not be acting.'

'Of course! Of course! Please call me Cherry, Mr Spinx.'

'Only if you call me Marcus, Cherry.'

That was it! The situation suited both lawyer and client. It was as if a contract had been signed and the two were now partners. At the end of the meeting, they shook hands and the skin contact was longer than required professionally. She felt the tingle of excitement, and he felt the seal of a deal.

'Goodbye, Cherry. I look forward to hearing more good news from you.'

'Goodbye, Marcus. I will be back tomorrow, and I will bring more details regarding the court date. It has been a genuine pleasure!'

She smiled in a manner that hinted at more than professional niceties, turned and walked to the door, swaying just the right amount on her heels. She knocked on the door and the guard opened it. One escorted Marcus back to the cell. The other escorted Cherry Jung out of the building. It was clear which one enjoyed the task more.

Marcus Spinx could hardly take the smug look off his face. He had provided Cherry Jung with some detailed instructions and he was confident she would carry them out. When he was alone in his cell, he allowed his true feelings to well up to the surface. He was disconsolate, and he shook with raw emotion. It took a while for him to regain control, as he truly loved Ariadne, and her loss was the biggest blow he had ever taken. It was even greater than his imprisonment. For a man in his position and power, he could not show weakness. He had been attacked, his power slighted, and if he was to keep his business empire together, he had to act, be seen to act, and the consequences had to be terrible. The first problem was discovering which of his enemies had been responsible. When he knew who it was, then he would strike. By using the swimming pool, the killer was sending a message to him. It mimicked Ariadne's trademark method. He wondered who it was. Ariadne had been about to kill the prosecutor's partner. He had always kept himself at arm's length from how she disposed of his enemies, but his wife had seemed to relish the experience.

Cherry should be able to pass the request to his contact in the local police force. Something as major as assassinating the wife of one of the major crime figures was bound to have created a lot of interest, and tongues would wag. If anyone could discover who was behind it, his informer would. He had instructed Cherry to offer inducements, and he had provided her with the location of a working cash fund. His worry was that she would not be trustworthy, but then, he had that in order.

Later that afternoon, there was a gentle tap on his door. Marcus returned the two finches to their cage with gentle, soothing words. Then he sat in his comfortable, non-issue chair and called out.

'Come in!'

The door opened slowly and warder Franco Paparone put his head around.

'I hope I'm not disturbing you, Mr Spinx?'

'No, Franco. Come in! Come in! I have something I wanted to ask you about.'

A LAUGHING MATTER

Miroslav Bilyk was not a man prone to laughter. In fact, there were many who worked for him, who despite regular business meetings with him, had never seen his face break into a smile. Today proved a first for many of them. He stormed into the boardroom with a wide smile on his face. A stunned silence fell upon those gathered there, and all eyes turned to him. This was a man who did not suffer fools, and when he spoke, he expected others to listen. They were not prepared for the smirk that appeared on their boss's face.

'Good morning, everyone. I hope you are all well on this fine morning. Today's meeting is cancelled. I have received some great news and so why don't you take the day off? Go out into our fabulous city and enjoy yourselves.'

There were stunned expressions on the men and women in the room. They turned at looked at each other. No one was sure what to do. Should they leave? No one wanted to be the first to act.

'Go on! Get out! I mean it!'

Miroslav didn't give instructions more than once, but on this occasion he would be magnanimous. The room filled with the sound of chairs scraping, papers being collected, briefcases snapping shut and then footsteps leaving the room.

'Not you, Pavle. We need to talk.'

The man who had been hesitating returned to the table and stood waiting.

'Take a seat, Pavle. There are some things we need to discuss.'

'Yes, Miroslav.'

'I just wanted to inform you that what we have spoken about

recently happened last night. I think we have made our point! That slag of a bitch and her men took a dip in the pool. I think we will have caught someone's attention. Late night dips can be so dangerous.'

He laughed, or at least the nearest he had ever come to laughing, and it was not a pleasant sound, but Pavle joined in. It was wiser that way.

'Now, one thing about last night, two people went to the house and came very close to going into the pool. They were lucky, but I need you to find out about them. I want them tailed. Who are they and why were they at the Spinx's house? You can do that for me, can't you, Pavle? They used a hire car. I have a name and address. I want them watched! Get back to me quickly. Go!'

He handed an envelope over and watched his man scurry out of the office.

Miroslav sat back into his chair and stared out across the city. The light was bright, and the skyline was filled with cranes and growing buildings. This city was changing! It was not the same place as when he had arrived. It was now his city. He controlled what happened, how it grew, and who would benefit. Of course, the biggest beneficiary was himself, Miroslav Bilyk, leader of the council, entrepreneur, a man with fingers in many pies!

Marcus Spinx had been a thorn in his side for too long, but now he had his revenge and would enjoy making an example of him. He pushed the button on the table and his secretary appeared within seconds.

'Yes, Mr Bilyk?'

'Dana, please me!'

Nothing more was said. The door shut behind the young secretary, and she walked provocatively across the room. The man pushed his chair back, and she stood before him, smiling.

'Of course, Mr Bilyk!'

She knelt down before him. Ten minutes later, she left the office, tidying herself and heading to the private bathroom.

Miroslav remained in his chair, and continued to gaze over the busy, thriving city. Leeds had become a city of wealth, but that wealth was not shared evenly amongst the population. Those that had it were happy to toe the line, and they looked out for themselves. There was no loyalty. That romantic notion of honour among thieves was a myth. It didn't exist! He had the power, and they would be happy to play along with him. Those of Marcus Spinx's circle would either join him, or they would disappear. They knew it! He knew it! Everyone knew it!

Later that day, he received the information he needed. Now he had the names of those who visited Marcus Spinx's house, and he arranged for their removal. The woman appeared of no significance, a Spaniard, but the man was more intriguing., ex-army, ex-mercenary, someone who might be a problem. Could he be working for Spinx? It would be of no consequence once he was eliminated. He gave the orders and they would be carried out. Up to this point, the day had been rather a good one. He pushed the button for Dana. She entered the room with the same enthusiasm as before.

'Yes, Mr Bilyk?'

'I'd like a large whisky, Dana.'

'Will that be all?'

Her face smiled as she spoke, but gave nothing away. A cold fish, he thought to himself, but God, she was hot!

She turned and left the room, but returned a few moments later carrying a drink. On the tray sat the whisky in a lead-crystal glass, and she put a serviette down on the desk and placed the glass on it.

She leaned forward as she did this, but Miroslav watched with only passing interest. He waved her away, and she left the room, unobserved by her boss.

He picked up his drink and savoured the first taste. A man of moderation, he had always been careful with his money. Yes, he rewarded those who served him well, but personally, he lived a relatively quiet life. He was not overly ostentatious, and didn't want to attract too much attention. Marcus Spinx, his onetime rival, had been much more flamboyant. A man seen out and about with the social set of the city, whereas the public viewed him as a hard-working politician and businessman, and that was the way he liked it. Miroslav saw himself as a spider, working hard, building an intricate web and then sitting, waiting to pounce when others got caught in it. This tactic had proved very successful so far, and he was confident that it would continue to be so. Marcus Spinx had walked into his trap, and with his imprisonment, Miroslav was now the dominant player in Leeds.

He led the council and had caused no scandals. Unlike his predecessor, he had improved the lives of the ordinary ratepayers and consolidated his power.

He had two further drinks whilst he waited the afternoon out. He expected news before too long. Dana answered his call and put one of his favourite pieces of music on the record deck. Jazz was his weakness, but not trad-jazz. He preferred something more challenging, and today it was Keith Tippett. Dana knew the exact volume her boss liked, and he sat back in his chair, eyes shut. Life really was good, he thought to himself.

Unfortunately, his good mood was to be short-lived. Pavle broke it to him in the late afternoon. The ashen-faced assistant arrived and when he entered, Miroslav knew.

Pavle expected him to blow up. He knew his boss's ability to erupt, but he recognised when fury overtook him. On these occasions, there was a deadly calm.

'They failed?'

'Yes, sir. Apparently, the targets saw something suspicious around the car and checked. They recognised the device and called the police.'

'I don't like failure, Pavle!'

'No, sir. It won't happen again.'

'Who was in charge?'

'Matija.'

'Let him know there must be no further mishaps. Make it clear!'

'He already knows, Mr Bilyk. The couple are back under observation and he assures me he won't let you down this time.'

'Go!'

Pavle fled the room. Even though he wasn't personally responsible for the failure, he knew the fate of those who were. Matija had been lucky. Miroslav had been in a good mood. Miroslav Bilyk was a good boss, when things were going well, but a terrible one if you let him down.

It was late that night that Miroslav was awoken from his sleep by his mobile ringing. His men and women knew not to disturb him unless it was vital. In the circumstances, he suspected the call wouldn't be good news.

He fumbled on the bedside table, disturbed his wife, lying asleep next to him, and swiped his phone to answer the call.

He didn't use the usual greeting, but just said 'Yes,' as he got to his feet on the way out of the bedroom. The voice on the other end spoke.

'It's me, Matija. I need to tell you something.'

The conversation was brief and cut off by another man's voice.

'Mr Bilyk, I have your man here. Yes, he is well at the moment. Standing on the very edge of a cliff. He took a bit of persuading, but he has confirmed what I thought. You murdered my ex-wife, Mr Bilyk. That was a mistake! A big mistake! I am coming for you, and I will kill you! I just thought I should let you know. He has told me all sorts of things about you and your business. I am coming! You won't know where or when, but I am coming! Goodnight, Mr Bilyk. I'll pass you back. See you soon!'

Miroslav remained silent. He felt an unnatural stillness. He wasn't scared, but he could tell from the voice that the man on the phone meant what he said. It wasn't an idle threat.

Matija spoke, and Miroslav answered him in Serbian,

'I have your family and they will die if you don't kill yourself!'

Silence followed, and in a matter of seconds, the phone went dead. Miroslav assumed his man was likewise.

He considered the man who had threatened him. He was more than a nuisance now. Was the man indestructible? Miroslav was the hunter and would not become the hunted. Now wide-awake, his brain worked overtime. He went down to the kitchen, poured himself a whisky, and added a couple of ice cubes before making a call. A sleepy sounding voice answered,

'Hello?'

'Pavle, it's me. He failed again! I need to see you!'

That was the whole of the conversation. Miroslav knew he wouldn't have to wait long, and he had a little time to think, but more importantly, he needed information.

He drank the drink in one go and poured another, which he left in the kitchen whilst he returned to his room and began to dress.

'What is it, Miro?'

His wife's voice muttered, still deep in sleep, and he replied,

'It's nothing, dear. Go back to sleep. Just work. You know how busy the council work can be. Go back to sleep. Nothing to worry about!'

In reality, he suspected this wasn't true. He was worried. It was rare for his men to let him down. By failing, one of them had stirred up a hornet's nest. It should have been plain sailing with Marcus Spinx in jail. Had it been a mistake eliminating Ariadne Spinx? She was a mad one, a sadist, and the world was a better place without her, but it was too late now. He would have to wait and see.

Whatever, he wasn't going to sit back and let someone come after him. There could be no failure. Mr Gordon Bennet had to be eradicated!

He was back in the kitchen, finishing his second drink, when he heard a car on his gravel driveway. Pavle had arrived. They had worked together for a long time, and his countryman had proven a very useful and reliable deputy. Miroslav had grown to trust the man, and nowadays left the finer details of any dirty work to him. He had never let him down, and the men he employed had carried out whatever was required to the letter. Something had gone wrong this time, and he had a niggling feeling the man they had been sent to eliminate was the issue.

Miroslav needed information, and he needed it fast.

He opened the door before Pavle had time to knock. The counsellor didn't want his wife disturbing any more tonight.

'Come in, and keep the noise down,' he said, holding the door open.

The two men walked into the kitchen. Miroslav poured another drink and handed it to Pavle.

'We have a problem,' said Miroslav, and he recounted the events of the night.

'Shit! I'm sorry, boss. I thought he was a good man. I can't think what went wrong.'

'We need to sort this out. I don't enjoy being threatened. I need to know everything about Mr Gordon Bennet and his woman. We still have our contact in the filth?'

'We do! I'll contact him and find out all I can. I'll do it as soon as we've finished.'

'Make sure you do! Now, what do we already know?'

By the end of the conversation, Miroslav was updated. He learnt Gordon Bennet was the ex-husband of Shelley Jones, the other murdered woman. He was ex-army, and had been living in Spain for a while. The two were staying in his place in Oakwood, and only been back a few days. They had arrived at Marcus Spinx's house during Ariadne Spinx's elimination. Shelley Jones was just unlucky to be there. She was of no interest to Miroslav, apart from her partner being the prosecutor who had put Spinx away.

His military and mercenary background suggested he could be trouble, and Miroslav couldn't shake the feeling of dread he had felt when the man threatened him on the phone. His calmness and certainty were unnerving. He tried to push this behind him.

After Pavle left, he returned to his bed to get a few hours' rest. Sleep escaped him and after a couple of hours, he gave up. He got up and readied himself for the coming day, hoping it would be better than the previous one had turned out to be.

TALLY HO

Gabriela was devastated by the death at the quarry, the suddenness and the finality of the man falling back into the darkness. She understood Gordon hadn't wanted it. He took the man there to frighten him, but not to kill him. Whatever the man on the phone said to him, their captive felt there was no choice, and the calm way he disappeared over the edge into oblivion was chilling.

Gordon had not spoken since he had torched the man's car. He had got back into the hire car and driven away from the Cow and Calf, away from Ilkley, and headed over the moors. He took a roundabout way, but he was heading home. Behind them, the night sky glowed, lit by the burning car. Suddenly there was a flash of light, followed by a rumble, as the fuel tank exploded. If there had been any doubt that the burning car would have gone unnoticed, it was now gone. It was only a matter of time before the fire brigade and police appeared, and Gordon wanted to be a long way away when that happened. The dead man was a different matter. He might go undiscovered for hours. The police would assume the burning car was the end of some joy-rider's escapade, and it would be daylight before anyone entered the quarry.

After twenty minutes, Gordon slowed the car down. He didn't want to draw attention. He hoped to avoid cameras until he was back in the suburbs and then there would be little, if anything, to link them to the excitement on Ilkley Moors.

For the first time since they arrived back, the gods smiled upon them. There were no incidents, and they re-entered the city suburbs unnoticed.

'I'm so sorry, Gabriela. I didn't mean for any of this to happen. I wanted this to be a holiday, that's all.'

'I know.'

Her voice was quiet and flat.

This worried Gordon. He had never seen her so down. Even after the Calpe incidents, her spirits had remained high. He drove back to his house, parked the car, and the two entered his home. As it was late, they got undressed and slipped into bed.

Despite her exhaustion, Gabriela kept reliving the night in her mind. Over and over again, she saw the man fall backwards into the quarry to his death. She wanted to stop him, but she was unable to move. As she relived it, he looked into her eyes and in his, she saw blankness.

She awoke, screaming, and Gordon jumped up. He held her in his arms, comforted her and told her she was safe, but she knew he was lying. She wasn't safe. Neither of them were. She was shaking, but she took comfort from his strong arms. Deep inside, she believed she would never be alright. She never wanted to fall asleep again.

They got up and decided a hot drink might help calm their nerves, or at least Gordon did. They sat at the kitchen table and Gordon reached across and held her hands.

'I'm sorry, Gabriela. This is a nightmare. Maybe we should go back to Calpe and leave this to the police. I don't think those after us will follow us there.'

'You don't believe that, Gordon. I know you don't. What's more, you would never rest knowing that Shelley's killers were still free.'

'I'd do it for you, Gabriela, because I love you. I feel, no, I am certain I have brought you nothing but bad luck. I don't want to lose you, and nothing I can ever do will bring Shelley back!'

'No! We'll see it through. I couldn't live with myself if I didn't and I think it would create a wedge between us. It is all so horrible, Gordon. I just want there to be two of us, no killings, and no danger. And I want to be able to sleep again.'

'When this is finally over, we will go back to Calpe and spend our lives together. No danger, no deaths, just the two of us, boring and ordinary.'

Gabriela smiled for the first time in a long while.

'You will never be boring, Gordon. There will always be something going on where you are, but I would rather be with you, no matter what. Can we go back to bed?'

He didn't argue, and left the kitchen with his arm around her, knowing he had brought her nothing but misfortune. She was emotionally drained, and he had to help her get through it.

This time she slept, and Gordon watched her as she struggled with the nightmares. She needed to recover and, even though tormented, the sleep would help her through it. Together, they had endured some dreadful times, but together they would come out the other side. She was right. If the person responsible for Shelley's death was free, he could never rest. He had told Miroslav Bilyk he was coming for him, and he was, but a man like that wouldn't wait for him to turn up. He would bring the hunt to Gordon and Gabriela.

This powerful man would stop at nothing, but Gordon equally would stop at nothing to bring Miroslav Bilyk to justice and Gabriela would be with him every step of the way.

The sleeping woman eventually calmed. She became more relaxed and finally Gordon allowed himself to fall asleep. The sunlight filtering through the curtains woke him. It was not bright, but had a watery hue, dull and pale. The seasons were changing and autumn was well on its way. He got out of bed, trying not to disturb Gabriela. She needed as much rest as she could get, and he feared they may struggle to get any over the next few days.

He made it to the kitchen and put a pot of coffee on the stove. The water took only a short time to boil. There was the hissing that signalled it was ready, and he turned the gas off as the kitchen filled with the heady aroma of fresh coffee. He searched for something he could prepare for breakfast, but finding nothing, he went to the shops quickly.

Gordon was nervous about leaving Gabriela asleep in the house. He had past form where that was concerned, but he reasoned it should be alright. He would be surprised if his nemesis would have been able to put a plan into action at such short notice.

As he closed the door behind him, he looked to see if anyone was watching. The road was deserted, apart from the man who lived across from his house coming back from the woods with his dog.

He came to a decision and almost ran to the bakery, bought a selection of pastries, and hurried back. If he had not been in such a hurry not to leave Gabriela alone any longer than necessary, he may have noted a familiar face watching him from a distance.

The man made sure he was hidden, but he kept Gordon in constant sight. He had been given a very early morning phone call, with orders he didn't like. Once he had started along this path, he couldn't leave. Twenty-two pieces of silver didn't seem worth the price anymore. He watched the man hurry back to his home and the woman inside, and he felt a mixture of envy and fear. Gordon Bennet, he knew, was not a man to be trifled with, but Miroslav Bilyk had unlimited resources he could deploy and, by sheer numbers alone, he would prevail. Thankfully, his task was solely to provide information. He had to confirm that the two targets were in the house, and leave the rest to others.

From a distance, he watched Gordon approach his doorway, but saw him stop, bend down and pick up an envelope. With the envelope in his hand, Gordon turned and scanned the street. The watcher dived behind a high gateway. When he felt it was safe to come out, he saw the door closed and the street empty. He assumed Gordon had gone back inside. Assumed, but he couldn't be certain. If he made the call now and it turned out wrong, he would be in deep trouble, but he didn't really have a choice. Taking out his mobile, he dialled and sent a text message.

'They are inside.'

After a brief pause, a message came back.

'Leave now.'

His part was complete. He was free to go. But why did he feel so guilty? It was never easy to betray a friend.

Gordon was surprised by the envelope. It hadn't been there when he left. Yes, he'd been in a rush, but he couldn't have missed it. That meant that someone had been to the door whilst he had been around the corner. They must have been watching. He didn't like this, and he hurried inside and ran up the stairs, opening the envelope. He pulled the white paper out and read three words.

'GET OUT NOW!'

'Shit! Shit! Shit!. Gabriela! Are you up?'

The stunning Spaniard stood in the kitchen, dressed and looking startled.

'What is it, Gordon? What's wrong?'

'I don't know, but we have to get out now!'

She rushed to grab her handbag and Gordon ran downstairs to get his pistol and ammunition. He threw them into his rucksack as Gabriela reappeared with her handbag and jacket.

'Come on! We must get out of here!'

The house had only one entrance and exit, and Gordon hesitated at the door. The car could be a problem. They had used a device before. Maybe they would try again.

'Come on. When I open the door, we are heading down the street to the wood. Don't stop for anything. If we can get to the wood, we have a chance. Are you ready?'

Gabriela nodded, and Gordon opened the door and dragged her out after him. He ran towards the end of the street despite it being deserted. The green sanctuary beckoned, but the hundred yards seemed a mile. The only sound was the clatter of their feet. No one followed, which surprised him. They had gone fifty yards when everything changed. There was an almighty flash and roar. His home, and those on either side, erupted in a bright light and then a cloud of dust. His ears were crashed by the sound-wave. He lost his hearing and his footing, staggered and fell, pulling Gabriela down with him. It then began to rain, but this was not a gentle shower, but stone, brick and metal rained down on the street and the cars. Anyone who had been near the explosion would be dead, and they had barely escaped. Gordon reacted quickly. Gabriela was already stirring, and the two stared back along the street, stunned. They got back on their feet and sprinted the rest of the way to the wood. There was no hesitation now. They were running for their lives.

The remaining distance seemed to take forever. Despite the two being shrouded in a world of silence, the surrounding area was springing into action in a shocked response to the explosion. The rain of debris had stopped, but the dust cloud hung like fog. This was probably what enabled Gordon and Gabriela to escape undetected, as there was no pursuit. They reached the trees and vanished into the dense greenery, before the cloud settled, covering the wrecked cars, gardens and fallen trees in a heavy grey sheet.

The two lay in the undergrowth, staring back, and as the cloud thinned they saw a gaping hole, like some extracted tooth. Where Gordon's home had been, a small pile of rubble remained, and the houses on either side lay in ruins, damaged beyond repair. Gordon didn't think that anyone in the neighbouring houses could have survived such carnage. The street looked like a war zone, and it probably was.

Neither of them could hear anything but a ringing in their ears. Speaking was pointless. They watched to see if they were pursued, but all they saw were bewildered residents staggering onto the street, dazed and confused. One or two had phones in their hands, filming the aftermath of the explosion, but it appeared someone was calling for the emergency services. This was major! Police, the fire brigade and ambulance service would all be on their way.

The numbness slowly faded, replaced with ringing that was almost painful. Gordon wondered if their hearing was permanently damaged. The chaos continued in the street, but eventually some residents got organised and approached the damaged buildings, looking for survivors.

The first sign that their hearing was returning was the muffled clamour of the sirens.

Gordon turned to Gabriela.

'Are you alright?'

'I think so,' she said, but the words were distant sounding. 'My ears! I think I am deaf.'

'Hopefully it will clear. God, we were lucky! Just a minute or two later and we would have been trapped inside, and that would have been it for us.'

'How did you know?'

'There was an envelope on the doorstep. It just said, Get out now! Someone knew what was happening and warned us, but who?'

Gabriela reached over and squeezed his hand.

'It seems you are a hard man to kill, Mr Bennet!'

'You too, Miss Morales!'

He leaned over and kissed her dirty face.

They stayed where they were and watched the unfolding drama. In a surprisingly short time, the first police-car and fire engine arrived. Even for the highly trained emergency workers, the scene was shocking. The firemen and women were the first to organise themselves and hoses were rolled out and the fires that were gaining hold in the ruins of the houses were tackled quickly. Firefighters were able to get on with their job as the police kept the crowds back. The ambulances arrived whilst order was being restored, but they were prevented from searching for survivors until the site was declared safe for them to enter. There were no signs of casualties, but the pile of rubble could have buried victims. Gordon knew the neighbours well, but he hadn't spoken to them since he had returned to Leeds. There were elderly couples on both sides, all retired. He prayed they had been out of their homes, but he feared they weren't. 'What are we going to do, Gordon?' Gabriela spoke quietly. The ringing had now faded in intensity and the initial shock had subsided.

'We are going to make whoever is responsible pay! This is becoming a war, Gabi. I need to speak with Peter. He might have some information. We will need to contact Inspector Glover.'

As Gordon said this, a figure strolled down the rubble-strewn street as if he were on a Sunday stroll.

'Talk of the devil! Come on, Gabriela. We can't stay here. Let's go meet the inspector. Before we do, we were just out for a walk when the blast happened. Don't mention the note. Ok?'

'I understand.'

'Come on, then!'

The two got to their feet and walked back along the street to where the inspector stood. They looked a right pair, faces covered in dust, clothes filthy and both had cuts from smaller flying debris. The cuts were not deep, but they produced a dramatic effect as the two zombie-like figures approached the inspector. A police officer stepped forward with her hand raised to stop them, but the inspector saw them and shouted for her to let them through.

'Well, here's a turn up for the books,' he said. 'I knew this was your house and feared the worst. I don't suppose there is any chance this was a gas leak?'

The inspector's face remained stoic, but his left eyebrow raised, and for him, this was a sign of concern and surprise. This complete catastrophe was not the usual work he was involved in and it would take a lot of manpower to get to the bottom of it. Initially, it appeared an accident, a gas leak, maybe, but as soon as he heard the location and the owner of the building, he had no such thoughts. Someone had tried to kill this couple, and they had tried again. They were becoming more desperate, it appeared, but Mr Gordon Bennet seemed to have more lives than a cat, and Gabriela Morales the same.

'Someone seems to want us dead, Inspector,' Gordon said, and Gabriela looked at him with a wan smile.

'So it would appear! You are both injured. I will arrange for an ambulance to take you to hospital, and afterwards I need to talk with you. Do not go anywhere!'

'Are you arresting us?' Gordon asked, and his voice held an edge.

'No. Not yet, at any rate, Mr Bennet. I dislike the way things are turning out. This is my city and murders, assassinations and explosions are not what I like. For some reason, they all seem to revolve around you two. I will get to the bottom of it, Mr Bennet. Have no doubt! Make sure you are ready for our talk when the hospital has finished with you.'

The inspector turned and called over a policeman in uniform.

'Take these two to the hospital and make sure they don't disappear. Take a couple of others with you. Do not let them out of your sight. Bring them to me when they are patched up.'

The officer nodded. He went and spoke to two colleagues and then returned.

'Goodbye, Miss Morales, Mr Bennet. I will see you shortly. Get the paramedics to have a quick check and take them to the hospital.'

The inspector walked back to supervise the rescue services. He didn't like so many people trampling all over his crime scene, but there was little he could do. A rescue mission would start when the fire service gave their approval that the site was safe.

He mopped his brow with his handkerchief and sighed. It would be a long day, a long week. He didn't like it and he would make someone suffer. Who was behind all this? He had no idea. His hope was that Gordon Bennet did.

A RINGING IN THE EARS

The check-up in the hospital was fairly uneventful. Despite the dirt, blood and destruction of the street, the doctors were quite pleased with Gabriela's and Gordon's condition. The cuts were superficial and required a clean and a dressing. The biggest concern for the medical staff was the damage to the hearing of the two patients. Much of their hearing had returned, but both felt it was still muffled. They had headaches, and the doctor wanted them to have a check in a week's time.

They were allowed to leave, and the police escorted them back for an interview with Inspector Glover. Their reception at the police station was less welcoming. The place was fairly chaotic with press gathered outside, police cars coming and going, and the officers inside wearing serious looks on their faces. This was a major event and was not something any of them had experienced in a long while.

They were checked through the front desk and escorted to an interview room where they were asked to sit and wait for the inspector. The room was like every other room in a police station the pair had visited in recent months, and they had visited a surprising number. They were offered a cup of tea or coffee, but both declined. They hoped they would not be in the station for too long.

It surprised Gabriela and Gordon when a woman came in carrying a camera and she took photographs of their head and shoulders.

'Why do you want these?' Gabriela asked.

'I don't know,' the photographer said. 'I just do as I am told. Ask the inspector when he sees you.'

After about ten minutes, the door opened, and the inspector

entered.

'I am told that you got off fairly lightly. I am glad about that Miss Morales, Mr Bennet. This was a very serious matter, and it is the second bomb attack on the two of you. Do you know how many we have had in the last thirty years, here in Leeds? No? Well, let me tell you. None!'

Gordon and Gabriela had nothing to say to this, but they waited for the inspector to continue, which he did.

'Someone wants you dead. I am sure you are aware of that, but I want to know who. We have recovered the bodies of four people in the wreckage. Four innocent victims. Your neighbours, Mr Bennet!'

'I am truly sorry about that, Inspector. I really am!'

Gordon knew the Sewels and the Backhouses quite well. They always spoke to him when they were passing in the street and they had kept a lookout for his house while he was away. Both pairs were elderly and certainly didn't deserve what had happened.

'I had hoped that it was a gas explosion. They are not uncommon, but the arson squad discovered chemical residue and the source. Apparently, Semtex and that is not something that is easy to get a hold of. They tell me it was a professional device, but luckily for you, the detonation was not as professional. I need you to tell me everything that happened this morning. Miss Morales, this officer will take your statement in another room. Please follow her.'

An officer held the door open, and Gabriela followed her out. The inspector remained with Gordon.

'It is not my business, Mr Bennet, but it is not safe for Miss Morales to be here. Send her home!'

'You're right! It's not your business, Inspector. Gabriela will decide when and if she returns home, not you nor me. I wouldn't try to tell her what to do, so I don't reckon much to your chances, but be my guest!'

'I am not trying to tell anyone anything, but it is something you and she should consider! Someone wants you both dead and they won't stop until they succeed.'

'I am a hard man to kill, Inspector. Many have tried, but none have succeeded. We will look after ourselves.'

'Maybe so, but I am offering you accommodation, temporary accommodation. It is a safe house. You won't be a prisoner and can leave whenever you want, but I would advise you to stay there for the time being.'

'That is something we might take you up on, seeing as my house and everything else has been destroyed. Thank you, Inspector.'

'Don't thank me. Apparently, there are people in certain circles who want you housed where they can keep an eye on you. Now! Tell me everything that happened this morning and anything that appeared out of the ordinary.'

They left the police station together and this time they were driven in a civilian car to a safe house. Gabriela had no idea where they were heading, but Gordon recognised the suburbs they passed through. The car stopped outside the main entrance to a large suburban hotel, very near to the Ring Road. Gordon smiled to himself. The inspector was no fool. The easiest place to hide is often in the most visible and therefore unlikely place. A young couple staying in a hotel room was hardly likely to raise any eyebrows. The car park of The Hamlet Hotel was large, and the hotel was more than just accommodation. It hosted a large gym, fitness centre, pool and was a busy centre for entertainment with its bars and restaurant. He knew the hotel and had spent many beery evenings there before he went to Calpe. Gordon had intended to take Gabriela there for a night out, but now it seemed they would they would be spending a while there.

The driver pulled up into a space, turned and spoke to the two in the back.

'Inspector Glover has instructed me to tell you the following. You are to check in under the names of Brian Johnson and Gabbi Romero. A large room is booked for you. I will be next door to provide security. I will swap occasionally and another officer will take over. He suggests you keep a low profile and do nothing to attract attention. You are not under arrest and are free to leave, but he advises you to stay in the hotel.'

The man handed the keys to Gordon.

'This is a hire car in the name of Brian Johnson. BRIAN JOHNSON, by the way, so make sure you sign in correctly,' he said, spelling each letter.

'In the boot are two bags. There is a change of clothes, but you might like to buy some of your own. I have a credit card in the name of Brian Johnson and a limit of ten thousand pounds.'

He passed a leather wallet over to the man in the back.

'That's very kind of the inspector!' said Gordon.

'No, it is not!' the plain clothes officer responded. 'They have arranged for your bank to link the card to your account. This is an emergency measure. Hopefully, it will see you out until we have made some arrests. There is a driving licence in your name and here is a passport for you both. These caused a lot of trouble, so take care of them. You will need to return them when this is all over. Apart from the inspector and myself and colleague, no one else knows your whereabouts. The rumour is that you both died in the explosion. The more people who think that, the safer it will be.'

'We'd like to thank the inspector,' said Gabriela.

'You might like to do that the next time you see him. Remember who you are? Brian and Gabbi. I would suggest you get a rest after such a shock. Whilst in the hotel, you can charge food and drinks to the room. I will get out here and leave you. When we see each other in the hotel, do not acknowledge me unless in an emergency. Good luck!'

The officer got out of the driver's seat and walked off to another part of the carpark. He stopped at a car, pulled out a key, opened the boot, and took out a small travel bag. After locking the boot, he hurried across the tarmac, up the flight of steps, and entered the hotel through the main doors.

Gabriela and Gordon looked at each other. They had been provided with clean, but not very fashionable clothes in the station and allowed to wash, so they had the crumpled look of weary travellers.

'Come on then! I need a shower, a change and a stiff drink, and so do you, Brian!'

Gabriela smiled as she said this.

'I've never slept with a Brian before. Guess there's always a first time.'

Her humour was an attempt to cover up the shock of recent events, but her use of his alias was a necessary reminder. Gordon knew it would be easy to slip up.

'Come on, Gabbi. We had better check in. After you, Miss Romero!'

The two got out of the car. Gordon opened the boot and there were two small suitcases. Gordon took both, and they walked over towards the front door and where the reception was. The hotel entrance was busy with both guests and people using the sporting facilities, and no one paid the new arrivals any attention. Gordon walked up to the reception desk and a young man welcomed them.

'Checking in?' the receptionist asked.

'Yes,' Gordon replied. 'Mr Johnson and Miss Romero.'

'Oh, yes. Booked today. We have a lovely room for you, and so I hope you enjoy your stay. Can I just see some ID?'

Gordon produced the two passports he had been given, and the receptionist gave a cursory glance at the names and the photographs before handing them back. You have room 213 on the second floor. He passed over a folder that held the key cards.

'Welcome to The Hamlet Hotel. I hope you will enjoy your stay. If there are any questions, or anything you need, you can call, or just ask at reception at any time. Do you need any help with your luggage?'

He gave the two small cases a disdainful expression and waited for a reply.

'No, I think we can manage ourselves, thank you.'

'Your room is on the second floor. The lift is just around the corner. Have a pleasant stay, Miss Romero, Mr Johnson.'

Gordon and Gabriela walked to the lift, carrying their cases. They were pleased to get away from the busy foyer, and the quiet of the lift, apart from the music, was a welcome relief. The lift was quick, and they exited on their floor and checked the signs, and then headed to their room. It was only a short walk, and they were on the end of the corridor. They assumed that room 211, the adjacent room, was where the police officer was, but they took no notice, and Gabriela slid the key card into the slot and pushed the door open. Gordon followed behind with the two cases and put them on the large double bed. Gabriela placed the key into the slot in the room and the lights came on. The door shut behind her, but she stopped and slid the security chain in place.

Gordon checked the room for any signs of listening devices and then checked the window. On the other side was a large flat covered open area. He assumed it was the roof of the central part of the building. There were some skylights, but they had stainless steel railings around them. He tried to open the window, but it only opened a couple of inches before a lock stopped it opening fully.

He would get the window restraint unlocked in case they needed an exit.

Gabriela sat on the bed and watched him work. In the past, she would have thought his behaviour was paranoid, but now she realised their safety relied upon his training and skill. In a short while, he seemed satisfied and sat next to her, and the two held each other for a long time.

Finally, they parted, and they took in their new home. The room was comfortable, but not overly large. There was the obligatory flat screen TV, bar fridge and tea-making facilities, a double sofa, a spacious bathroom and a serviceable wardrobe, particularly as they had so little luggage. Gabriela had opened both suitcases and was inspecting the clothing they held. There were several sets of underwear, and someone had done a reasonable job of matching the clothes to the size of the two of them.

Gabriela frowned at the uninspiring clothes, but she realised it was better than nothing.

'We will have to go and buy some basics,' she said. 'I can't put up with these for more than a day.'

Gordon smiled.

'I'm sure we can do that. I have a credit card.'

'And I know how to use it,' she added.

There hadn't been much to smile about recently, but Gordon and Gabriela both did. He knew, once again, why he loved this woman. Nothing seemed to hold her down for long.

'I'm having a shower,' Gabriela said. 'You check the fridge for a drink. I could do with something strong. It's not every day that your home gets blown up!'

'Will do!' Gordon answered, and he opened the fridge whilst Gabriel entered the bathroom, a bundle of clothes in her hands.

The fridge was pleasantly stocked with a wide range of overpriced spirits, beers and soft drinks. Gordon ignored those and found two small bottles of red wine. Taking two tumblers, he divided the first bottle of chateau plonk into the glasses. He took a sip and winced, but shortly a warming of the throat and stomach confirmed it was at least alcoholic.

With his drink, he sat on the couch listening to the shower and Gabriela's movements in the bathroom. He pictured the scene, but at the moment his need for a drink and time to think overruled his natural desire to join the beautiful Spanish woman.

He was worried. He would only admit this to himself, and for the first time he wondered if he should take Gabriela back to Calpe and forget all about what had happened. He knew he couldn't. He hadn't wanted this. Trouble had found him out. He pictured the pool with the victims tied to their chairs. He wondered what their feelings were in those final moments. The fear they had felt. The knowledge that all the things they had hoped to do in the rest of their lives would never happen. He thought of Shelley. The two had shared some good times before he had fallen apart and driven a wedge between them. He had cared for her, but he realised now he had never loved her. At least, not in the way he loved Gabriela. He had always wished his ex-wife well. She had sought his help when her partner, Paul, had disappeared. He failed to solve that mystery, and she had been killed.

He had suspected Marcus Spinx was behind it all, but Spinx's wife, Ariadne, was also murdered, so it looked as if someone else was behind it. Someone had provided him with a name, and that was the only real clue. The man following them in Leeds market led them up the chain and now he had threatened Miroslav Bilyk.

Clearly, Bilyk didn't like threats. They bombed his house the next morning. He and Gabriela would be dead, if not for the warning message. This just gave them the minutes to get out of the house.

His ears were still ringing, and there was a dull muffling to his hearing. He took another drink of the red wine, grimaced, but welcomed the warm glow.

He needed time to think. Everything had been such a rush since they arrived back in Leeds. He was lost in thought when Gabriela appeared. She was dressed in a plain t-shirt and tracksuit pants. He smiled at her, and she smiled back.

'Not the most glamorous outfit, but functional,' she said.

'Maybe not, but you make anything sexy!'

And she did.

'Go have a shower. You'll feel better. Is that drink for me?'

She looked towards the full glass sitting next to the kettle.

'It sure is, but don't expect too much. It is certainly vin ordinaire!'

He grabbed a few clothes from his bag and disappeared into the bathroom, giving Gabriela a quick kiss as he passed.

He stripped off his dirty clothes and got into the shower and ten minutes later returned to the bedroom a new man.

Gabriela had almost finished her drink, and she pulled an

exaggerated grimace as the wine passed her lips.

'I told you so!' Gordon said. 'Would you like another?'

Gabriela held out her glass, and he filled it and did the same to his own.

'Cheers,' he said.

She touched her glass to his and then took a drink, pulled her face and laughed.

'You look good,' she joked at his tracksuit and t-shirt. 'Quite an improvement on your usual outfit!'

'I thought you'd like it,' he laughed. 'We'll need to do some shopping, but that will wait until tomorrow. Are you hungry?'

'Starving!'

'How about we go down to the bar and get a decent drink and something to eat?'

'Will that be alright? Is it safe?'

'I should think so. We have the boys in blue looking out for us, and no one knows we are alive. Come on. Oh, where is the laundry bag? We can get our clothes cleaned for the morning, and then we can buy some replacements.'

Gabriela passed him the bag. Her clothes were already in it. He added his and phoned down to room service, and reception told him to leave the bag outside the room.

Picking up his wallet, he took the key and opened the door for Gabriela. She walked out into the corridor and stared nervously around. Gordon shut the door behind him, left the bag of laundry, and looked up and down the empty corridor.

The room next door where the policeman was staying was silent.

'Come on,' he said, loud enough so that if anyone inside was listening, they would know they were leaving. They didn't bother using the lift, as there were only a couple of flights of stairs to go down.

They reached the foyer and walked into the busy bar. It was a sports bar, with several televisions showing soccer matches. There was a raised seating area with tables, and a lower tabled section, but the bar extended further into the back. On the outside, they saw a terrace that romantically looked over the car park.

They walked to the bar, ordered drinks and bar meals. Then they took the drinks and went to sit at a window table in a quieter part.

'This seems so strange, Gordon. Do you think we are safe? Is anyone watching us?'

'I think we are as safe as we can be at the moment. Give me five minutes, and I'll tell you if our bodyguard is here. See if you can find them.'

SHOPPING

It didn't take Gabriela long to have a go at identifying the officer keeping an eye out for them. A man of about thirty was sitting at the bar, on his own, drinking a pint slowly. His place at the end of the bar enabled him to have a clear view as he sat sideways on the bar stool. A newspaper was open, and he made a show of reading, stopping every few minutes to scan the patrons. She pointed him out to Gordon.

'Good try, but I don't think so. Have you noticed the young woman sitting in the coffee bar?'

Gabriela followed Gordon's gaze outside the bar area and into the coffee lounge. A woman of about mid to late thirties sat in fitness clothing, resting, enjoying a drink after working out.

'It can't be her!'

'I think you'll find that it is. If you look carefully, there is no sign of perspiration. She came down the stairs, not up from the gym. She has been watching us off and on since she arrived. Why don't you go and ask her?'

'I can't do that!'

'You could, but why spoil her afternoon? If she is still here when we have finished our meal, then we will know. Just keep an eye on her.'

The meal arrived as they finished talking. Both felt so hungry that they didn't speak for a while. The meal was plain, but welcome, and Gordon returned to the bar to supplement their drinks. Gordon looked at how he was dressed and became a little self-conscious. The clothes provided were certainly not his, nor Gabriela's usual style. In fact, he bet whoever chose them had a laugh on their behalf. He looked back towards Gabriela and realised she was attracting some interest from some of the males in the bar. She could dress in a sack and still look good and he realised how blessed he was to have her love. She was exquisite.

The red wine from the bar was a superior drink to the one from the bar fridge in the room. They both enjoyed the first glass, and it was having a mellowing effect on them.

As he walked back to the table, Gordon deliberately made eye contact with their guardian. He smiled and nodded, and she looked embarrassed, knowing her cover was blown.

'I think I won,' he said. 'She looked mortified I'd sussed her out.'

'Poor woman, she has a job to do, keeping us safe. Why would you embarrass her?'

'Just wanted to check I was right. Anyway, I am pleased someone is keeping us out of harm. Don't rely on anyone, though. We need to keep our wits about us at all times. Cheers!'

'Cheers!'

They enjoyed each other's company for the rest of the night, but they were both weary. By the time they headed for their room, the woman was gone, replaced by the officer that drove them to the hotel. They avoided any eye contact and, arm in arm, climbed back up the two flights of stairs and along the corridor to their room. Once inside, Gabriela put her arms around Gordon and kissed him hard.

'Time for bed!'

'Yes indeed. Time for bed!'

The next morning, coming to terms with what had happened was difficult. Sleep helped, but the shock was still real for them both. Death had been just seconds away, but Gordon's neighbours hadn't been so fortunate. He carried a sense of guilt that he could not shake. In each other's arms, they'd escaped the reality for a while, but when they awoke it returned.

'Good morning, my love.'

Gabriela's greeting was precious to him and he would be happy to remain with her for eternity, but knew they had to plan and avenge Shelley's death.

First, there were more practical things to do. Breakfast, followed by a trip into Leeds to buy some replacement clothes. He hoped it would be safe to venture out. The inspector had not forbidden it, but he would avoid his usual haunts. These would be the places someone might look for him. If they were believed dead, Miroslav Bilyk would call off his dogs and Gordon and Gabriela could act without fear. It was his best hope.

Fed, watered and clean, the two left the hotel, but their eyes scanned the car park for anyone or anything suspicious. The first concern was figuring out which car was theirs. They had an idea where it had been parked and, with the help of the remote entry button, discovered which one it was when the lights flashed and there was a beep.

Gordon had taken little notice the day before, but this time he checked the vehicle before opening the door for Gabriela.

'It seems safe, but we must remain on our guard.'

'It's Ok, Gordon. I understand. Come on. Let's go shopping!'

She beamed at him, and he smiled back. Her resilience was remarkable, greater than his own. His past had scarred him, but Gabriela seemed less affected, or at least he hoped so. They couldn't carry on this way much longer. They had to see it through.

'I never thought I'd ever say this, but great. Let's go shopping.'

Leaving the hotel car park, they headed towards central Leeds. The traffic was busy, but they had missed rush hour. He wondered if the police were following them, but he saw nothing.

The day was partly cloudy and patches of greyness fell and lifted like their moods. They didn't speak about anything but shopping, but Gordon pointed out places of interest such as Headingley Stadium, which didn't get much of a response from Gabriela.

He knew where to find a parking spot on a busy day and within twenty minutes he entered a multi-storey car park. He drove up a narrow ramp to the higher levels and found a space.

In a short time, they were walking into Leeds centre, arm in arm. A chill wind blew through their barely functional tracksuits.

Despite not knowing Leeds, Gabriela seemed to have a natural knack for finding fashionable clothing shops. Within a couple of hours, their arms were full of shopping bags. They stopped to enjoy coffee and cake inside a lovely arcade of shops and, for a moment, both forgot the terrible things that had happened. It was a too-short moment of pleasure.

Neither had given any thought to how much they were spending. Fortunately, most of Gabriela's best clothes had been left behind in Calpe.

Gordon bought the Yorkshire Post newspaper and stared at the front page.

FOUR KILLED AND TWO MISSING IN GAS TRAGEDY.

The two missing were enjoying their afternoon, but they knew the calm wouldn't last much longer.

Gordon was sitting close to Gabriela so they could both read the paper. He glanced over the top and thought he saw a face he recognised. He wasn't sure, but it looked like Peter, his friend. This worried him, but he relaxed. Peter was probably part of the contingent guarding them, and that made him feel better. Peter was the sort of man you needed in a crisis, he thought. When he looked again, there was no sign of him.

'What is it, Gordon?' Gabriela asked, concerned he had frozen and was not listening.

'Oh, nothing! I think I saw part of our support team.'

They finished their coffees. Gabriela wanted to make one or two visits to stores she had seen, but not yet visited, and Gordon was happy to indulge her. One smile and he would agree to anything. She smiled, and he did!

Gordon kept a watch for anyone tailing them, but he saw nothing and certainly not Peter. Weary and heavily laden, they made their way back to the car. It was later in the afternoon and Gordon wanted to return before the worst of rush hour. They took the lift up to their level. They were alone in the lift and when the doors opened to let them out, both were on edge. The level appeared deserted, and the car was still where they had left it, but now alone, as the spots on either side were empty.

They checked the car for anything suspicious, but there was nothing. After the near misses, they didn't want to fall victim to laziness. Gordon unlocked the car, and they threw the bags onto the back seat. They climbed in. Gordon had already paid for the parking and the ticket let them out onto the city roads.

The drive back to the hotel was uneventful, but Gordon kept checking if they were being followed. There were no signs, and he relaxed a little. They parked back at the hotel, and carrying the bags, went up to their room. The room next door was still silent. They just had to trust the police were doing their job.

For the rest of the afternoon, Gabriela tried on her new clothes and Gordon made appropriate and appreciative comments about each revelation. In truth, he enjoyed it tremendously. What was there not to enjoy about watching your beautiful partner modelling lovely clothes? Gabriela even insisted he try on his and he obliged her, making his best attempt to be a male model. Gabriela fell about laughing at his efforts, but he smiled in response.

When they finished, it was dark. Gordon looked for his wallet and couldn't find it. He had put it in the glove compartment of the car when they headed back. He needed it to pay for the meal and drinks.

'I've left my wallet in the car!' he called to Gabriela, through the bathroom door. 'I'll just go and get it. Be back in a minute.'

'Ok, darling!'

He left, taking the spare room key.

By now, the afternoon crowd from the gym had gone and, shortly, the evening patrons would start arriving for the bar and restaurant. There was nobody in the car park, but he noticed a few service vehicles and a white transit van parked in the space next to his car. Two men in overalls stood next to it, chatting, but he only gave them a cursory glance.

He edged past, and they gave him room to open the passenger door. He reached and opened the glove compartment. The wallet was where he had left it and as his hands reached for it, he felt something prod him in the back of the neck. He took his hand off the wallet.

'Now be a good chap and I won't shoot you. Just back out and don't try anything!'

The voice was quiet, calm, and had a foreign accent. Gordon realised his mistake. He could have kicked himself. He had been too eager to get back to Gabriela and had not been paying attention.

'Back out now!'

Gordon did as he was instructed, and as he turned, he faced the two men in overalls.

'Into the van.'

The man gestured to the open side door and Gordon knew he had better do as he had been told. He climbed in and sat on the bench seat. From behind, an arm reached around his head. A pungent cloth was pressed to his face as he was thumped in the stomach. This forced him to gasp for air and as he inhaled, he was overcome by the chloroform. The world went black!

ALONE

Gabriela enjoyed her shower, and she was looking forward to a relaxing and uneventful evening. She spent some time putting on makeup and she put on one of the dresses she had bought. It was the ultimate little black dress, and she was certain Gordon would like it from his expression earlier in the afternoon. As she finished her final touches, she suddenly wondered why he was taking so long. It didn't worry her at first. She thought he must have stopped to have a coffee, but after a further five minutes, she realised this was unusual. She grabbed the keycard and hurried downstairs, out through the entrance and into the car park.

Gabriela looked around and checked if the car was still there. It was a little difficult in the dark, with only a couple of lights illuminating the area, but she caught sight of the car and felt relief. She walked over, ready to give Gordon a piece of her mind for worrying her, but as she approached, she realised the passenger door was wide open. She ran the last few yards, and the car was empty. The glove compartment was open, and his wallet was still there.

Panic hit her like a tsunami! Where was he? He wouldn't have left the door open unless something had happened to him. She was beside herself with fear. Gabriela stood alone in the dark, shaking. Her brain was a quiver of indecision. What should she do? Who could help? Should she go to reception?

She had no answer, and her brain was working against her. Time was important, and this was not helping. To save Gordon, she had to act and act quickly. The room next door, she thought. The police were supposed to be guarding them. They should be able to help, do something, anything. She almost screamed with frustration, but that wouldn't help anyone.

That was it! She rushed back into the hotel, trying not to attract attention. She hurried back up the stairs and along the corridor and thundered against the door to room 211. There was a sound from inside, and then a voice.

'Hello. Who is it?'

'It's me!'

She was about to say Gabriela Morales, but then realised she was meant to be under a pseudonym.

'The woman from next door!' was the best she could do under the circumstances.

The door opened slightly, and a face appeared.

'What's the matter?'

'It's Gordon! He's vanished!'

She almost fell through the door and the woman officer caught her as she almost tripped.

'Come in! Sit on the bed. Tell me what's the matter.'

The officer looked shocked. She realised something dreadful had happened, whilst she was responsible for their safety.

'Gordon went to the car. He'd left his wallet when we came back from shopping. I worried when he took too long, so I went down to find him and the car door was wide open. His wallet was still there, and he's vanished! I'm frightened they've got him!'

She almost screamed this last sentence as she realised he could well be dead. They had tried before and only just failed.

'Calm down! Calm down!'

'How can I calm down? You were supposed to make sure we were safe. Why was nobody watching out for him?'

'They were! Wayne was down in reception in case either of you left. He should have seen Gordon pass. I'll try calling him. I'm Amahle by the way.'

The police woman took out her mobile, dialled and waited. After a few seconds, a voice said he was not available and did she want to leave a message?

'Shit! Shit! Shit!' The policewoman paled, and she looked frightened. 'Where is Wayne? He should be ready at all times. I'll have to call Inspector Glover. You're sure they are not in the bar?'

The look Gabriela gave her left her in no doubt. She dialled, and a familiar voice answered.

'Officer Aysi? Why are you calling? Is everything alright?'

To say all hell was let loose would be an understatement. In a remarkably short time, several police cars roared into the car park and within a few minutes more, the inspector pushed the door open and strode into the room. His face showed both concern and anger. He looked as if he wanted to kill someone, but the small, but strong looking officer before him was clearly as worried as Gabriela. Whilst they had waited for the inspector to arrive and take charge, she had explained that Wayne was her boy friend as well as her work partner. The two women shared fear for their men, and Inspector Glover calmed down and started questioning them.

Gabriela explained what had happened. Before she had finished, he turned to the officer waiting outside the door. Get access to the cameras that cover the car park. Do it now. I will be down in five minutes and I want to view the film. If there are any objections, tell them I'm on my way! Understood?

The officer gulped, turned, and vanished from sight. The inspector followed them out and spoke with the officers in the corridor.

'Check all vehicles trying to leave. Search every one! It's probably too late, but you never can tell. I want the hotel searched. Every room, every cupboard. I don't care if anyone objects, I want the place screened. I also want the names and addresses of everyone here. Check their identities. No one is to leave before we are sure. Understood?'

The message was clearly understood, and the two officers hurried downstairs to get it started.

Inspector Glover walked back into the room.

'We will do everything we can, Miss Morales. Now, I need to know everything that has happened since you arrived here. Don't leave any details out. Anything, no matter how small, might be important. I'll get to you in a little while, Officer Aysi! You have some explaining to do.'

A groggy, confused and disorientated, Gordon Bennet slowly became aware of his surroundings. He was rocked and bumped on a hard metal floor of a van. With this realisation, the memories of what had happened as he reached into the hire car to get his wallet flooded back.

His mouth had a metallic tang, and he had a thundering headache, but apart from those inconveniences, he was unharmed. There was someone else on the van floor next to him. His immediate fear was that it was Gabriela, but he turned his head and he was lying next to a man. He recognised the police officer who had driven them to the hotel whose job it was to guard them. Clearly, he had failed miserably.

Gordon tried to move, but he couldn't. He was trussed up, with his hands bound behind his back and his legs fastened at the ankles. It was dark, but the streetlights kept illuminating the back of the van sufficiently for him to see. The swaying made him slide, pressing him into the still unconscious man in the back with him. He heard talking from the front, and he could just see the back of a bench seat that was behind the driver and front passenger seat. He saw the silhouettes of three heads. Two captives had a chance of overpowering three men, whereas it would be impossible for one.

The man next to him stirred. He watched his eyes flicker and open. They stared at him. Both men's mouths were taped, but they looked into each other's eyes with a clear understanding of what had happened. There was nothing that either of them could do. They were helpless, but not entirely hopeless. Gordon had been in dire straits before and survived against the odds, and he understood how important not panicking was. His face was pressed against the ridges of the van floor and each bump banged his head against the metal and added to his headache.

There was a sudden braking and Gordon slid forward and his head went under the bench seat and a sharp stabbing pain bit into his lip. The tape over his mouth slipped with the friction and released his bottom lip. The copper tang of blood filled his mouth. It was only a minor injury, but it added to the discomfort and his growing belief that his luck had run out.

The van sped up, and he slid back an inch or two, only to be shot forward as the van suddenly braked. This time, his lip rested on a loose, shiny metal surface. The van slowly sped up again, and he remained where he was. He used his tongue and felt a small piece of metal and another nick to his tongue. It told him what he needed. It was a section of a box-cutter blade.

Delivery vans would carry cartons and a piece of blade had snapped off. Gordon recognised an opportunity, and he took it. He reached his tongue out as far as he possible, touched the piece of blade, and tried to draw it towards his mouth. His wet tongue slid off and the blade frustratingly remained unmoving, stuck to the van floor. He tried again. His tongue had dried a little, and he got some traction. It moved the merest of distances, but non-the-less it moved. Once again, he stretched his tongue out, but the blade remained stubbornly stuck. His tongue hurt, and he had to rest for a moment. He couldn't be long, as any movement of the van could take it beyond his reach. His next attempt proved more successful, and he dragged the blade to his bottom lip. Using his lip, he tried to lift it off the metal, but he couldn't. He tried again, getting more desperate and frustrated with each attempt. It seemed impossible, and he pressed his face into the floor, angry, frustrated and unsure what to do.

The duct tape covering his mouth hung loose, but remained tacky. As he raised his face slightly, the blade stuck to the tape and dangled above his bottom lip. Gordon couldn't believe it. Maybe luck was on his side.

He reached for the hanging blade with his tongue, fearful it might drop and any hope be lost. He edged his tongue around it and pulled it back towards his mouth. As he did this, he closed his bottom lip and held the blade. He almost cried. Almost, but didn't. He didn't want to risk letting it drop and clenched his lips together. He worked it between his lips, making tiny movements to try to edge it further back into his mouth. Slowly, he worked the blade back sufficiently for his teeth to clamp it. He held it firm and allowed himself a moment to relax.

The next part proved delicate. He had to get it into his cheek where it wouldn't be seen. As he worked it with his tongue, he flinched, as a sharp slice cut the tip of his tongue and he tasted blood again. At least he had it fully inside his mouth.

As he struggled, the policeman watched. He wondered what Gordon was doing, but eventually realised. His eyes opened wide, in frustrating agony, watching the man next to him struggle. He would get so close, but fail over and over. When he finally got the blade into his mouth, the officer's eyes watered with emotion.

There was no time for either to do anything more, as the van came to a stop and this time, it didn't move off again. The front doors opened and the two captives heard voices and some laughter. The side door opened, and they were dragged out with little care or consideration. Gordon kept his mouth clamped shut on the blade piece, and struggled not to swallow it.

Gordon was partially blinded by the bright light, but as his eyes adjusted, he saw they were in a large warehouse. He was standing next to the officer, and both struggled to keep on their feet as their ankles were bound together.

The two men from the car park were standing with a third man and grinning at the bound pair. Finally, they became silent as a well-dressed man walked in through the main entrance. He was flanked by two very large men and one attractive woman.

'Good evening, gentlemen. I hope the trip wasn't too arduous for you, but I wanted to see you off personally. At least I wanted to meet you, Mr Bennet! You, I'm afraid,' he said to the officer, 'are just collateral damage. Mr Bennet, I am so pleased to meet you under these circumstances. I know you are a dangerous man, and I don't take too kindly to threats from dangerous men. Anyway, you'll be out of my hair shortly. Your ex-wife enjoyed a swim and you'll be going for one as well. I thought you'd want to know how you will die. The anticipation will make it so much more enjoyable. Goodbye, Mr Bennet, officer!'

The man's voice had an eastern European accent. He stopped, turned to the three in overalls.

'You know the drill. I hear the park is lovely at this time of year. Enjoy feeding the ducks, Mr Bennet!'

The woman standing next to him looked uneasily at the two men trussed up. Miroslav saw her expression and spoke.

'Don't worry, my dear. There's nothing going to happen. Just two men who need to learn a lesson. They'll be, how do the English say it, as right as rain afterwards. Just a little roughed up. Come on, Dana.'

The woman's face relaxed a little. She stared back at the two bound men for a brief second and then followed Miroslav out of the warehouse. They didn't turn as they left, but Miroslav smiled at the scraping of two chairs on the concrete floor. Finally, it looked as if the day was going to end well for him.

JAILBIRD

News of the explosion travelled fast and even in the prison, Marcus soon heard about it. Franco knocked on his cell door, a pleasantry that very few inmates enjoyed.

'Come in, Franco,' he called.

The inmate held one of his finches and was feeding it by hand. He looked at the bird lovingly, and stroked its back, before returning it to the cage with its partner.

'Mr Spinx, sir. There's been a development!'

'Did you pass on my message?'

'I did, sir, but I wasn't in time!'

'What do you mean? What happened? Tell me everything!'

The guard did exactly that. He told of watching the house where the man, Gordon Bennet, lived, as instructed. He told Marcus that a woman rang him and told him to leave the warning.

'I hope I did right. She said she worked for you.'

'You did the right thing, Franco. What happened?'

The guard explained that the man had briefly left the house.

'I think he went to the shops. I had written the message on a sheet of paper and slid the envelope under the door. The woman told me to post the message and to get away fast. She seemed worried, so I did as she said and then walked back to my car. It was parked near the old clock. I just got to the car when there was a mighty explosion. I got in my car and left as quickly as I could.'

Marcus' face turned grey.

'It was on the news headlines, Mr Spinx. They said a gas explosion destroyed one house and the two on either side were badly damaged.

Apparently, no one in the houses survived!'

'Damn! Damn! Damn!'

Marcus was clearly not happy.

'It seems I won't be using Mr Bennet. Shit!'

He paused and appeared to be deep in thought for a while. Neither man spoke, but the finches cheerfully chattered away. After five long minutes, Marcus Spinx appeared to come to a decision.

'Right, Franco. I need you to get a message to my lawyer. Can you do it?'

'Of course, Mr Spinx. Anything you want.'

'Good! Good! Come back in half an hour? I'll have the letter ready for you.'

'Sure, Mr Spinx. Half an hour.'

The guard turned and left the cell, closing the door behind him.

When he returned later, Marcus had the letter ready and sealed in an envelope. It was addressed to his lawyer, Cherry Jung.

'Can you make sure she gets this today?'

'Of course, Mr Spinx. I will deliver it by hand.'

'Thank you, Franco. I knew I could trust you. There will be a small gift for you later. I have instructed Miss Jung in the letter. It is important no one reads it, so make sure you deliver it only to her hand. Is that understood?'

'Perfectly, Mr Spinx!'

'Then thank you, Franco. That will be all.'

The way Spinx dismissed the guard from the cell was most peculiar, but then much of what happens inside Her Majesty's Prisons is peculiar to those who have never entered.

In the evening, Franco made the journey to the house of the lawyer. It proved further away from his home than he had hoped, but he had been promised a large gratuity, so felt it wasn't too much of an imposition. He was curious about what was inside the letter. Inmates can send letters to their briefs without having to use such secret methods. This intrigued Franco. He considered steaming open the envelope, but then he knew Marcus Spinx would not take kindly to it if he found out. Franco had heard rumours about what happened to those who let Mr Spinx down. People disappeared after crossing the man. He was notorious and no less dangerous because he was in jail.

Franco parked his car on the roadside and walked along the gravel path to the Art déco house. Its white rendered and painted walls, with a curved turret and round window, had an air of sophistication and affluence. Low box hedges edged the lawn and Franco experienced a pang of jealousy. This is how the other half live, he thought, but then amended it to how the other five percent lived.

He felt small and out of place as he approached the front door. He saw a button, and he pushed it. From far away, an answering chime sounded, and he waited, letter in hand, for the door to open.

It seemed no one was at home. Suddenly, the handle turned, and the door opened, but only partially. A security chain preventing it from opening wider.

'Yes?' said a woman's voice.

What a fabulous voice, Franco thought. No, a really sexy one. In truth, most women's voices sounded sexy to Franco.

'I'm Franco. From the prison. Mr Spinx asked me to deliver a message to Cherry Jung.'

'Cherry's inside. I can give it to her.'

'No, I've been instructed to give it only to Miss Jung myself.'

'That's a bit annoying! Can't you bend the rules?'

'I'm sorry, but I can't. Mr Spinx was very insistent.'

'Oh, in that case, you'd better come in and give it to her yourself. Make sure you wipe your feet on the mat and then take your shoes off. We can't let you dirty the white carpet.'

She shut the door. There was the rattle of a chain and then the door was opened fully, and there stood a stunning woman of about thirty years. She had long, dark, straight hair that shone with vitality and pampering. She had a slightly annoyed expression on her perfect face and was dressed in a red silk dressing gown that was tight enough in all the right places to make Franco speechless.

'Stop gawping like a trout, wipe your shoes, leave them on the mat, and wipe that look off your face. Follow me.'

She moved ahead down the wide corridor with a sway that nearly caused Franco to have a heart attack. He smiled to himself and tagged along like a puppy.

The woman ahead approached a curving staircase covered by a thick white carpet as immaculate as the woman he followed. The entire experience made him realise how shabby and grubby he was, which was exactly what the woman intended. He didn't like taking his shoes off for a start and he hadn't changed since work. His socks would smell, and to make it even worse, he had a hole in one and his big toe poked through. Franco was completely out of his depth, but the sight of her swaying hips took his attention.

She turned at a bedroom door and called through.

'Cherry darling, there's a....'

She hesitated, turned and looked at Franco, with the expression she would give to a slug on her salad.

'There's a man here for you. Says he has a letter he has to deliver to your hand!'

Franco stood like a schoolboy outside the headmaster's office, waiting to be caned, when another vision of beauty appeared.

Cherry Jung had just come out of the shower. Naked, apart from a towel wrapped around her torso, her hair damp, she looked exquisite. With no makeup, she was still stunning and, if anything, more impressive than the other woman. She approached and leaned on the other woman's shoulder. The two women looked at each other, turned their heads and kissed, in a way that stunned Franco.

He nearly fainted with such overt sensuality. All his fantasies were coming to fruition in this house. The two women became lost in each other and gave no thought to the shabby man standing there. If they remembered him at all, there was no sign.

Finally, their lips and hands separated, and Cherry turned and looked at the fidgeting man.

'You have something for me?'

The voice was sensuous, deliberately so, and even Franco realised the pair was toying with him.

'Mr Spinx sent me to give you a letter.'

At the name of Marcus Spinx, Cherry changed. She was no longer playing.

'Thursday, be a darling and go make some coffee!'

The other woman smiled, nodded, and slid back down the staircase to the kitchen.

'Forgive our quirks. I didn't realise you were Mr Spinx's messenger. Well, give me the message!'

Franco pulled out the envelope, now more crumpled than when it started out.

She took it in her finely manicured fingers, slid a long nail along the flap and pulled out the white folded paper. She read the letter, never looking at Franco, until she finished reading it.

'Well, Franco! It seems Mr Spinx wants me to reward you for your services.'

She reached out and took hold of his hand and led him into the bedroom.

'Through there is the bathroom. Be a good man. Go have a shower. I'll be back in a minute.'

Franco was stunned. What the hell was going on? He didn't understand it, and he didn't care. He almost ran into the bathroom. The opulence was amazing, but he shrugged his clothing off in a hurry and got into the shower. He just couldn't believe his luck.

In five minutes, Cherry and Thursday returned, and the two shed their clothes and joined the embarrassed, but at least clean and fresher smelling warder in the shower.

They scrubbed and rubbed him till he shone. Franco rose to the occasion and the next, disappointingly short, space of time became forever etched into his memory. The two women worked professionally at an art they excelled in. All the time, a series of very candid and incriminating photographs were being taken.

In no time at all, he was told to dress, thanked for delivering the letter, handed a plump envelope he hoped contained cash, and sent on his way. He almost staggered out of the door, struggling to fasten his shoes, and walked away from the house.

He got back into his car and sat there for a long time, whilst he gathered his thoughts, and took in what had just happened to him.

The drive back to his flat was a haze as he relived the dream.

Marcus knew Cherry would follow his instructions. He wanted to control the guard, and a compromising video and photographs would ensure his compliance. He was aware of her partner. The two would provide all the leverage he would ever need. Franco would do almost anything for money, but some things might require more pressure. Without Ariadne, he had to work with those whose trust was uncertain.

Miroslav Bilyk was behind Ariadne's murder and he wanted revenge, wanted to re-establish his influence and get out of prison. He had to play smarter than the brutal Bilyk. He thought he had had the perfect tool with Bennet, but that option had gone. Franco was a poor substitute, but he had to make do with what was available. Fortunately, his lawyer, Cherry Jung, was ruthless, amoral and would carry out his wishes as long as she believed he could win.

Marcus Spinx stroked the soft feathers of the little bird on his finger. Its grip was delicate but firm, and it felt safe. Apart from Ariadne, the finches were the only things he loved. At the moment, these were all he had left. His love was limited, but his hatred unbounded and it was all directed towards Miroslav Bilyk. He would make the man suffer.

This thought made him smile, and he looked adoringly at the little life in his hand. Another setback, but he was nothing if not resilient. His mind was a whirl, busy calculating the way forward. He would make his man on the inside earn his money. When Franco returned on duty, he had another task for him.

He placed the bird back in the cage and put his finger out and the other finch jumped eagerly onto it.

AN INSIDE JOB

Dana tried her best to remain calm. Steady nerves were an essential attribute for anyone in her professional field. It was certainly not a nine-to-five job, and it prevented a normal family life, but she was totally committed. Since she was a child, she had held a firm belief in fairness. She used to become incensed when she saw people flout the rules and get away with it. This anger burnt into her psyche with increased passion after a drunk driver killed her sister and parents. They were walking home after a family meal when a car mounted the pavement and killed the rest of her family. To make matters worse, no charges were ever brought. She found this impossible to accept. The driver claimed diplomatic immunity as a member of a foreign embassy. She railed against this injustice and the unfairness changed her.

The police were sympathetic and supportive and the female officer spent time with her, explaining some frustrations she and her colleagues faced in their job.

Her grandmother became her guardian and tried her best to provide a loving home, but when Dana was seventeen, her grandmother became seriously ill and died a year later. Now left on her own, Dana managed to get by, but her formative years hardened her. She remembered the police officer who had supported her and when she became old enough, she joined the police. She became a capable student and excelled in her training. Her thoroughness and skill eclipsed the best of the men and her movement up through the ranks had nothing to do with positive discrimination, but everything to do with merit. She wasn't well-liked, but her fellow officers respected her. And when the opportunity came to work alone, undercover, she jumped at it. Anything she could do to bring the bad guys to justice, she would willingly do. She volunteered to become Miroslav Bilyk's personal assistant, and do whatever was necessary, even if it disgusted her.

It didn't take her long to discover his criminal activities, but finding compelling evidence meant she needed to become close to him. The man had no scruples and was frighteningly clever when dealing with enemies. He destroyed his opposition by leaking hard, but false, evidence to the police and the prosecution. It was this that led to Marcus Spinx's conviction. Dana shed no tears for Spinx's imprisonment for a crime he hadn't committed, as he was an equally nasty piece of work. One less criminal on the street and that seemed fair to her.

Most of the victims were other criminals and so few in the police or legal profession lost any sleep, despite some knowing the evidence came from Bilyk and his organisation. As a PA, she learnt more about her boss than his wife knew. His desire, the price she would pay, if it led to his downfall. Until today, she believed he trusted her, but he rarely trusted anyone. She needed to be careful and convincing, particularly as his behaviour had changed.

As his long-time PA, Dana proved efficient, patient and thorough. Her insight into his business and council work equalled his own. Knowing the fate of his enemies was one thing, getting sufficient proof, another. Their deaths made the city safer, so at least she wasn't too concerned.

Tonight, though, was different. Two innocent men were to be executed. This had never happened before. To make matters worse, she recognised one of them. They were students together at the police academy, a fellow officer. The shock had nearly blown her cover, and it proved difficult to hide. She worried he would recognise her, but neither man looked at her. What was Miroslav doing? He usually kept her apart from the criminal side of his business. Was he testing her somehow?

She regained her composure and hoped Miroslav missed it. She needed to carry on as normal. The dilemma was, if she did nothing, the two men would die tonight. Could she live with herself if she didn't act? She had heard rumours about Miroslav's killing ground. She risked breaking her cover by alerting her supervisor, but time was short. The murders were imminent.

She was confused and drawn between doing nothing and doing something, anything that might save the two men. There was also the question of how.

All the time, her mind spun. She had to pretend and carry on as if everything was normal. From the corner of her eye, she glimpsed Miroslav watching her strangely. It lasted only a fleeting second, but alarmed her. Dana had played the part for so long and become adept at remaining calm in difficult situations. She felt sure her facade held. Her heart hammered, but she gave no outward signs. She turned to Miroslav Bilyk.

'I could murder a drink,' she said.

Miroslav looked almost startled at her comment, unsure if she was being funny, or whether it was just a poor turn of phrase.

He had received information about an informer in his organisation and he had been working to find out who it was. It couldn't be the delightful Dana. She was so good as his PA and she had other benefits he didn't want to lose. He had decided to test her by bringing her to see the two men destined to die and he caught a brief shocked expression. It had vanished quickly, replaced by the indifferent look she usually wore. However, he doubted she was the leak, but he would be happier when he discovered who it was. At this pivotal time, he couldn't afford mistakes.

If not Dana, then who? Pavle? Surely not! Whoever it was, he would make sure that they suffered long enough to regret it.

'A fine idea, my dear. Back to my house for a quick drink. My wife's visiting her mother for the night, but I can't be too late. I have a council meeting tomorrow. A servant of the community never rests. Yes, a drink sounds just right after this evening's business. Come!'

He led the way, and she and his minders followed. The clearing up and sorting out, he left to his men. He got into the car, and the two sat in the back, not speaking but looking out onto the city suburbs.

The journey to his home took only a few minutes and soon they were driving through a much quieter area of suburban Leeds. The houses were grand and partially hidden from view by expansive grounds and many trees. This wasn't accidental. The people who lived in this area wanted to keep their presence and their wealth out of the public eye.

As they neared the gate, the car slowed whilst it slid smoothly to one side, allowing them access. They moved forward, and the gates shut behind as they entered the impressive driveway. Dana had been there before. It had always given her a strange feeling, one of foreboding, and tonight her unease was even greater. The tyres crunched on the gravel, but once the car stopped, the doors opened and she and Miroslav walked up the steps to the front door, already opened by one of his men.

They made their way along the corridor and into the lounge. Miroslav sat down in the armchair. Dana walked over and opened the cocktail cabinet, turned and looked questioningly at him.

'I'll have a scotch on ice, Dana. Make it a large one and have whatever you would like.'

Dana made his drink and poured a very generous scotch onto the bed of ice. She walked over to him and placed it in his waiting hand. He missed the glass and firmly grasped her wrist. The pressure was strong, and she almost cried out in surprise. He pulled her face close to his.

'Do you know, my dear? A little bird tells me there is a snitch in my organisation. Someone high up! Someone trusted! You wouldn't know anything about it?'

It startled her. Even her ice-cool temperament couldn't hide her shock. He looked into her eyes from mere inches away, and his expression was anything but friendly. He searched for something in her eyes. Maybe he saw, or failed to see, what he was looking for, but his demeanour changed and he smiled. He released her arm, took the glass and sat back, smiling.

'Of course you wouldn't! You're too smart a cookie for that. Dependable Dana! Get your drink, woman. I needed to check.'

Dana walked a little unsteadily back to the bar and poured an even more generous drink for herself.

As she turned, she saw him relaxed on the sofa and the way he was looking at her told her she was going to be busy for a while.

Eventually, she had to go to the bathroom, and this was her opportunity. She was sure it was too late, but she had to try. She ran the shower and under the cover of the noise, she sent a text message. It was risky, but she had to do something. Miroslav had been told someone had infiltrated his organisation. That information could only have come from a handful of police officers, and even then, only people high up. This forced her hand. It was probably too late to save the two men, but she wanted to try.

Her GP, Dr Freeman, was in her contacts, but she had two numbers. The second one was her emergency link to her superior. The messages were encrypted, but there was always a risk. She used language that was ambiguous, so if anyone intercepted it, it would be difficult to understand. She typed:

I NEED TO SEE YOU. I'M NOT FEELING WELL. WASN'T HAPPY WHEN I WENT TO ROUNDHAY PARK.

That was the best she could do. She got in the shower, happy to wash the man from her, but worried. This was serious, and it wasn't only those two men in trouble. Her whole position was vulnerable. The sooner she got out, the better, but she wanted to bring Miroslav Bilyk's empire down. She was so close!

BREATHLESS

Gordon couldn't say anything with the blade between his teeth, but as he appeared gagged with gaffer tape, he wasn't expected to. He watched Miroslav and the woman with him. The man looked evil, cool, clearly intelligent, but without a scrap of humanity.

The policeman bound next to him had wide-eyed disbelief at what was happening, and what they were going to do to him. All he had been doing was keeping a watch, making sure that the two in protection stayed out of trouble. He had no reason to expect that this would be a particularly dangerous mission, but rather one where he would enjoy spending time with Amahle in the hotel, and the expenses were all being covered by the police department. Now he knew his future would be measured in minutes rather than hours and certainly not the many years he'd expected. He tried not to collapse with fear.

He looked at the man next to him, the one he was supposed to be protecting. The man had a calm, calculating look in his eye. Wayne couldn't believe how still he seemed. There was no sign of panic, even when they slid about. At first, he had wondered what he was doing, but then he had seen the man's gag come adrift. Wayne watched him trying to get the small blade into position with his tongue to pull it into his mouth. Any hope vanished, as the man had done nothing.

The stranger addressing them was a face he had seen in the local papers. Wracking his brain, he tried to remember who it was, and then it came to him. He was the leader of the city council, Miroslav Bilyk. If true, then this was serious indeed. He was well respected in the city, and had a reputation for getting things done. He wasn't an obvious criminal. Wayne was terrified by the man's hard expression and ice-cold eyes. A stunning woman stood beside him, but he kept his eyes on Bilyk. The council leader ignored him, but he spoke to Gordon Bennet. After the short, one-way dialogue, Wayne realised his fate had been sealed, and he despaired.

The couple left and the policeman's heart sank. He wanted to cry, to beg for mercy, but gagged and bound as they were, there was nothing he could do.

As they left, the others, no longer wearing overalls, bundled the captives back into the white van. The door slammed shut and within seconds the engine started and the van reversed out in to the night. Wayne struggled, trying to break the cord that bound him, but it was hopeless and after a few minutes, he stopped.

Gordon Bennet made no such efforts, and he just lay calmly face down in the van's rear. He stayed unmoving for a little while, but then he shuffled towards the policeman on his side. Wayne had his back to Gordon, which helped. Trying to get the position right, the time lost shuffling became an agony of frustration. He was too high up to reach his target and to edge backwards was difficult. His legs prevented him from moving down, so he had to bend them to create space. Gordon rocked backwards and forwards and with each movement, he edged mere fractions of an inch further back. It was exhausting. Gordon could only breathe through his nose, which meant stopping regularly to get his breath back. The man next to him lay still. Gordon continued to work his head down the other man's back until finally he reached the point where his face pressed against the man's hands. The policeman's fingers flexed, but they remained where they were.

The next part of Gordon's plan was the most critical. If he failed, then all hope would be lost. He had to reposition the blade between his teeth, so the blade's edge faced outwards. The only way for him to do it was to push it with his tongue, whilst releasing his teeth slightly. Too much and the blade would fall out and that would be the end. Gordon understood this was their one chance. He pushed with his tongue. The sharp pain almost caused him to lose his grip, but he held on. Blood filled his mouth, and this time, the cut was deeper. Trying again, the blade turned slightly. Catching his breath, he tried once more. The drive to Roundhay Park would not be a long one. Time was pressing, like the blade, but on the next attempt, he got the blade where he wanted it. He swallowed blood and drew his lips back and pushed his face into the cords that bound the policeman's hands. It was impossible to exert firm pressure as he held the blade. Gordon moved his head up and down and the policeman responded by pushing back against the blade.

Strand by strand, the cords parted, but it was a clumsy, not effective process and twice the blade slid and cut the policeman's wrists. He flinched, but continued to give Gordon assistance. Gordon was getting a cramp in his jaw from holding the blade so tightly. He needed to rest, allowing a spasm to subside. There was no choice, but the wait was frustrating as time was running out.

The pain ebbed, and a fraction at a time, he made progress. He could see he had slashed through half the cord, but the cut was shredded and uneven. Hope was just appearing when the van turned a corner and the two in the back slid to the right. Gordon was squashed by the other man's body and the blade cut into his lip. Without intending to, he released the blade, and it fell onto the floor of the van. With the loss of the blade, hope had gone, and he almost wept with frustration and anguish. He didn't have time to dwell on it, as the van stopped. The front doors opened and the driver and the other two men got out. There were some muffled words before the side door slid open.

Gordon could have screamed, and in other circumstances, he probably would have. He was hauled out of the van and stood next to the policeman. Both men stared at the three men before them and their surroundings. Gordon saw the Boathouse Cafe, but the place was deserted, as it was the early hours of the morning. The air was icy and the man next to him shivered, but Gordon wasn't sure if it was the cold air or fear.

The sky was clear, with just a sliver of a moon, and they could see the pewter surface of the large lake. One of their captors pulled out a large knife and cut the ropes binding their legs.

'Just a little walk,' one of them said nastily, and they all laughed.

Their arms bound behind their backs, the two were led down a narrow path to the edge of the lake, underneath the cafe. A rowing boat was moored to an iron ring, and the men helped Gordon and the policeman unceremoniously onto it. He tried to break free, but all he got for his efforts were blows to his body, which winded him, but barely delayed the inevitable. They lay on the bottom on top of some iron chains and Gordon realised the intent. A weighted body could spend years at the bottom of the deep lake, and time and decay would leave little evidence.

One of their captors rowed whilst the others kept watch on Gordon and Wayne. It took only a few minutes to reach the centre of the lake. Gordon readied himself. Their legs remained unbound, and he knew it was now or never. Without warning, he jumped to his feet, braced his feet against both sides of the rowboat, and rocked. He put all his force into that movement. The others panicked for a moment, getting to their feet. This made the rowing boat more unstable and one side went below the water, and the lake rushed in. The boat capsized, tossing everyone into the icy black water. The two bound men fell together.

Gordon heard shouting and some very unpleasant language as he took a deep breath and disappeared below the surface. The shock of the water was intense, but he held his breath, as the policeman slid past him down into the darkness. With their legs free, they kicked and headed towards the surface. Their heads breached, and they stared around. Several yards away, silhouetted in the moonlight, the upturned boat still floated with three men clinging to it. They gasped the fresh air and trod water, trying to avoid detection. One man on the hull pulled out a pistol. A flash and a splash, followed by a bang, filled the night as the bullet hit the water, but missed both men.

'Dive! Now!'

Gordon didn't shout the instructions, but the policeman understood the urgency. Both men took a deep breath and duck-dived into the depths. The waters covered them and they vanished into the darkness. Wayne knew what to do, and he tensed his arms in an attempt to break the partially cut cords around his wrists. He strained his arms apart. The cords held, and he was on the edge of panic. Trying again, there was a sudden release as the rope broke. The cords unravelled from around his wrists and he was free. Gordon was nearby, and he felt around for him. His hand touched something, but there was no movement. It felt like a body, so he pulled it up to the surface. He needed air and his chest ached with holding his breath. The man in his arms was limp, and it was only when he got his head above the water and saw the face that he realised his mistake.

He held a bloated face, with eyes partially eaten, inches from his.

The policeman stifled a scream and released the cadaver, his stomach retching. The nightmare disappeared back into the depths and Wayne heard splashing sounds from his left. He turned. The silhouettes of three men still on the upturned boat argued with each other as they were searching for the two escapees. There were flashes and small splashes, but the shots were a long way from him.

He feared Gordon had drowned by this time. He didn't know where to search and didn't want to face another corpse. The lake was a place of horror, so he turned and slowly and quietly swam, breast-stroke, away from the arguing men and the danger.

He'd barely started when a head exploded out of the water and gasped for air. This man was clearly alive, and the two faced each other. Gordon was struggling to keep his head above the icy water as his wrists were still bound. Wayne reached for his wrists and felt the knot. Stiff with the cold, he struggled to untie it. Painstakingly slowly, he felt the cord move.

Gordon slid below the water and would have been lost if Wayne hadn't reached down, caught a handful of hair and pulled him back to the surface. He tried again to untie the knot. This time, he felt the rope give a lot. He unwrapped the cord off Gordon's wrists, and with a wonderful relief, his arms came free.

Despite being in agony, he could now support himself in the water. The two men stared back at the upturned rowing boat and saw their assailants give up trying to right it. One had grabbed a floating oar and started paddling his way slowly back to the boat shed, sitting astride the hull. Wayne and Gordon headed in the opposite direction towards the far bank in the distance.

The swim seemed endless, and they made slow progress. The darkness hid the two. Bound by the wrists, it would be a miracle for anyone to keep afloat for long, so they hoped the three killers would believe they had achieved their mission, just not in the intended way. Even with their arms free, both swimmers were exhausted, and hypothermia was a genuine threat. If they didn't reach shallow water soon, they would be in trouble.

A PRESSED MAN

Franco did not understand what had happened to him, but for the rest of the day, it was impossible to wipe the smile off his face. True, the women seemed to want him to leave fairly quickly after the deed, and they showed no interest in his suggestion of catching up, but even so, it was the greatest moment of his life. This wasn't saying much, as he endured a miserable existence. Life as a warder was bad enough, but when even your fellow guards did not like you, then your life was pretty bad.

The next time he entered Marcus Spinx's cell, he walked in with a spring in his step, which Marcus noted.

'I take it you delivered my message, Franco?'

'Yes, Mr Spinx. Just as you instructed. Do you want me to take another?'

'No, Franco. One will be enough for now, but maybe later.'

The warder smiled at the prospect and again Marcus saw it and smiled back.

'Do you need me to do anything else, Mr Spinx?'

'Well, I do. I have something special I need you to do for me, if you don't mind.'

'Anything you ask, Mr Spinx.'

'That's good. I will ensure you are well rewarded, Franco!'

Again, Franco couldn't keep the smile off his face. Things were truly on the up for him. This work might be a little dangerous, and not approved by the authority, but so far he had done nothing illegal. He delivered messages, kept a lookout, nothing criminal, but he had come close to being caught in the explosion when he was too late delivering the warning.

'Come back before you finish your shift. I'll tell you what I need you to do.'

The warder left the cell and got back to his monotonous workday.

Later that evening, shortly before he finished his shift, Franco returned and Marcus was ready with his instructions.

'I may need you to be a little more active this time, Franco. I know! You could easily have been caught by the explosion, but you weren't, and I have made sure you were well rewarded.'

The prisoner stressed the words, 'well rewarded'. Franco noticed an amused smile cross the man's face, and he felt himself turn red with embarrassment, as he realised Marcus Spinx was aware of his encounter. If Marcus was, he made no further allusions towards it, and Franco listened to what his instructions were.

The guard left the prison and drove to the city. He found a parking spot, left the car, and walked to where the City Council offices were. He sauntered into reception and over to the desk. There was a well-dressed man sitting there, and he looked up.

'I have a letter for Mr Pavle Mugosa. Can I leave it with you?'

'Of course, sir,' the man said to Franco. 'He's not in tonight, but he will be tomorrow. I will put it in his mail, so he gets it when he arrives.'

'Thank you,' said Franco.

He passed the envelope over and left the building. That was all that he had been asked to do. It hardly seemed a fuss, but it seemed important for Mr Spinx. He didn't care as long as he got paid. All in all, these had been a good couple of days.

CALL FOR ACTION

Inspector Glover got the text message. He knew immediately who had sent it and that she would only contact him in an emergency. He was about to meet with the superintendent when the message arrived. These had been troubling times. The disappearance, the murders, the attempted bombing of Gordon Bennet's car and then the destruction of his home and the killing of the two sets of neighbours. Not the ordinary run-of-the-mill week by any stretch. His superiors were worried, and he shared their concerns. He didn't understand what was happening, and whatever was playing out, he didn't like it. The week began so well with Marcus Spinx's guilty verdict and imprisonment, but had rapidly gone downhill since then. To make matters even worse, Gordon Bennet had been kidnapped and Constable Maisonet had also disappeared.

Sitting back in his chair, he stared at the mobile in his hand. He read the message and tried to understand it.

I NEED TO SEE YOU. I'M NOT FEELING WELL. WASN'T HAPPY WHEN I WENT TO ROUNDHAY PARK.

He understood how important the message must be. 'I need to see you,' the agreed panic code, telling him her cover was blown, and she needed to get out. The rest of the message puzzled him. He paused, got on the phone and made the arrangements for her speedy removal from Bilyk's circle. The text let him know she wasn't in immediate danger, but it needed to happen as soon as practicable. He organised for her to be collected that evening. He couldn't risk losing another colleague.

That sorted, he puzzled over the second part.

WASN'T HAPPY WHEN I VISITED ROUNDHAY PARK.

What did it mean? He thought about this. The location was clear enough. She wouldn't have added it to the message if it wasn't important, but what did it mean?

He wondered if it had anything to do with the kidnappings. Somehow, he felt in his guts that it had. His instincts had served him well over the years. If he acted now, maybe Gordon Bennet and Constable Maisonet could be saved.

'Damn it!' he said to himself. 'The superintendent will have to wait!'

He got out of his chair, opened his office door and called to those of his team busy at their desks.

'I need six of you. You will need arms. Be downstairs in ten!'

Glover then returned to his office, got what he needed and went to organise the group.

Half an hour later, a car and white van sped towards Roundhay Park. The inspector was playing his hunch, and he decided to start by driving down to the main car park. A smaller group was to investigate the main gates near Canal Gardens. The park was one of the largest in Europe, so luck would really have to be on their side if they were to discover what Dana's message hinted at. A needle in a haystack, but he had few other leads. He would never live with himself if he didn't try. He liked Mr Gordon Bennet, but the ex-soldier appeared to have run out of luck in the end.

Carpets of leaves were building up under the trees that lined the road to the car park. The Soldiers' Fields were deserted and soccer posts had replaced the cricket squares of summer and they were silhouetted like servicemen on parade. A crescent moon provided only temporary light, as clouds scudded across the sky and a chill wind stirred the leaves. The car and van assisted the wind, and the leaves took to the air and fell in a dance like a snowstorm.

The car turned the corner at the top end of the sport grounds and headed down the steep hill and the car park came into view. Inspector Glover saw a van near the cafe. Maybe luck was with him tonight.

As they got closer, three dark figures appeared out of the night. They turned to face the headlights, dripping with lake water, icy cold and shivering. Suddenly realising it was the police, they turned and ran away from the approaching vehicles. They sprinted up the rise and into the darkness.

One turned and pointed a pistol towards the approaching van and fired. The flash was followed by an almost instantaneous crack, and the shattering of glass. The van screeched to a halt, skidding sideways and rocking violently, and the doors opened and several armed officers jumped out, returning fire.

The police car pulled up, with tyres screeching, and Inspector Glover got out and followed up the hill after the fleeing men. His instincts were reliable. Whatever these three had been doing, it was nothing good. The use of firearms was rare, and the police being shot at an even rarer occurrence. Penalties were severe and few would risk life in prison. Now they had to arrest them and find out what they were doing.

The men were disappearing into the darkness. One turned, stared back at the pursuing police officers, and fired again. The police were well-armed and wearing bullet-proof vests, but instinctively they ducked. This allowed the fleeing men to increase the gap.

Inspector Glover arranged backup and the police helicopter. He couldn't allow them to escape. They were his only lead. It was possible that Maisonet and Bennet were somewhere in the park, and still alive. Dana's message had brought him here, and he wouldn't let this chance slip. This might be his opportunity to link Miroslav Bilyk to the recent murders. He continued after his colleagues.

The moonlight kept disappearing, and without it, the park was as dark as death. As he reached the top of the hill, the clouds parted around the crescent moon. A gentle light provided an opportunity to see what was happening. Distant black shapes were approaching the end of the lake where there was a castle folly. Beyond this lay a wooded and shrub-covered hill. Rhododendrons created dense areas that would provide cover for those trying to escape. Glover knew the park. He'd been brought up in the city. Over the hill lay a narrow valley, known as the gorge, and further on lay the busy Ring Road.

The inspector paused again and called for reinforcements to block the Ring Road exit. Bugger the expense, he thought. I won't let them get away.

He set off again, making headway, as gunfire halted the chase. The fleeing men reached the corner of the lake and stopped for a second. He could see them turn back, look around and there was waving of hands as if they were having an argument. It lasted only a second or two, and then two headed up past the folly and the lone man ran around the lake edge, heading back along the opposite side of the lake.

The clouds covered the moon and once again darkness fell, making it difficult to see what was happening, and the figures disappeared.

The fleeing men had the advantage and splitting up gave them an even better chance. Glover only had half a dozen officers until backup arrived and that was half an hour away. He rushed down the hillside to the end of the lake. His fitness was not what it once was, and he was out of breath and he suffered the first twinges of a stitch. The sound of his men came from just ahead, and he caught up with them and took control.

'You four follow the two up the hill. Be careful, there are places they can hide. I want them, preferably alive. Go! You two follow me. We'll go after the other one. He can run quickly on the path, but then so can we. Come on!'

He knew the man they were after was wet, and that would slow him down.

Whatever the fleeing man intended made little sense to the inspector. Running along the open track was faster in the dark and avoided tripping and falling, but was easy to follow. He must have known backup would be arriving. The inspector expected him to turn and make a dash up the hill into the woods, but it didn't happen and the fugitive just kept on along the track.

Those chasing occasionally saw his silhouette as the moon temporarily broke through the clouds. They were about halfway along the length of the lake when the footsteps stopped and there was silence.

'Shit!' the inspector said. 'Where the hell has he gone?'

They took their torches out and searched for any signs of where he'd gone. There wasn't much choice. On the right lay the dark and unappealing waters of the lake, and to the left the steep wooded hillside and out to the Ring Road. Beyond that was open countryside.

They thought he must be hiding. Maybe he planned to backtrack, but there were no obvious hiding places. A stone wall edged the lake with a short drop to the water. They checked, but there was no sign of the fugitive.

'You two go on along the track and I'll go up the hill. Call on the first sign. Remember, be careful.'

The two officers continued along the trail and he watched their torch lights pick out their path. Inspector Glover listened for the fleeing man, but apart from the stirring of the leaves in the breeze, the park remained silent. After running, the sweat chilled him, and he shivered. This night was not going his way. He couldn't let this man escape.

Glover scanned the hillside with his torch beam. There was nothing.

Shit! Shit! Shit! He thought to himself. This was turning into a fiasco. He was angry with himself. Angry with his men! Angry at the fugitives, and worried that he had been too late for Bennet and Constable Maisonet.

'I'm just getting too old and too slow for this game. Maybe I should leave it to younger men!'

For the first time ever, the prospect of retirement seemed a pleasant option. He considered climbing up the hill to the Ring Road, but then thought not. There would be reinforcements soon, and the helicopter. He would leave it to them and he pulled out his packet of cigarettes, took one and put it to his lips. His wife, Angela, had been on at him to take the offer of retirement. She wanted them to spend time together, go on holidays. She had ideas for the garden and the decorating of their home. He took out his lighter, flicked it, and was dazzled by the sudden light.

He knew the park well. The gorge was a good choice to get away from the police, but he had an even better idea. But it would only work for one man. The others weren't happy about splitting up. With only a handful of police and the enormous park, they had the advantage. He had fished this lake countless times, and what lay hidden in its waters didn't put him off. With his rod, keep net, thermos, sandwiches, and flask of whisky at his side, he would sit on the bank and be in heaven. What more could any man want? He wondered if the people in the lake would agree.

It was whilst angling that he had first noticed the drainage pipe. He couldn't really say why he had paid it any mind, but he had. A water vole had scampered along the muddy water's edge and disappeared into it. He investigated and pondered whether he could fit in it. As a lad, he would not have hesitated, he would have been in it in a heartbeat, but as a man, it was more a conundrum, a puzzle for his restless mind. Now, as he fled, the memory had bubbled up into his consciousness and offered a solution. If only he could find it. He remembered there was a lifebuoy on a pole near it, unless someone had vandalised it. Could he find the right spot and get into the pipe without being seen?

It turned out easier than he had thought. The lifebuoy was still there, and so was the pipe. It was wet, but he was soaked anyway and the pipe took him out of the wind. Sliding backwards into the pipe, he waited in silence. He hoped those after him would just pass by. If they did, he'd head back and get out of the park. It might not be the best of plans, but it was the best he had.

There was just one snag! There were three coppers after him. He heard them stop and talk on the footpath. After a short time, two carried on, but one was still there. He heard the policeman standing directly above where he was hiding. He could hear the man's breathing, but then silence.

The silence lasted a long time, but then he heard feet shuffling on gravel and the policeman was just above him.

This night had been a mess. If the police had turned up a few minutes later, they would have been well away. Someone must have tipped off the police. Relja had shot at them. Another mistake. The night had been one after another. He wondered if his mates had got away. Rodavan lay in the pipe, becoming frustrated. Police reinforcements would arrive soon and then he would have no chance to escape. Even if he stayed where he was, the dogs would eventually find him. Because he was still soaking wet, hypothermia was likely to kill him first. He had to act.

He wormed his way slightly out of the pipe. Lying on his back, he looked up. In the darkness, it was difficult to see, but he heard the man's breathing and his fumbling in his pockets. Rodavan pulled out his pistol. It was no longer wet, but it might not fire after being in the lake. The figure above him moved on the gravel and he knew it was now or never. In as quiet a motion as possible, he edged out of the pipe and crouched, with the pistol in his hands.

The inspector flicked the lighter in his hand. There was a flash, and he put the flame to his lips and drew in a deep breath. A second flash appeared just beneath him and oblivion swallowed him.

Rodavan watched the man fall. This was his chance. The gunshot would draw the two policemen back. He sprinted up the hillside. He needed to get as far away as possible.

The slope was wet and slippery, but he put in an extraordinary effort. He heard cries and the sound of running feet. Up he went, and his breathing was ragged and laboured. The banking was steep and in places he had to pull himself up by exposed tree roots and clumps of ragged grass.

He had a chance. Not a good one, but a chance if he could get over the hill and across the Ring Road. The sound of the police was getting louder and nearer. The shot man and the hill would slow them. His hands stung from cuts from the grass, but he reached the crest. There was a rough wooden fence, and he hauled himself over, stumbling down the abrupt drop onto the road. There was no one in sight and no cars. He was exhausted, but he rushed across the road to where there was a hedge, and beyond, a fallow field.

As he made the other side of the hedge, lights approached and two police cars screamed past. He waited, anxious that they had seen him and would stop, but they hadn't.

He continued along the hedge line and he heard sirens and racing engines. Adrenaline kept him going. He was frozen despite running, and his wet clothes made it difficult and uncomfortable. He could see little. The sky was now completely hidden by cloud. This gave him the best hope and when rain fell steadily, his chances improved.

He was putting a good distance between himself and the park when he heard gunfire. It didn't last long. A series of short bursts, and then there was silence. The police must have caught up with Relja and Miro, but what was the outcome? If cornered, he didn't give his friends much hope. Police don't take kindly to anyone who shoots at their colleagues. He hoped all the attention would be directed towards them, and he continued further into the countryside. The rain became heavier. It was now a downpour and storms rolled in and it became torrential. Lightning streaked through the skies, briefly illuminating the land below. Rodavan was fortunate. The helicopter could not fly in such weather, and even the tracker dogs could not get a scent. Despite his exhaustion, he eventually found a disused barn that offered shelter for the rest of the night.

Rodavan had covered five miles, and his luck remained with him. The police had cornered his friends, and they were both shot. Three men were taken to the hospital. Two were badly wounded, and the third was dead.

The next day, Rodavan awoke in the ruined barn. He had mostly dried out. With luck, he hoped he could get home unnoticed. He followed the hedge line until he reached a road. It was only a minor one, but a mile further, it joined a major one and there was a bus stop. He crossed his chest. God was with him. He waited at the bus stop. His crumpled clothes wouldn't attract too much attention. The pistol was in his jacket pocket and he still had his wallet. Even after the soaking in the lake, the cash and notes were fine, but his cigarettes were a lost cause.

At least the morning was dry, he thought. Dark clouds scudded across and foretold of rain to come, but it held off whilst he waited for a bus. More than anything, he wanted to be home. He needed a hot bath, a good meal, a cigarette or two, and a bottle of wine. The thought of this lifted his spirits. But then he realised, if Relja and Miro were alive and in custody, the police would soon come for him. He hoped they were dead. Dead men can't speak, he thought, and smiled.

He waited patiently for the bus, and after an hour, it arrived. It was almost empty. Two old ladies sat at the front. The sign said it was heading to Moortown Corner. He asked for the ticket, gave the correct change, and went and sat halfway along the single-decker bus. It seemed so strange, so ordinary, and he was back in civilisation. His mood became buoyant, until he realised he would have to report back to Miroslav Bilyk, and that was something he wasn't looking forward to.

NOTHING TO LOSE

Gabriela was beside herself with worry for Gordon. She was alone in her room, with armed guards outside in the corridor. Amahle was in the adjacent room, and Gabriela had heard her crying. She could think of two reasons: Wayne, her police officer partner, had been kidnapped. Inspector Glover had vented his unhappiness with her work.

Gabriela had spent some time crying herself, but self-indulgence would do nothing to help rescue Gordon. She had pulled herself together and come up with a plan of action. Gordon had blamed a man called Miroslav Bilyk for Shelley's murder. If he was behind this, then perhaps Gordon and Wayne would be held there. It wasn't much of a hope, but all she had. She had to do something, anything, despite the inspector telling her to remain in her room. She couldn't just walk out. The police were there to keep her in, as well as keeping her safe.

Gordon had left his mobile on the bedside cabinet when he went down to get his wallet. The inspector hadn't asked, and she hadn't realised until now. She reached out for it and tried to open it. The request for the pin number came up, and she froze. She had never needed to use Gordon's phone before and she didn't know his pin number. What would it be? She tried his birth year, but that didn't work. Next, 1234, but it blocked her. Another couple of tries was all she had left before it locked her out. Time was important. She tried to think about what he would use. It wasn't his year of birth, but maybe it was hers. She entered 1997 and this time it opened. You romantic old fool, she thought, but then had to stifle a sob.

She looked in his contacts and finally found what she was looking for. Peter, and there was only one, Peter Falkirk. She hoped it was Gordon's police friend, and she speed-dialled his number. A familiar voice answered.

'Hello?'

'Peter? It's me Gabriela!'

'Hi, Gabriela. How are you? What can I do for you?'

'I need some information, Peter. Where does Miroslav Bilyk live?'

'Bilyk? Why do you want to know?'

'I just need to, Peter. Do you know where he lives?'

'Why, yes. It's no secret. It is public knowledge. He lives in Manor House Lane. The Stables! What's going on, Gabriela? Are you okay?'

'Nothing, Peter. That's all I needed. Thank you for your help!'

She then rang off. Something didn't seem quite right. Peter hadn't asked about Gordon. Did he know he was missing? Of course he did! It must be common news amongst the force. But, in which case, why hadn't he mentioned it? This puzzled her, but she pushed the thought aside. She knew where she was going. It was just a question of how to get there.

She went to the window and pulled it upwards. The stop preventing it from being raised more than four inches had been unlocked, as Gordon had asked. She pushed her head through and looked out. It was dark and all around lit windows cast their light onto the flat roof. Some windows opened into rooms and some onto corridors.

Gabriela paused and started thinking. She had no transport, didn't know where Manor House Lane was, and had nothing to defend herself with. However, she did know who did. Pulling herself through the window, she edged along to the next lit one. This was Amahle's room. She looked in and the policewoman was sitting on the bed. Gabriela saw her face was streaked with tears. She was alone and Gabriela took her chance. She tapped gently on the window. There was no response, so she tried again, a little louder. This time, the woman on the bed looked up. A shocked expression filled her face, but changed when she recognised who was there.

Amahle walked over and pushed the window up.

'Gabriela? What are you doing here?'

'Just coming to see you. We need to keep our voices down. We don't want to attract the guards outside. I need to talk to you.'

Gabriela silently climbed through and into the room.

'Do you have a car?' she asked.

'Yes, yes, I suppose so,' the policewoman answered, but she didn't sound sure. 'What are you planning?'

Gabriela kept her voice as quiet as possible so that the police in the corridor wouldn't hear her, and she explained she was going after Miroslav Bilyk and needed Amahle's help. She finished with a question.

'You have a pistol, Amahle? You should bring it. I believe we have a chance of freeing Gordon and Wayne, but these men will stop at nothing. I know it is against your regulations, but it's our only chance. If we wait for the police, we will be too late!'

Amahle stood thinking, her face lined with worry.

'Where are we going?'

That was all that Gabriela needed. Amahle removed a pistol in a holster from her wardrobe and strapped it onto her waist. Her jacket hid it.

'I have the address where Bilyk lives. It's in Alwoodley, Manor House Lane. Do you know it?'

'Yes! Come on. Let's go!'

This time, it was the policewoman who was climbing out through the window first. Gabriela followed her out into the night and they carefully passed several lit windows. They came to a window that looked into a corridor, but they couldn't open it, so they hurried on to another. This time, the window was unlocked and Amahle poked her head through. The corridor was empty. She quickly climbed through. Gabriela followed, and they headed for the staircase down to reception.

Reception was busy with people moving between the restaurant and the bar and the two wormed made their way through without drawing any attention. Guests were arriving and some leaving, and they just filtered through and out into the darkness.

The car was where Wayne and Amahle had left it. The lights flashed as they approached and Amahle got into the driver's seat. She started the car and turned right at the entrance and turned onto the Ring Road. Amahle knew where she was going.

'You know the place?' Gabriela asked.

'I sure do. You don't spend time in the force and not provide security to those that live in Manor House Lane. It's where the very rich and powerful live.'

'It's where Miroslav Bilyk lives.'

'I know his house. We've been called out a couple of times. There were reports of prowlers, but we saw nothing.'

True to her word, Amahle knew the way and at this time of night, there was very little traffic about.

'What are we going to do when we get there?' she asked.

'I've been thinking about that,' said Gabriela. 'We should try to get up to the house unnoticed and then we can see what's going on. Is that possible?'

'Possible, but not easy. They have security cameras, but not constantly monitored.'

'That'll have to do!'

The two were wearing dark clothes, but neither was skilled in breaking and entering.

They parked on the tree-lined street. The night was dark, and the moon broke through, only infrequently casting its pale light. There was a chill in the air and the possibility of rain later. The street was deserted. Amahle led the way, her pistol hidden. They hurried to the gate of a large house, set in expansive grounds. There was a sign, The Stables, just to the left of a white gate. There was a communication panel so that visitors could have the gate opened.

Patchy streetlight produced pools of dim illumination at intervals along the street. The drive was edged with lights and there were security ones on the house. It looked nothing like any stables. They stared at it, and it appeared like a Hollywood haunted house. There was a tower standing above the rest of the building. There was something ugly about the house, not helped by gargoyles on the four corners of the tower. They stared down as if watching for anyone who dared to approach. It was the creation of a twisted mind, and it suited the reputation of the man who lived there.

'We can't stand here gawping. We need to move!'

Gabriela led the way this time. She looked along the wall, but decided the easiest way was over the gate. She climbed up and vaulted over, landing softly on the other side. Amahle followed suit and they were in the grounds.

They skirted around the edge of the lawn under the shelter of the tall trees and shrubs that shielded the occupants from the neighbours and other prying eyes. The house was mostly in darkness, but there were one or two windows with lights.

'At least someone's at home,' Gabriela whispered.

They squatted at the edge, behind a flower border, and they stared at the house, wondering whether Gordon and Wayne were inside.

Whilst they were out of sight, they heard a car approaching. Lights moved along the road and stopped by the gate. There was the sound of metal on metal as the gate slowly slid open. They lay flat on the ground, watching the headlights move through the gateway and approach the house. The car stopped and two figures got out. They were silhouetted in the security lights. A man and a woman went up the steps. They opened the front door and disappeared inside.

Gabriela and Amahle watched the driver follow the drive around behind the house.

'That was probably Bilyk, but I don't know who the other one was.' Amahle whispered.

'Yes, and there is at least one of his men,' Gabriela added.

'Do you want to turn back?'

'Not a chance,' she replied. 'Come on! Let's go see what's happening.'

Gabriela crawled forward, keeping as low to the ground as she could. She moved from one well of darkness to another. She hoped everyone in the house was too busy to check the cameras, but even if they did, it would be difficult to see them.

The blow when it came was strong, sudden, and she felt her nose snap with the force. She would have screamed and fallen to the ground if she hadn't been bound to the chair by her hands and ankles to the frame. When the second blow came, the chair toppled with the force, and blood welled in her mouth. She would have spat it out if her mouth hadn't been taped shut. Miroslav stood panting. There was anger in his eyes and a sneer on his lips. There was one of his men with him and he leered at the naked woman. He liked what he saw, and he hoped he might have a little sport with her later.

The next blow came, and the woman lost consciousness, frustrating Miroslav. He wanted to inflict pain and punishment, and now he would have to wait for her to come round before he could start again. Her right eye was swollen and almost shut, and her nose was clearly broken. It was a blessing she had passed out. Miroslav turned to the man and said, 'I'm going for a drink. Get a bucket of water! I want her awake so I can continue.'

The man nodded his understanding, and Miroslav left the cellar and went up the stairs to the lounge. He poured a large drink and sat down on the white leather sofa, sinking into its comfort and luxury. Finishing his drink in one go, he got up and poured another.

He was enjoying his whisky when his mobile rang. He pulled it out of his back pocket and checked who was calling him at home in the middle of the night. Few would dare, and those that would, would have a good reason. Probably his men confirming they had got rid of Mr Gordon Bennet, he thought. He checked the screen. It was someone he hadn't expected. It was his insider, one of his trusted men. He would only call if it was urgent.

'Yes?'

'It's me. There's a major incident. Police are all over Roundhay Park. There's been some shooting. Two men are dead and another in hospital. Thought you should know.'

'Thank you.' Miroslav's voice was slow, controlled, but he was struggling to keep his composure.

'Two dead, you say? Roundhay Park. Let me know if you have further details.'

Miroslav knew better than to say anything that could implicate him.

He drained his glass, got to his feet, and walked over to fill it again. Three shot! Could those be his men? If so, what had happened to Bennet and the policeman? One wounded! If that was one of his men, it would be a problem. Better that man died, too. He would have to make enquiries. This was getting out of hand, and he needed information to stop it. Miroslav walked back and sat down. He made a couple of quick calls. He organised some of his contacts. They were clearly not fully awake, but they soon sharpened up when they realised who was calling and what he wanted.

Finally, he put his phone away. What was happening with that damn woman? Surely she's come around by now! As he thought this, something touched the back of his neck. It was a gentle caress, cool like a gossamer breeze, but the hairs stood to attention and his heart missed a beat.

'No! I don't want to kill you, but I will if you make any sudden moves. Put your drink down and put your hands behind your head!'

The voice was bitter, chilling, and left no doubt that the speaker meant what they said.

The prod was more insistent. Miroslav had no choice. The voice was that of a woman. Had the bitch somehow escaped from the cellar? Had his man helped her? He didn't recognise the voice, but maybe she had just been acting all along. He placed the glass on the side table at the arm of the sofa, raised his hands, and linked them behind his head. Someone took hold of one wrist. He felt cold steel, and then there was a click as a tight metal band closed. The prodding at the nape of his neck did not stop, and he suspected there were two people. The process repeated on the other wrist, and then he was cuffed. That was the last thing he was aware of, as a powerful blow caught him on the side of his head and darkness swallowed him.

The man in the cellar filled the bucket. He wondered if he had time for some fun with the woman. She was impossible not to notice. She was magnificent. Proud, athletic, had legs that any woman would die for, and a figure that he could barely keep his hands off. Even in her battered state, there were still the remnants of the beauty, and he became aroused at the thought. Miroslav wouldn't mind if he played a little.

He unfastened his trousers and his fun began. Before long, there was a low moan from the bound woman. Not one of pleasure, but a signal she was regaining her senses.

The two women were standing in the room, a little unsure what to do. The man on the sofa lay with blood dripping down his forehead and drops had stained the white carpet and leather sofa.

'Have you killed him?'

'No, he's still breathing, but I hit him harder than I planned to. I know it's not easy to knock a man out.'

'Well, you did a bloody good job. Go, girl!'

Their voices were whispers as they knew there were others in the house. They looked in the kitchen and found some scissors. Gabriela returned to the room, cut a thin strip of fabric from the gorgeous curtains and gagged the man.

Gabriela searched the ornate desk, but there were only papers. She rifled through the drawers, but there was nothing. However, in the bottom right-hand drawer was a silver pistol and a box of ammunition.

'Bloody hell! Look what I've found.'

Amahle joined her, and both women smiled.

'That's good. If I use mine, then I will be in real trouble. Take it. It's his gun. There is at least another man about.'

'Come on, let's go see!'

Gabriela picked up the pistol. Checked it was loaded and headed out into the corridor. There was an open door and a flight of stairs leading down. Amahle followed, but she stopped by the fireplace and picked up the heavy iron poker.

Pistol in hand, Gabriela stood listening. She could hear noises from below, and then the sound of footsteps approaching the staircase. The two women stood back on either side of the doorway, waiting as the steps led up to them.

The man came through the doorway. He was a powerfully built, had short, razor-cut hair, and a physique that showed the benefits of regular hours in the weight-room of the gym.

'Hello!'

Gabriela spoke with a husky, sexy voice and the startled man turned to stare at her, unsure what was happening. He never found out, as the hard, cold, iron poker hit his skull, with sufficient force to fell him without a murmur.

Gabriela bent down and checked his pulse in his neck. She felt nothing.

'You might have done it this time!' she whispered to Amahle. The two women took hold of his ankles and dragged him out of sight from anyone coming up the stairs. The women tied him up and left him in the corridor.

They carefully crept down the stairs, unsure if there were any more of Bilyk's men about, so the pistol and poker were kept at the ready. Neither said it, but they both hoped to find Gordon and Wayne in the basement.

At the bottom of the steps, they heard nothing. They looked around the corner. There was a single lightbulb hanging from a chord and it cast a yellow light around the room. What they saw both disappointed and horrified them. There was a lone woman tied to a chair. They stood there, shocked. She was naked, and so badly beaten that her face was unrecognisable. Their hearts sank. Gordon and Wayne were not there. This woman needed their help, so there was no time for disappointment.

TREADING WATER

Three women were in the room when he stirred. Bilyk was confused and tried to move, but he was bound in place on the chair. His eyes showed anger tinged with fear as he understood what had happened and his eyes landed on Dana as she pressed a pack of ice onto her swollen face. Her gaze bore into his. Her look was freezing cold like the icepack and for the briefest of seconds he flinched and looked away.

The room itself was unusually hot, and he stared at the fireplace and saw a roaring fire that he hadn't remembered from before. There were two other women there that he didn't recognise, and they looked at him with hatred.

'The bastard's awake!' Dana spoke with some difficulty through her damaged mouth.

'Good,' Gabriela said. 'We haven't time to waste. Mr Bilyk! You don't know me, but you have tried to kill me a few times. Now I need you to answer our questions. Is that understood?'

The man looked straight at her and gave no indication he had even heard.

'I thought you might be reluctant, so I have something that will help. By the way, don't expect your man to help you. He is unconscious, and tied up nice and tight, so he won't be stopping what we are about to do!'

Gabriela's voice carried menace and anyone listening would have no doubt she meant every word. Bilyk's mouth was taped so he couldn't speak even in he wanted to.

'I need to prove my sincerity, Mr Bilyk, so just watch a while.'

The Gabriela went to the fireplace and removed the iron poker from amongst the blazing logs. She turned and looked at the house owner, trussed and helpless. The man's eyes stared and, despite knowing what she was threatening, did not show fear.

The iron glowed yellow at its tip that changed to red and then black along its length. Dana and Amahle stared at Gabriela as she carried it carefully to hold just before the bound man's face. A white chalky look appeared on the yellow end, but it was clearly frighteningly hot.

Gabriela held the tip close enough to his skin that he flinched in pain, but he was unable to move more than an inch or two.

'I don't think you believe I will hurt you, so I'm going to show that I will.'

With no warning, she lowered the tip onto the top of his hand. He screamed and his eyes flooded with tears, but bound and cuffed, he could not escape, and his taped mouth meant that his scream was silent. Gabriela held the point just above the surface of the skin and the flesh seared and smoked. She wanted to convince him and despite wanting to remove the iron, she held it for what seemed, to her and the man, an age.

There were stifled screams as his body shook and the three women wanted to look away, but their eyes remained fixed on his hand. Eventually, Gabriela removed the poker and returned it to the fire.

'Mr Bilyk, I hope I have convinced you I will not hesitate to burn you again and next time, it will be somewhere else. Now I have some questions and I would advise you to answer them truthfully and honestly. Where are Gordon Bennet and policeman Wayne Maisonet?'

Amahle ripped the tape off Bilyk's mouth so that he could speak.

'Fuck off, bitch!'

The tape was slapped back over his mouth, stifling his words, and Gabriela returned to the fire.

Five minutes later, when the tape was removed, Bilyk was far more cooperative. The three now knew where the men had been taken. Bilyk was sobbing on the floor, and Dana contributed to his discomfort with a swift kick to his groin. It didn't add a great deal to his suffering, but it made her feel a little better. She had recovered her clothes from the bathroom. Dana was clearly badly hurt, and they insisted on taking her to hospital. They couldn't call for an ambulance.

The drive was not a long one, and they helped her through the doors of the emergency department of St. James' Hospital. At reception, the horrified look of the nurse resulted in her being wheeled through for treatment. Gabriela and Amahle told the nurse they had found her wandering the streets. They gave their own contact details, but then left hurriedly, knowing lost time could cost Gordon and Wayne's lives.

They got back into the car and headed towards Harehills and then along Roundhay Road to the park. Gabriela had warned Bilyk they would be back and that if their men were dead, then they would return and kill him.

The roads were almost deserted until they approached Roundhay Park. At the main gates, they could see flashing lights, ambulances, and lots of officers. Gabriela knew they wouldn't be allowed in and asked Amahle if there was another way. The police officer drove back a little to Oakwood and then straight past along a main road that was empty of traffic. After a short drive, they pulled into a small car-park and the two women got out. Amahle led the way, off to the right, up a steep incline where they had to scramble on all fours. Dark and with rain falling, they got to the top of the bank.

'This is the lake,' Amahle said, staring out into a black void. 'It is big and parts are deep, but in this dark we won't see anything. If they're out there, we won't find them.'

'We have to find them! We have to!' Gabriela was desperate.

As she stared out, she saw moving lights in the distance and realised she was looking at torches. She thought this was probably the police searching. The rain continued to fall, but there came a break in the clouds and a sliver of moon cast its reflection on the surface of the water. It was a vast expanse. If they had thrown Gordon bound into the water, he would have little hope of surviving. She broke down into a shuddering despair. She couldn't have lost him! She couldn't manage without him! Amahle put her arm around her and together they stared out across the water, before it disappeared into darkness once more. They were not sure what to do. They couldn't just walk away, but what was the point of remaining?

'We need to know what's going on, Amahle. Can you find out?'

The police woman took out her phone.

'I'll call some of my friends and see what's happening.'

Someone answered, and there was a detailed conversation. Gabriela tried to listen but couldn't hear much. Amahle put the phone away.

'Well?' Gabriela asked.

'Three men acting suspiciously shot at the police and there is a major manhunt. No one knows all the details, but there have been no signs of anyone else.'

'Oh, no! Are they out there?'

'No, they can't be!'

The early morning wind was icy, and the two women needed each other's body heat. In the dark, the distant lights kept moving and in the boathouse's direction, others joined them and sirens and flashing lights moved from higher in the sky. Gabriela realised they were cars moving downhill to the lakeside.

She could only put up with inaction for a short while. The cold and the misery spurred her on.

'Come on! At least we can skirt the lake. Maybe they've got away. Gordon isn't an easy man to kill! I bet they've swum to the shore.'

Amahle didn't believe this, but doing anything was better than doing nothing.

Wayne was tiring fast. His strength was waning. He was not a good swimmer at the best of times. He had hated swimming lessons at school. The water was just so cold. His clothes were weighing heavily on him and the cold cut deeply into him. Even the man near him in the water, the man who had seemed so superhuman and resourceful in facilitating their escape, was struggling. Wayne could hear his breathing, laboured and tired, and he had stopped encouraging him and fallen silent.

Neither man could see anything. They had headed away from the men and the boat, but they couldn't see anything now. Rain was falling, and the moon had disappeared. The hope that had sprung when they had freed themselves was now gone. Wayne had to fight against surrendering to the cold, to the inevitable, and just slipping away beneath the water.

His mind agreed, and he stopped struggling when he was grabbed by the hair and pulled back from below the water.

'No, you don't! Swim, you bastard! It can't be far.'

The words struggled to penetrate, but he hadn't the power to argue with them, and his arms moved and his legs kicked a little.

Despite the strength of Gordon's words, the man himself was nearing the end. Lost, exhausted, the cold was slowing him. His brain was not working logically, and he feared they were swimming in circles.

The two carried on a few yards more, but he saw Wayne disappear beneath the water next to him, and the water lay smooth where a second before his head had been.

Gordon knew he should turn, but he no longer had the strength. He trod water, ready to give up, when a head burst from out of the depths. Wayne's head and torso appeared, and the policeman stood waist deep, spluttering, teeth chattering. Gordon was stunned. Was he hallucinating? His right foot jarred with pain as he stubbed his foot on something hard. Reflexively, he put his foot down and felt ground, or at least mud and rock. They couldn't believe it and turned, throwing their arms around each other, laughing hysterically.

It took a while, but they stopped. They were weak and so cold.

'Are we dead?'

Wayne's question was genuine.

'It'll take more to kill us than that! But not much more!' Gordon said. 'But if we don't get out of the water and get dry, then we soon will be.'

They stared around. There were pinpricks of light away to their right and others behind. Gordon did not know if was the attackers still hunting, so he set off in the other direction. He supported Wayne by the arm and they struggled to keep their feet. They fell several times as they walked, but Gordon realised the water was becoming shallower.

Soon it was thigh deep, and then calf deep, and finally there was a stone wall before them. It was the lake's edge. They didn't have the energy to climb out and just leaned on the cold stone, catching their breath, their heads resting on their hands. They were cold, very cold and Gordon knew the dangers of remaining soaking wet, but he was too tired to care. His eyes closed and he would have drifted off into oblivion if he hadn't heard approaching footsteps on the gravelly pathway. Should he call out? Was it the men who had dumped them in the lake? Had they found them? Wayne was too lost, and too exhausted to notice, and Gordon prayed he wouldn't speak as the footsteps got nearer.

They were below the path level and in the dark, someone could well walk past without noticing them. There were the sounds of two people, but he couldn't see anything. Closer and closer the steps approached, and grew louder. They were barely five or six yards away when he heard a voice and shadows appeared.

Gabriela and Amahle walked with no real purpose. If Gordon and Wayne were in the lake, then they were dead, but Gabriela couldn't accept it.

'They will be alright! Gordon wouldn't leave me!' she said.

Just after she spoke, there was a voice in the dark. It wasn't loud, but it was familiar. She thought it was a trick of her mind, but then she heard it again, and this time, she was certain.

'Gordon? Gordon!' she called. 'Gordon, is that you?'

A voice called back to her.

'Gabriela, Gabriela? Good god! Gabriela, you are my angel!'

The women hurried over and saw two shadows. Their prayers were answered.

Amahle and Gabriela jumped down and after the initial flurry of hugs and kisses, they realised Gordon and Wayne were in danger. It took a lot of struggling, but eventually, the men were dragged over the wall and onto the pathway.

Amahle took out her mobile phone and called for help. It took a little while to convince the operator that she was a police officer, but eventually, she was put through. She gave their location, and the condition of the two men. She was told that emergency vehicles were in the park and to stay where they were.

They waited, keeping Gordon and Wayne talking and not allowing them to fall asleep. They wrapped them in their jackets to keep the icy wind from lowering their core temperature any further, and waited, frantic with worry. Where was the help?

Finally, vehicle lights appeared along the far side of the lake and moved around, getting nearer to where they were. Gabriela got up and walked towards the lights, waving her arms. When the first ambulance arrived, Gabriela ran to the driver's window and explained what was going on. The paramedics and the police took over and Gordon and Wayne were stretchered into the ambulances and quickly driven away, alarms sounding and lights flashing.

The two women were taken to the police station, reassured that the men would be well taken care of, and that once they had given a statement, they could visit. It would be St James' Hospital and they would be told immediately if there was a change in their men's condition.

They had no choice and soon were leaving the park and heading towards the police station.

NEW DAY, OLD WAYS

The rest of the night was spent explaining what had happened. Amahle and Gabriela had agreed between themselves not to mention anything about Miroslav Bilyk's house, nor anything that had happened there, at least for the time being.

They were surprised when, instead of inspector Glover, it was another officer who interviewed them. This one had been brought in to take over the inquiry. She was well briefed and understood who the two women were. Her first questions concerned why they had turned up at the park, and how they had found Wayne and Gordon.

Despite being interviewed separately, they both told the same story. Amahle had heard about the report of the shooting at Roundhay Park. Fearing that it could involve their missing partners, they left the hotel and arrived at the lake. It was just by chance they stumbled upon the wet and exhausted men climbing out of the water.

The likelihood of such a fortuitous encounter caused the officer to raise an eyebrow. She gave the two the same knowing look that said,

'I don't believe any of this, but it will wait.'

She didn't tell them what else had happened at the park that night and gave no explanation as to where Inspector Glover was, but the station was unusually hectic and there was a sense of tension.

After having their statements taken, the two women were allowed to leave, and driven back to get Amahle's car from the park. They then drove hurriedly to St. James' hospital. It wasn't far, and they parked and rushed into reception. They explained who they were and were shown up to the ward.

The duty nurse spoke with them before they could see the patients. Apparently, both had suffered quite severe hypothermia. It had been touch and go for a while, but they were now stable. The two women burst into tears with relief and held each other. When they composed themselves, they turned to the nurse.

'Can we see them?'

She smiled and told them they were sleeping, but she would allow them to go in for a while.

The two patients were in adjacent rooms. Gabriela went to Gordon, who was lying asleep on the bed. Various monitors measured his vital signs, and he looked very pale. She kissed him on the forehead and then sat down on the chair next to him. He didn't stir and his breathing was regular, but shallow. She just looked at his face, concerned how close she had come to losing him. The nurse appeared at the door and gestured time was up. Gabriela squeezed Gordon's hand, looked once more into his peaceful face and left the room.

Amahle was in the corridor and the two women walked out of the hospital and into the carpark. The nurse had told them that the police were posting guards outside the rooms.

The pale light of the new day was now the dull grey of autumn. Both women were exhausted, and they headed back to The Hamlet Hotel. Amahle still had a role, keeping Gabriela safe, despite all that had happened. They went up to their rooms, and arranged to meet for lunch after a sleep. Gabriela was too tired even to shower and just fell onto the bed. As her head hit the pillow, she was fast asleep. Dreams of what might have been haunted her slumber and tormented her heart.

When she finally woke, the light from outside was dim, and it was late in the afternoon. She had slept much longer than she had intended to. She got up, went into the bathroom, and took a long, hot shower. Afterwards, she sorted out some clothes to wear. When dressed, she went out into the corridor and knocked on Amahle's door. The policewoman opened it and smiled at Gabriela.

'I can't believe how long I slept,' the policewoman said. 'Come in.'

She stepped aside and Gabriela walked in.

'I'm starving! Shall we go down to eat at the bar?'

'Sounds good to me.'

The hotel was its usual hive of activity and the bar was doing a roaring trade, filled with mainly young men and women. They walked up to the bar. The barman noticed them and came over to take their orders. Two large glasses of red wine were poured, and the women checked the menu and chose what they wanted. The barman told them he would bring the order over when it was ready.

They found a table and enjoyed their first drink of the wine. They were sitting next to a low window that looked out onto the car park, but in the dark, it was mostly hidden from sight. All they could see were a couple of patches of light where the floodlights in the car park cast their brightness. The two women had become quite close after all that had happened.

'Once we've eaten, we'll drive in to see how they are. They would have called us if there was a problem.'

Amahle's voice showed her relief and Gabriela realised she had been as frightened as she had. To have lost Gordon would have been unbearable, and she still felt that fear in the pit of her stomach.

'They will be fine,' Gabriela reassured the other woman. 'We'll see them soon. Hopefully, they'll be awake. Come on, finish your drink and I'll buy you another.'

Gabriela drained her glass, and Amahle followed suit. The young Spaniard picked up the glasses and carried them over to the bar. Smiling to herself, she remembered she was still a barmaid at heart. She wondered how her friends were back in the Morena Bar in Calpe.

It was the same barman who served her, and she ordered the two drinks. He told her the food should soon be with them, and she headed back, carrying the two glasses. She placed one on a beer mat in front of Amahle and put hers on the table. She sat down, but nudged the table. Her glass teetered on the edge and, as if in slow motion, the glass tipped and gravity took a hold. It was about to fall, when with quick reflexes, she dived to catch it. As she leant forward, she was showered in glass. The window above her exploded sharp shards onto her and she fell to the floor. The cacophony lasted a mere second or two, and then there was a stunned silence. This was broken by the sound of a car's engine revving, and then a screech of tyres. Every eye in the room stared at the window, their table, and the bloodied bodies that lay on the carpet.

Gabriela was confused and hurt. She staggered to her feet and looked around, unsure what had happened. She stared at Amahle. The policewoman lay unmoving, her body torn by the glass and pierced by the hail of bullets. She didn't move and Gabriela watched as a black pool formed around the woman's chest.

In a wave, a sound tsunami rushed over her, and she was overcome by the enormity of it all. There was shouting, screams, cries, and confusion. The barman had been on his way over with the meals, but he had dropped them as the window broke. He hurried over to help, but the black woman lay there unmoving. Bending down, he checked for a pulse, but there was nothing. There was no doubt she was beyond help. Gaping wounds showed there was little point in trying to resuscitate her and vacant eyes stared upwards, accusing and lifeless.

Gabriela instinctively knelt down and closed her friend's eyes, giving her some privacy. Gabriela's ears rang from the sound of shattering glass and her face, head and hands were bleeding. She didn't think the cuts were serious.

'Your friend is dead.'

It was the barman that spoke, and she already knew the truth of his words.

'What happened? Why would someone fire at the hotel, for fuck's sake?'

This was said more to himself than to Gabriela and he stared around seeing others who were injured. He pulled out his mobile and called for help. The woman on the line told him help was on its way.

He went back to Gabriela and moved her away from the window and her friend. He found her a seat and sat the shocked woman down. In the bar, there were those injured and stunned and others who were helping and providing first aid. Gabriela was unaware what was happening. She looked for Amahle, but a hotel blanket covered her friend. Some of the hotel staff were moving people out of the bar and herding them into the restaurant. The chaos that had been initially present was becoming organised.

A single police siren cut through the night, followed by others, and within a short while, arrived at the entrance to the carpark and a convoy of emergency service vehicles flowed in. Car doors clattered, and many feet pounded up the steps to the front entrance.

Gordon woke up, and it took him a second or two to realise where he was. He remembered the freezing water, the tiredness that overcame him, and the sweetest sound, Gabriela's voice. He was in a hospital. Lying in the bed, he felt warm and comfortable. He had no idea what time it was and or how long he had been there and he ached all over. He wondered where Gabriela was, and how Wayne was. The policeman had nearly succumbed to the cold water, but he remembered they had both made it out of the lake. Gordon lay back in bed and shut his eyes. He was safe and in one piece and he was thankful for that, but he was a man with a mission. He had to make those responsible for his ex-wife's murder pay. The police had failed to protect him and he was worried about Gabriela.

As he lay with his head on the pillow, he heard the door opening. He didn't open his eyes. He assumed it was a nurse, and he was deep in thought and drifting back into sleep. Without warning, something soft pressed down onto his face with powerful pressure. He couldn't catch his breath. Every instinct cried out that this was not right. He was being attacked. There were voices of two assailants. One stopped him breathing, and the second held him down, preventing him from moving. Most people would panic, but not for Gordon. His training and experience kicked in. With a swift and fluid motion, he swung both legs upward and over. His knees came into contact with something hard. The force hurt him, so he hoped it did even more to the back of the head of the man pinning him down.

The man holding Gordon was thrown forward and his head struck the man pressing the pillow on Gordon's face. Both let go. Gordon rolled to the side and fell off the bed. He gasped for air, but was on his feet and faced his attackers. One was lying face down on the bed, not moving. The second turned to look at Gordon, reaching inside his jacket. Gordon dived over the bed in a swift movement, colliding with the assailant before he could draw a weapon. Both fell back on the floor, and Gordon was on top and followed with a series of swift and powerful blows into the man's face. Once! Twice! Three times! And then once more. Gordon held nothing back. He knew his life was on the line once again. He felt the man's nose break and blood flowed, but he didn't stop. Each blow spread more blood and caused more damage, until his attacker's eyes rolled upwards, and he went limp.

Gordon was kicked in his side before he could get to his feet. The force lifted him off the ground and felt his ribs crack. He fell back onto the floor, but rolled to the side under the bed. For a moment, he was out of reach of any more kicks, but blindsided and couldn't see where his attacker was or what he was doing. He was a sitting duck if the man fired into the bed.

Before Gordon, or the attacker, could act, the door opened and an angry female voice shouted.

'What are you doing?'

Before anything more could be said, there was a dull pop and a thud. Gordon knew the sound of a body falling and that of a silenced gun. He had a choice, left or right. He rolled to the right and hoped the gunman wasn't on that side. If he was wrong, he was dead. There were three more pops, and he felt the force of bullets striking the mattress where he had been and he was hit by fragments off the floor. He heard shouting from the corridor outside and an alarm went off.

'Shit! Shit! Shit!'

The male voice had a strong accent, but if English wasn't his first language, he had certainly mastered profanity, Gordon thought. Two more pops. Gordon knew he was still out of sight of the man, but for how much longer? Before he could react, there was the sound of footsteps hurrying out of the room and then running away.

Gordon got to his feet and realised he had blood on him, but he wasn't sure if it was his or from the man he'd beaten unconscious.

He stumbled around the bed and saw the body of a young nurse. Blood was still spreading on the lino around her and he checked to see if she was alive, but he felt no pulse. Gordon turned to the unconscious man. He was where he had left him, but now there were two gaping wounds in his chest. The man's eyes were open. Gordon leant over.

'Who sent you?'

Gordon shook the man, heedless of his injuries.

'Who sent you? Speak, you bastard! He's done for you, so you might as well say!'

The glazed look in the man's eyes cleared, and his lips quivered. Gordon put his head near to the man's mouth to catch the words, but he couldn't hear anything.

'Bilyk? Bilyk?' Gordon said to the dying man. The empty stare returned and then a rattle left just Gordon alive in the room. He staggered to the door in a state of shock. There was pandemonium. Two police officers approached with guns drawn. Gordon couldn't see any other casualties, but as he passed the adjacent open door, Wayne's stunned-looking face appeared.

'They had another go,' Gordon said. 'Fortunately for me, they failed, but they killed the nurse.'

Gordon and Wayne raised their hands and backed into Wayne's room. They waited there whilst the police checked the nurse and the dead assassin.

Order was eventually restored. Large numbers of police arrived and questions were asked, particularly why the police guard was not at his post. He had left to get a drink from the dispensing machine on the lower level. This had probably saved his life, Gordon thought, but not his career. The man was a wreck and guilt was plain on his face.

Wayne and Gordon were discharged, and the ward was closed. They were taken to the station to give full statements. The building was a scene of hectic chaos. Something else had been happening. A manhunt was taking place for the escaped assassin, but he had disappeared into the city.

Gordon expected to be interviewed by Inspector Glover, but another officer carried out the interview. When the two men arrived, the new inspector had taken Wayne into one room and Gordon was put in another.

After a while, she came in.

'I am Inspector Salisbury. I must let you know, Mr Bennet, that your partner, Miss Morales, narrowly escaped an attack earlier this evening. Yes, she is alright, Mr Bennet! Unfortunately, Constable Maisonet's friend, Constable Aysi, was not as fortunate. She was killed. I have just told him the news.'

'Where is Gabriela? I must see her!'

Gordon's voice was frantic with worry for Gabriela, but also devastated for Wayne.

'In good time, Mr Bennet. In good time! We are not used to such events in Leeds, Mr Bennet. This city is a busy one, but we don't have wholesale killings and assassinations. Trouble follows you, and I don't like that. On this occasion, it seems you are the victim and somehow you've survived another attempt to kill you. You must have some dangerous enemies. You really must have pissed someone powerful off! I believe that Inspector Glover told you to return to Spain. It is a shame you didn't listen to his advice.'

Eventually, Gordon was taken to Gabriela. They were relieved that they were alive, but devastated by all that had happened.

'It's so unfair, Gordon!'

'I know!' Gordon's voice was raw with emotion, and he didn't know what to say. There was nothing that would make it any better.

They were to return to yet another hotel. It was not far from The Hamlet, but as that was now a crime scene, they couldn't go back there. Their luggage was taken from The Hamlet to The Parkside.

After checking in, and being provided with another hire car, they were told to remain at the hotel. There was no guard this time, as all officers were needed.

When they got to their room, they held each other and the guilt they both felt for Amahle and the nurse overcame them. They couldn't image how Wayne was managing.

'This is a nightmare! We have to do something, Gordon!'

There was steel in her voice and Gordon knew she was right. They had to end this, and they needed to do it now.

'It's Bilyk!' she said.

She explained what had happened the previous night. Gordon's eyes opened wide with surprise when he heard how they forced him to say where Gordon and Wayne were being taken.

The more she told him, the more his eyes opened with admiration for this brave young woman. Gabriela told him about Dana and what had happened to her.

'They hurt her, Gordon. They hurt her really bad!'

'They've hurt a lot of people, but we need to put a stop to it.'

ALL GOOD THINGS COME TO AN END

Rodavan knew he was going to have to face Bilyk and explain what had happened. This was not something he was looking forward to. His boss was violent to a point that was psychopathic, and he didn't respond well when people failed him. He had seen what had happened to others, but he had no alternative. Miroslav Bilyk had power and contacts, so running away was unlikely to work. The only thing in his favour was that he had escaped, and he was pretty sure the two men were dead at the bottom of the lake.

It was mid-morning when he drove over to Bilyk's home. Normally, he wouldn't have gone there, but his boss needed to be told what had happened. He had tried phoning, but the call rang out to an answer machine, so it was with a great nervousness that he parked in the street. The houses in this area were impressive and Rodavan felt insignificant. He had listened to a local news report, and that said that there had been a shootout with three armed men in Roundhay Park the previous night. One police officer and two of the three gunmen had been shot, but they were unsure of their condition.

The gate was open, which struck him as odd. When he had been at the house before, the gate was always shut. As it was, he strolled through and made his way towards the house. He walked on the lawn that edged the gravel driveway as his steps sounded so loud on the loose surface. Like a man walking to the gallows, he approached the house with little enthusiasm. As he got nearer, the only sign that anyone was at home was the front door being ajar. This was very unusual. Mr Bilyk was a man who was very security conscious.

No one appeared, and as he reached the door, he called through to anyone inside.

'Hello? Mr Bilyk? Are you there?'

There was no reply, and he cautiously pushed the door wider and tried again.

'Are you there, Mr Bilyk? It's me, Rodavan!'

Again, nothing, but he thought he heard some movement further in the house.

'I'm coming in, Mr Bilyk. I hope you don't mind, but I need to report back on what happened last night.'

Still no reply, and so he walked in nervously. The inside of the entry hall was fairly dark, and he could see and hear nothing. He almost tripped on a bound man lying on the floor.

His heart was pounding, and he feared what else he would discover as he stepped over the man. From an open door, he heard a faint sound.

Not being armed, he retreated into the kitchen. There was a knife on the worktop and so he took it and returned to the room as quietly as he could.

He found a man bound and gagged, sitting on a chair. Clearly, he had been badly tortured. There were large fluid-filled blisters on his face, and his hands had deep, straight, red burn lines. The victim was alive, in great pain, and needed hospital treatment. The tortured man's eyes opened and stared at Rodavan. He knew those eyes. He had seen them many times, and they always made him uneasy, but today they pleaded for help.

This was Miroslav Bilyk, and someone had hurt him badly. His boss was at his mercy and he thought about killing him. He would then be safe, but as he stood facing Miroslav, the knife in his hand started shaking. The eyes looked back at him as he looked down at the brutalised face. The opportunity would never come again, but fear stopped his hand. He cut the bonds holding his boss's arms to the chair and then slashed through those holding his ankles.

As soon as his wrists were free, Miroslav reached out, flexed his hands and screamed a silent scream. His mouth was still taped, so it was his eyes watering and heaving chest that showed his pain.

'I will remove the gag, Mr Bilyk. I think it will hurt a lot. Do you want me to do it?'

The seated man just nodded. The gaffer tape was stuck firmly and blisters edged up to fabric and Rodavan knew removing the tape would rip them.

'This will really hurt, Mr Bilyk. Are you sure you don't just want me to call an ambulance?'

The head shook, and Rodavan acted. Grasping a loose edge of the tape, he pulled in a continuous and forceful way. There was a ripping sound, a blood-curdling scream as skin came with the tape and watery fluid flowed down the man's face, mingling with his tears. Bilyk sank onto his hands and knees, shaking. His rescuer was unsure what to do. Bilyk's injuries appeared more painful than life-threatening, but even he felt a tinge of sympathy for his boss' suffering.

He rushed to the kitchen and opened cupboard doors and found a glass, filled it with cold water, and hurried back. Miroslav had regained some control, and was on his feet. He took the glass of water and drank a little. He spoke, but it was more of a mumble as moving his face was agony.

'Get Dr Johnson.'

It was difficult to hear, but Rodavan knew the doctor. Bilyk had used him to deal with injuries they didn't want to explain. The doctor did private work and the authorities never knew about it.

'My phone!'

Rodavan looked around for the mobile and found it on the carpet near the fireplace. Bilyk took the phone, dialled a number, and handed it back.

'Get him here! Tell him, burns!'

The voice spoke through gritted teeth. Rodavan listened. A voice answered.

'Dr Johnson here. Is that you, Mr Bilyk?'

'No, it's not. Bilyk's hurt. Badly burned. He needs your help. He's at his home. Get here quickly!'

There were more words said and then the phone went dead.

'He's coming right over! Can I do anything?'

Rodavan made some phone calls for his boss as he was treated by the doctor. Painkilling injections, dressings and an intravenous drip stabilised his injuries and were the best the doctor could do without Bilyk going to hospital. Dr Johnson made the patient comfortable. Bilyk was sedated, and in his bed. The unconscious guard had recovered, but had a headache.

The doctor was tidying up and promised that he would return in a couple of hours. A nurse would arrive in a short while to take over. The doctor made it very clear that Miroslav was not to leave the house, not to move and should rest as much as possible. He told Rodavan to stay with the patient.

The doctor left the house, passing a man arriving. The two had met before, and the doctor briefly explained what had happened to Bilyk. He reiterated that Bilyk was not to move, must stay in his bed and then the doctor left.

Pavle walked up to the door and entered. He knew the house, and he went straight to the master bedroom. His boss's condition shocked him. He had never seen him other than in total control. This was a man who wielded power ruthlessly, and to see him maimed and vulnerable was shocking. Miroslav's eyes told another story, though. They looked at him with an intensity that made him shiver. Despite all outward signs, this was not a man who had been defeated, and he wondered what he intended to do.

The discussion that followed was slow and painful, but at the end, Pavle knew his orders. Leaving the house with the recovered guard, he made a call. Bilyk wanted people eliminated that very day. Pavle was not happy about it. It was too rushed, too brazen and could only lead to trouble, but he had his orders and he knew to carry them out to the letter. This time, he would take charge. The male target was in the hospital and the woman back at the hotel.

The first part went to plan. They had hung around the carpark watching for the opportunity. He hoped she would come down to eat at some point. If she didn't, they would have to find her room. Their informer provided the information. He couldn't believe his luck when the women sat by the window in the bar. There was another with her.

Guess it's not your lucky day, he said to himself, and he started the engine. His partner fired a quick salvo through the window, as they drove past and out of the carpark.

He smiled as they got away from the hotel.

'Next,' he said.

They drove towards the hospital, men on a mission. To kill the troublesome Mr Gordon Bennet.

It had been a cock-up! He had been lucky to get away, and he had had to kill Serge.

'Shit!'

He had been fortunate not to be caught by the police, as he had driven away. There was a car at a rendezvous spot and he drove there, trying to avoid attracting any attention.. That bastard Bennet took some killing. His mind was a whirl, and all he could do was follow the prearranged plan. Dump this car, set it alight, and report back to Bilyk. Facing his boss was something he didn't want to do, but he had no choice.

He pulled up in a lay-by where the other car was and drove in behind it, leaving a few car lengths of separation. Sunrise was a few hours away, and the sky was full of dark clouds. Getting out, he walked over to the other car, and opened the boot, rummaged around, and emerged with a glass bottle full of petrol, trailing a rag. He looked about. There was no sign of anyone about. He flicked his lighter. The spark shone, star-like, for a second, before the gas lit and the small flame dazzled.

Pavle tossed the bottle through the open door. It shattered, and the petrol exploded in a fireball, lighting the night sky and searing his skin.

He hurried back to the car, but as he was about to get in, a voice called to him.

'Good evening! Pavle? I hear things aren't going too well for you.'

'What the hell are you doing here?'

Pavle wasn't pleased. The well-oiled machine that his boss had created was coming apart at the seams. Why the fuck was this man here? Inside, he panicked, but his voice did not reveal it.

'I know your boss, Pavle. How can I put it? We had an arrangement that was mutually beneficial. It appears times are changing, and I need to ensure I am kept clear of the fallout when his house of cards collapses. I guess I'm cleaning up.'

Pavle went for the pistol in his belt, but the stranger was faster. His gun was in his hand and three rapid shots were drowned out by the explosion of the car's fuel tank. Pavle was dead before his body struck the road. There were two holes in his chest and a third through his forehead. The stranger smiled.

'Bloody good shooting,' he said to nobody but the night. 'It's a good job someone can do the job right.'

He walked down a narrow lane to where he had left his car. He whistled jauntily and was feeling better than he had for a couple of days.

The car was still engulfed in flames as he drove past, heading away into the darkness, his work almost over. There were still a few loose ends before he could relax and carry on, knowing he was safe. It was a shame it all had to end, as it had been so lucrative, but all good things come to an end.

TWO TO TANGO

Gabriela was in a state of shock as she arrived at the hospital. Despite her protestations, the police insisted she went to be checked out. They arrived in the middle of a major incident. Police cars with lights flashing filled the car park and entrance. Her first fear was for Gordon. Gabriela walked into reception, but in the chaos, she slipped the police escort and went straight up to Gordon's room.

She arrived at the entrance to Gordon's ward, stopped and asked the nurse what was going on. It was mayhem! Medics and police were rushing here and there and she saw a sheet covering a body in the doorway to Gordon's room. A voice called out.

'Gabriela! Gabriela! Thank God!'

She turned and saw Gordon hurrying towards her. Clearly unhurt, he appeared to have recovered from the hypothermia.

'Gordon! Gordon! What's happening?'

'Someone came to finish the job! Two men came to kill me, but I'm a hard man to kill.'

He smiled at her, and she smiled back, but he let his smile drop and replaced it with a sad expression.

'They shot the nurse, Gabriela. She's dead and one gunman.'

'You killed him?'

'No, not me. The other hit man shot him before running off. I can't tell you how lucky I was!'

'Oh, Gordon. How long can our luck hold?'

It was her turn to tell him her dreadful news.

'The police woman guarding us at the hotel, Amahle. She was Wayne's partner. She and I were having dinner when she was killed.

194

They shot through the window. If I hadn't bent down at the right moment, I would be dead too.'

Gordon held her tight, realising how close they'd come to losing each other.

'We will stay together now, Gabriela, and we must put an end to this madness.'

Whilst they stood there, a stern faced officer approached.

'Mr Bennet, Miss Morales, I am sorry to break up your moment together, but I need to speak with you now! Follow me!'

She turned and walked away. She clearly assumed they would follow, which they did. Gordon was now dressed, having changed out of the surgical robe. The policewoman led them into an empty office in the hospital. She shut the door behind them and they all sat down. The officer's face looked like thunder.

'Do you realise how much trouble you have caused since you have been in Leeds? How many deaths? There have been more killings in these last few days than in the last few years. Bombs, drownings, assassinations, kidnappings, the list goes on and on. Innocents have been caught in the crossfire of something that is inexplicable. There is just one common factor, you two.'

'I'm not sure what to say. We came on holiday. I wanted to show Gabriela my hometown. We had only arrived when my ex-wife's partner disappeared. We found Shelley, my ex, and three others at the bottom of a swimming pool and ever since, someone has been trying to kill us and we don't know why!'

Still looking furious, the woman spoke again.

'Well, they've made a complete hash of it! Maybe if they'd done it properly, it would have saved all the others!'

She sounded exasperated, maybe tired. Gordon could only imagine the stress she must be under.

'Where's Inspector Glover? I thought he was in charge of this case?'

'He is, was. That is until he got shot whilst you were in the lake! I'm Inspector Salisbury!'

'Is he ok, Inspector?' Gabriela asked, worried for the dour policeman.

'It was touch and go, and still is. Someone shot him at point blank range. They've operated, and he lost a lot of blood, but he is still alive. Which is more than I can say for Constable Aysi. I have had to break that news to her partner, Constable Maisonet. They were to be married later this year. I am not sure he will ever get over it. You are bad luck. Bloody bad luck! Now what is going on? Inspector Glover thought Marcus Spinx lay at the centre of this. Revenge for his jailing, but it appears to have gone way beyond this. Tell me, what do you know?'

It was a long interview and Gordon and Gabriela told the officer what they knew.

The inspector's mobile rang and the Gordon and Gabriela sat listening to the one-sided conversation. When the call ended, she turned to them.

'Another! Another! Will it ever stop?'

She glared at the faces of the two sitting opposite her. It was a rhetorical question. There was nothing they could add.

'This is getting serious, Mr Bennet. There is a burnt-out car and a body next to it. He has three holes in him. One through his forehead and two in his chest. This is no amateur's work. It is a professional hit. The victim matches the description of the man who attacked you tonight, but we can't be sure. Go back to the hotel and stay there. Leave this to us! Do I make myself clear?'

'Perfectly clear, Inspector. We are happy to leave it up to the police. We only wanted a holiday!'

'I warn you, Mr Bennet, Miss Morales, keep out of it! Believe me! I do not joke! Go! Be assured, I will speak to you both later.'

The door opened, and a constable walked in.

'Take these two back to the hotel!'

'Yes, ma'am!'

Gordon and Gabriela followed the police officer out into the corridor and then down the stairs and out to the car park. He approached a squad car and opened the back doors for them.

It was almost dawn when they arrived back in the car park and the police car stopped at the front steps of the hotel. They got out and walked up the steps to the front entrance. The officer watched them go into the building and then he drove off.

The reception desk had a gentle light, but the rest of the foyer was in semi-darkness. They nodded to the bored-looking woman at the counter and walked around to the stairs, and they headed upwards.

When they were back in their room, Gordon spoke.

'We've got to put an end to this madness. Did you say you'd left

Bilyk at his home?'

'Yes, but he won't be going anywhere. He didn't want to speak, and he took some persuading. In the end, he told us they had taken you to the lake in the park. Unless he's in hospital, he'll be at home.'

'We are going to go and get him and sort this out. If only my gun hadn't gone when the house exploded. This could be tricky.'

'That's not a problem. I've got one.'

Gabriela went over to the bedside cabinet and opened the drawer and she removed a pistol and a box of ammunition. Gordon looked at her with a mixture of surprise, love, and admiration.

'Is it any wonder that I love you?'

'Not to me! I guess I'm just perfect! This is Bilyk's pistol. I took it from his house.'

'Only fitting that we take it back to him. Is the car still in the carpark?'

'It should be! They returned the keys after your kidnapping. They'd been left in the car, so it should be there.'

'Let's have a few hours' sleep. We'll need our wits about us.'

Gabriela was exhausted. She had been living on adrenaline for days now. They got onto the bed and instantly fell asleep.

Gordon woke her with a cup of instant coffee. It was the best he could do. She took it, pulled a face, but drank it.

They both showered and dressed.

'We have a house call to make. Are you ready?'

Gabriela nodded. They left the room and passed the reception, through the doors and out into the morning.

They found the car just as it had been left, but Gordon still checked to make sure it hadn't been booby-trapped. It was clear, so they drove out of the front gates and headed towards Alwoodley. Gordon had driven there many times. The roads were busy, being rush hour.

It took longer to arrive at Manor House Lane than the last time Gabriela had driven there. The pavements of the tree-lined street were empty, but the road was busy with cars pulling out, heading for work. Gordon drove along the street towards Bilyk's house. He slowed down as they passed, and the two stared across to see what was happening.

When he arrived in the street, he knew he would have a wait. It was essential that whatever happened, Bilyk must not involve him in this sorry mess. The Serb must keep him out of it.

From his position, he had learnt a great deal about the council leader and businessman. He investigated the man's relationships, his lovers, and his family. Bilyk also gathered similar information on all who worked closely for him. An insurance policy, he thought. You could never be sure when it would be needed. Bilyk had a wife and family, and they were unaware of his non-legitimate business dealings. They only knew of his council role and his legitimate businesses. His drug dealing, his extortion rackets, and prostitution, he kept hidden. Bilyk's wife was either in denial, or simply tolerated his sexual dalliances. She had met some of those who worked for him, and he couldn't believe she was that naïve. The woman enjoyed the trappings of wealth, and ignorance was the price she paid.

It was Miroslav Bilyk's wife that he was waiting for. She had been away, but was expected back that morning. She had become a woman of habit, and that played into his hands. Information was power, and he would use it.

He waited out of sight and, sure enough, as expected, a taxi pulled up outside. Karika Bilyk got out of the car. Middle-aged, she carried a few extra pounds, and may once have been a beauty, but age had left its mark. She was a nice lady, he thought. It always seemed to be the nice people who had to suffer. He pushed this thought aside.

She could have asked the taxi driver to drive into the property, but she didn't want a fuss, and the short stroll gave her time to gather her thoughts before she met Miroslav. It was a dangerous game she played. Her husband still loved her, but he desired young flesh. She suffered the humiliation, played the dutiful and dumb wife, and raised her three children. But she harboured feelings and passions too, and as long as he never found out, life was tolerable. In fact, she lived for the moments when she could be with her lover. He was old, like her, cared for her, and was prepared to take the risk for the few hours they spent together each month. Her sister provided the excuse and the alibi.

Karika loved being with her man. They spent most of the time talking, laughing, happy in each other's company. Mostly innocent, but her husband wouldn't see it that way. She feared what he would do if he ever found out, but he hadn't yet. She smiled. It really had been a lovely break, but now she was back and she had to face reality.

At least until next time.

The man stepped out in front of her. She hadn't seen him, lost in her daydreams. The face looked familiar. Friendly, not at all threatening, but she saw him take something out of his coat pocket. He held it up, and she looked at it, at him, and blinked in surprise.

'Mrs Bilyk, I am glad to meet you. Please follow me!'

'What, now?'

'Yes, right now. I have a car over there.'

They walked over to it. He opened the passenger door, and she got in. As he got into the driver's seat, he threw her travel bag onto the back seat and drove off. Ten minutes later, he phoned Miroslav.

'Mr Bilyk, it's me!'

'What do you want? I warn you, I'm not in the mood for anything today.'

'Oh, you'd better be in a listening mood, Miroslav. I can call you that, can't I?'

'What do you want!'

'Well, I have a hunch the police will be calling on you today. It appears you've been a naughty boy. Anyway, I just wanted to tell you that if anyone asks, you don't know me and we have never met. Alright?'

'Why should I do that?'

'Well? If you love your wife, you will! She is here with me now. A lovely lady.'

'I want to talk to her, you bastard. Put her on! If you've harmed her, you will pay!'

'Oh, I don't think so! You are in no position to threaten me. But I'll let her speak.'

'Miro? Are you there? He's got me? I'm frightened.'

'You'll be fine, Karika. He won't hurt you!'

'She's no longer on the phone, Miroslav. She is gagged again. Now listen, I will keep her safe until your trial ends. Any link to me and she will die. Is that clear? I am to be kept out of it!'

'I'll kill you if you harm her!'

'No, you won't. I hope there is nothing linking us. If there is, then you'd better make it vanish quickly. I would say you have, maybe half an hour! Goodbye, Mr Bilyk. It has been nice not knowing you!'

Dana came around in the hospital room, confused and unsure

how long she had been unconscious, but she realised she had undergone surgery. She lay in a bed with tubes going into her and machines surrounded her, bleeping and displaying numbers and lines. She struggled to gather her thoughts. As she did, memories flooded back, and she screamed.

Two nurses rushed in and administered a sedative, and Dana drifted back into sleep.

The second time she awoke, she wasn't alone. A stern-looking woman was sitting facing her.

'Dana, I am Inspector Salisbury. I know who you are and that you are a serving officer. You were working for Miroslav Bilyk. Are you capable of telling us what happened?'

'They hurt me!'

'I understand, Dana. I want to arrest the man and men who did this to you. For me to do it, I need to know if you have hard evidence. The doctors have treated you, Dana. They have taken DNA samples, but I need more. Can you give me more?'

The woman in the hospital bed looked the inspector in the eye and nodded.

For the first time in a while, the inspector smiled. She finally believed she might have the evidence, but it needed to be solid and irrefutable.

She spent an hour listening to the undercover policewoman. It was hard, but she learnt how the woman had suffered at the hands of Bilyk and his men. She heard about the two men who were sent to die in the lake at Roundhay Park, and she learned of a paper trail that Dana had collected and stored that linked Miroslav to other crimes and murders.

At the end of the interview, she had grounds for a warrant. As she left the hospital, the inspector called the station and arranged for an application to be made. She went out of the front door and into the waiting car, which sped away. It was still dark, but she wanted everything ready for the raid later that morning. This was her opportunity to rid the city of a corrupt councillor, crime boss and serial killer. If she could bring Miroslav Bilyk down, then everyone would benefit. Despite all that had happened in recent days, she began to think that finally things were going her way.

The police cars sped down Manor House Lane, and the front car stopped before the gates. Two police officers got out, one carrying a heavy crowbar. They forced the gate open and slid it across, and the cars streamed into the grounds, sirens blaring and lights flashing. The tactical armed squad was ready for any eventuality. They didn't expect anyone to resist, but experienced told them to be prepared.

The door gave way to their rams and inside the house they discovered the badly injured owner receiving medical treatment. His assistant, Pavle, looked ready to put up a fight, but his face changed, and he surrendered. Bilyk's condition made him incapable of being difficult, and when presented with the warrant, his only demand was to be allowed to contact his lawyer. The inspector laughed. She read his rights and formally placed him under arrest.

An ambulance arrived within ten minutes and the Serbian was taken to the hospital for medical treatment. Pavle was taken to the police station for questioning, but they released the nurse, pending further inquiries.

They searched the house and grounds and in the cellar were signs someone had been tortured. They also found Bilyk's safe and, when finally opened, there were accounts of his illegal activities. This hard evidence was something Miroslav Bilyk wouldn't be able to talk, or bribe, his way out of. Dana had been held in the cellar and the DNA would confirm it. It was now up to forensics to do their work and find conclusive evidence that linked the city councillor to the killings and other crimes.

The inspector couldn't help believing she held all the cards. Inspector Glover would hopefully recover, but she would oversee the end to Bilyk and his web of crime.

She wanted to interview Bilyk as soon as possible, but understood that wouldn't be until the doctors said he was fit. From the extent of his injuries, that might be a while, so she would make a start on his right-hand man, Pavle. She needed to break his spirit. With his boss heading to jail for a very long time, he might talk. It was surprising how the possibility of a shorter sentence could get a man to open up.

FRUSTRATION

As they drove past Miroslav's house, Gabriela and Gordon saw the police, the cars and the flashing lights. They were too late. It was out of their hands. Gabriela couldn't help but experience a sense of relief. She feared what she and Gordon might have done. She frightened herself with how badly she had hurt Bilyk.

Gordon almost screamed with rage. Somewhere, a part of him demanded revenge. An eye for an eye, for the murder of his ex-wife and the innocents like the police woman. Ego and Id? In the end, the city leader had avoided his justice. Like Gabriela, Gordon also felt a sense of relief. Losing his freedom and Gabriela was a price he didn't want to pay. Much as it hurt him, it appeared he had no option other than leaving Miroslav Bilyk to the law.

There was nothing more he could do. It was over. He had lost his house, his neighbours, friends and almost Gabriela. What a homecoming! He had put Gabriela through purgatory. It didn't matter that he just wanted a holiday. Fate, it seemed, had different plans. The thing he couldn't understand was the reason she stayed with him. Anyone else would run a mile, but the beautiful young Spaniard at his side just took it in her stride. He loved her more than anything and yet all he did was bring her trouble.

She turned and looked at him. A smile crossed her face.

'There's nothing for it, Gordon,' she said. 'Take me back to the hotel. I want a long shower, a good sleep, good food and someone to make all this disappear. If I can't have that, then I guess I'll make do with you!'

Her smile turned into a broad grin, and she leant over and kissed his cheek. He almost lost control of himself and the car, but just prevented it from running off the road.

He didn't care. The world was a better place because of Gabriela. He was a better man. The old Gordon Bennet wouldn't have allowed the law to run its course. He would have searched for a way to ensure Miroslav paid the ultimate price, but the new one wanted nothing more than to live his life in peace.

'Your wish is my command, fair lady!'

He laughed, even though new demons were to join his nightmares. People he felt responsible for and yet failed them. Gabriela's eyes searched his face, and she seemed to read his thoughts.

'I know, Gordon. But there was nothing you or I could do. We will both have to live with it. It will always be there, but if you are with me, I can face it! Take me back. I want some time alone with you.'

He drove back to the hotel and to a few hours of bliss, a pressure release. The danger was now a thing of the past, or at least, so they believed, and they started the recovery.

When finally they stirred, the sense of frustration remained. Gordon understood it would be a long time before they could return to their own lives. Ahead lay hours, if not days, of interviews and questioning by the police. There was a distinct possibility they might be charged. Gabriela was partially responsible for Miroslav Bilyk's injuries. Gordon hoped the police would see it as justified self-defence. With Amahle murdered, only Dana and Gabriela could account for what had happened. Dana suffered torture and rape, and Gabriela had been trying to rescue her.

This sense of limbo wasn't helped by Gordon's home being destroyed. All his history dwelt in that house, and now he had nothing. Even his ex-wife was gone. It was as if his life had been wiped clean.

Gabriela looked at him, and she took his hand and squeezed it. She didn't say anything. She didn't need to. That simple act reminded him she was there. They had each other, and that was something to look forward to.

He turned to her and smiled. She reminded him of what they did have, and that was worth more than all they'd lost.

The telephone on the bedside cupboard rang. Gordon reached

over and lifted the receiver to his ear.

'Yes?'

'Mr Bennet? Inspector Salisbury here. We will need to interview you and Miss Morales this morning. I will send a car around in about an hour's time. Can you be in reception waiting?'

'Yes, Inspector. We'll be there. We have nowhere else to be. Thank you.'

His manner was polite and cooperative. He knew the police had a job to do. Complex and very serious cases needed careful unravelling, and Gordon wanted the investigation to be completed thoroughly. He didn't want to give Bilyk any opportunity to get away with his crimes. He had the satisfaction that Marcus Spinx was in jail and he wanted Bilyk to join him for many, many years.

'They want to speak with us in an hour. We just have time for some breakfast.'

'We'd better get moving then,' said Gabriela.

There was a flurry of activity, and before long, they were in the restaurant, eating heartily. They weren't sure when they'd get the opportunity to eat again, and so they tucked in with gusto.

Gabriela pulled her face when she tasted the coffee, but she managed to drink it.

'This is horrible, Gordon!'

He agreed with her, but it was slightly better than nothing. After finishing, they waited at reception until a police car pulled up. They walked down the steps and, within minutes, were whisking their way to the station and the long day ahead.

NEWS GETS OUT

Marcus Spinx had waited for good news from Franco, but the guard had little to report. Luckily, Cherry Jung, his lawyer, was more informative. She made regular visits as required to keep him up to date with the appeal, the situation regarding the murder of his wife, and anything else she thought would be of interest.

He listened to what she had to say, as well as passing an appreciative eye on the way she looked. She was fully aware of her impact and, with this in mind, she chose her attire for each visit. She didn't have to worry about anything happening. Some things were beyond his influence in the prison, but anything that kept her in employment and paid well was a tool for her to use.

'There was a report in the papers of an incident in Roundhay. Apparently, the police arrived after a tip-off to find three men acting suspiciously. The three shot at the police and the police returned fire. Two of the three men are dead and an officer shot.'

Marcus' ears picked up on this.

'Did it say what the men were doing there?'

'No, no further details, apart from the name of the officer shot. I believe you know him. Inspector Glover.'

Marcus Spinx leapt to his feet.

'Oh, there is a God! That old bastard. I hope he's dead. Is he?'

'No, Mr Spinx. They say he was seriously injured.'

'Well, at least something's going right. I can only hope he takes a turn for the worse. The old bastard put me here. I will forever be in debt to whoever shot him. Oh, good news indeed!'

It was at the end of their meeting, and she left Marcus in a much better mood than when she first visited. The next day when she returned, she had more news for the inmate.

'Mr Spinx, I hope you are well. I have some more news.'

'Do tell me Glover is dead.'

'Sorry, Mr Spinx. No, he is still alive. But I can let you know the police raided Miroslav Bilyk's house this morning, and the man has been arrested. Evidently, it is linked to the missing lawyer, his partner's murder and the death of your wife, Ariadne.'

'They've arrested him!'

He jumped to his feet and shot across the room in a heartbeat. He grabbed and kissed the lawyer fully and passionately on the lips. Startled, caught off guard for a moment, she didn't respond, but then she entered into this business opening with gusto. Never let it be said that she didn't seize her opportunities. Marcus Spinx was still a wealthy and somewhat powerful man. His wife had been murdered, and she was a free agent, so why not? He was older, locked away, and in need of people he could trust. She was happy to be that person, and she would play it her way.

The two parted and he smiled.

'I think I might enjoy working with you, Miss Jung.'

'The feeling is mutual, Mr Spinx,' and she laughed and tossed her hair in a dramatic and well-practised manner.

'I need you to find out anything and everything regarding this case. Keep me updated daily. If you can't get here, contact Franco, the guard. You have met the man. He will do whatever you ask. I want, no need, to be sure that Bilyk is going down!'

'You will hear everything the moment I do, Mr Spinx. There is one further thing.'

'What is it?'

'I thought you might like to know that the police found him badly beaten and burnt when they arrived.'

'Oh, Miss Jung. You truly are the harbinger of good news! Thank you. I am in your debt! Go! Keep me updated!'

She nodded and turned and left the interview room.

When Spinx was back in his cell, he took his precious finches out of their cage and told them all the good news. He was like a child on his birthday, and his grin was a permanent fixture. The birds responded with their usual lively chatter and movement. He fed them extra, spoke to them, and shared their joy in living. The three of them were caged, but that didn't mean that their lives were empty.

The finches' kisses were pecks, but Cherry's, whilst initially hesitant, was not. He didn't fool himself that she was after more than his wealth and influence, but he needed someone and he would play her. What was more, he would have fun doing it. He had three pets now.

SEALED LIPS

When Bilyk came round in hospital, his pain was now a little less agonising than before. The surgeons treated his burns and kept him sedated sufficiently so he didn't really care. His condition had been serious, but not life-threatening. He would be scarred, but the doctor who visited said he should make a full recovery otherwise. The good news ended there.

His eyes opened, and the face that looked at him showed scant regard for his wellbeing. In fact, if looks could kill, he would be a dead man. The stern face of Inspector Salisbury stared at him.

'Miroslav Bilyk, I am arresting you for the murder of Ariadne Spinx and Shelley Jones. You do not have to say anything, but anything you say can be used in a court of law. You know the drill, Mr Bilyk. We are also investigating several other deaths, and further charges may be laid later. You are advised to appoint a lawyer, but if you don't have one, we can provide one for you. I hope you are feeling better after your ordeal.'

'I have nothing to say until my lawyer is present.'

'That's your right, Mr Bilyk. I believe he will be waiting for you when we arrive at the station. The doctors tell me you are out of danger and fit to be interviewed. The officers here,' and she nodded to two standing by the door, 'will arrange for your transport to the station when you are dressed. Good day, Mr Bilyk. I will be speaking with you shortly.'

She got to her feet and went to open the door, when she turned and spoke again.

'In case you didn't understand. You will be a very old man, if you ever leave prison, Mr Bilyk. A very old man!'

Inspector Salisbury wore a broad smile as she left the hospital room. This was the part of the process she loved. The look on the face of someone charged for an offence they thought they had got away with. The even better part was when the jury found them guilty and they were sentenced. It was only a matter of time, but it was coming for Miroslav Bilyk. Oh yes, it would surely come for him!

The sad part for the inspector was the loss of a colleague. Constable Amahle Aysi had been killed whilst on duty, and it was a devastating end to a promising career. Even worse for her partner, Wayne Maisonet. The man suffered badly, traumatised, both by Amahle's killing and by what happened in the lake. His testimony would prove vital in ensuring Miroslav's conviction. He and Gordon Bennet saw Bilyk give the order for their slaying. This was condemning evidence. She organised police divers to scour the lake and a number of bodies were removed. Some were recent and some badly decayed as they had been in the water a long time. It would take considerable time to identify them all, but they had a long list of possibilities.

The newspapers and television had loved it. It remained the major news for days. The park remained closed for a protracted period, which the cafe and other businesses weren't pleased about. As the biggest case in years, reporters, local, national and international, descended and the city council featured daily as Bilyk's web of crime unravelled. Several councillors also faced arrest, and their faces appeared in the daily papers. A provisional new leader for the city was appointed and elections organised. The population of the city were shocked by how their elected leader had failed them, and how much corruption there was.

Miroslav Bilyk's wife had vanished and her children were desperate for her welfare. Stories and reports of her being seen on the continent, living the high-life, filled the less reputable tabloids. The inspector was concerned about her, though. She wasn't sure Karika Bilyk was aware of her husband's dealings. Nevertheless, she had all ports out of the country put on alert for her.

All of this took time and, meanwhile, Gordon and Gabriela remained in a new hotel. At first, they were busy giving statements and appearing regularly at the police station, and there were meetings with Gordon's insurers, but eventually they were left to themselves. They considered returning to Calpe and coming back for the trial, but Gordon had a lot to do regarding the rebuilding of his house and the neighbouring two houses. There were Shelley and Paul's funerals to attend, and later Constable Amahle Ayisi's. Paul's body was one of those recovered from the bottom of the lake. Gordon had to formally identify it, as there were no close relatives.

On the day of the funeral, the weather reflected the sombre mood. The grey skies were threatening and winter had arrived. Lawnswood Cemetery was where Gordon had said goodbye to several of his friends and relatives, and the double service was mercifully short, but more emotional for it. Colleagues gave eulogies, and despite never meeting him, Gabriela and Gordon realised how well respected he was. Gordon said a few words about Shelley. He was generous in his praise, and his sadness was genuine and heartfelt. Gabriela felt proud of him and afterwards told him so.

As the two coffins were lowered into the earth, the heavens opened and it added to the sombre occasion, but forced people to leave for the wake. Gordon and Gabriela attended the function with the mourners, but didn't stay long. Gordon felt awkward with Shelley's relatives and he was worried for Gabriela, so when they had remained for a polite period, they gave their excuses and left.

Amahle's funeral took place a week later, and this proved an equally sad occasion. The young policewoman was given a full-police funeral with an honour guard and many officers from her station. Inspector Salisbury was present, and the Chief Constable gave a moving address to those present and to the media and camera crews. One surprise attendee was Inspector Glover. The policeman appeared, looking very pale, and he leaned heavily on a walking stick, supported by his wife. To Gordon's and Gabriela's relief, his rumoured death was clearly exaggerated. The dour man looked even less happy than normal, but they understood the responsibility he felt for the policewoman's death. They watched him shuffle his way over to Wayne Maisonet, place a hand on his shoulder, and speak to the bereaved officer. Gabriela wondered if he regretted the way he had scolded Amahle after Wayne and Gordon's kidnapping, but understood his genuine regret for her death.

After the conversation, he turned, saw Gordon and Gabriela looking and he and his wife slowly made their way over.

'Inspector Glover, Mrs Glover. I am glad to see you are on the mend,' Gordon said to the wounded police inspector and his wife.

'This is a tremendously sad occasion.'

'It is, Mr Bennet, Miss Morales. It appears your luck continues to run.'

'So it seems, Inspector.'

'Even cat's run out of lives, eventually, Mr Bennet. Take my advice. Go back to Calpe. You are still a marked man. I would sleep happier knowing you were both out of the country. Trouble really does follow you, and I want a quiet life. I'm getting too old for being shot.'

'There's nothing I'd like better, Inspector. I want to see justice for Shelley and the others. Miroslav Bilyk and his associates have to be put in prison for the rest of their lives. When that's done, I promise I'll be out of your hair.'

'I hope so. I wish you both well, and I am sure we will meet over the next few weeks. Goodbye, Miss Morales, Mr Bennet.'

'Goodbye, Inspector Glover, Mrs Glover,' Gordon said.

'I'll keep him safe, Inspector!' Gabriela added.

'Make sure you do!' and with these words he turned, and helped by his wife, shuffled back to his car and the waiting driver.

TIME HEALS

Time heals physical wounds, and Dana made a remarkable recovery. Within a few weeks, she was out of hospital and she arrived one afternoon at the door of Gordon and Gabriela's room. Gabriela invited her in. Dana refused, but asked Gabriela to come down to the coffee shop. After a quick introduction to Gordon, the two went down and gave their orders. They found a table and there was a brief silence before Dana spoke.

'I wanted to come and thank you.'

'No, there's nothing to thank me for,' Gabriela replied.

'That's not true. If you and Amahle hadn't come, they would have killed me.'

'We were there to find our men. We didn't know you were there. It was just chance, Dana. You would do the same for me, so no thanks are needed.'

'Thank you anyway.'

'How are you feeling? You look well.'

'I'm getting there. Some days are better than others, but it is the nights that are a problem. I keep reliving what they did to me. I hate them!'

'It's not much of a compensation, but they will be in prison for a very long time. They won't be able to harm you.'

'I can't get them out of my dreams. I hate going to sleep! They haunt me. Maybe time will help. How are you?'

'I'm fine, but Gordon is still struggling like you. I hear him talking in his sleep. He's seen some dreadful things, we all have, but it will get better. We are both waiting for the trials to start, for Bilyk to be found guilty and sentenced. After that we want to get on with our lives. We are going back to Spain. I have a job to get back to, some studying, and Gordon has to decide what work he wants to do.'

'That sounds like a good plan. I am on leave from the police for quite a while, and they are insisting I meet with the psychologist and then get counselling. They want me back, but not in undercover work.'

'Well, the trial should start soon and then hopefully we can put all this behind us.'

Gabriela and Dana chatted and to any observers they were just two women talking about their lives, their loves and their hopes. But in reality, it was much more. They shared a traumatic experience, one they would never quite escape, and they were a sisterhood, linked by the death of Amahle. The police woman had become Gabriela's friend and Dana's saviour, one that she could never thank.

They spoke, drank coffee and occasionally laughed for the rest of the afternoon, but eventually Dana had to go and she made her farewells. As she was about to leave, she spoke once more about her suffering.

'I wanted to kill him, Gabriela, the man who raped me. I still want to kill him!'

'I understand, Dana. I wanted to hurt Bilyk, and I did, but it didn't make me feel any better. I thought he had killed Gordon. Nothing I could do would have made any difference, but I am glad I didn't kill him. If I had, I would have lost Gordon, anyway. I hate the man for what he's done, but we just have to make sure he is found guilty. That will be justice, and I know you believe in justice.'

'I know you're right. We'll need to ensure justice is done. See you in court!'

With that, the woman left the hotel and got into a waiting car. Gabriela watched her go and wondered if she would ever get over the trauma of recent days, whether Dana would find peace and whether Gordon's nightmares would continue to plague his nights.

Gabriela was about to return to the room when Gordon appeared.

'Fancy a drink in the bar?'

'Why not?' she answered, and together they walked over to the bar. It was a quieter, much more sedate than the one at The Hamlet and she was pleased it was so different. She didn't think she could face being there again. It held too many ghosts for her. They got their drinks and sat on a soft, curved sofa near a large open fireplace.

'Peter called me,' Gordon said. 'He wants to catch up and have a drink with us. He's coming round in half an hour. Is that all right?'

'Of course, why shouldn't it be?'

'I didn't think you'd mind.'

'What's there to mind about having a drink with your handsome, charming and single friend?'

She laughed as she said this and Gordon laughed too, but maybe not quite as enthusiastically as Gabriela.

They got lost in their conversations and were starting to think about their return to Calpe. Gordon had always said he wanted to be based there, and that was even more important, after all that had happened. They spoke about the Morena Bar, and they both thought wistfully about sitting staring at the wonderful beach and Mediterranean.

'I wonder if that drunk is still at the bar?' Gabriela said. Her thoughts were interrupted as Peter arrived and called across the bar.

'Red wines?' he called.

'Go on then, force us,' Gabriela called back, laughing.

Gordon was pleased to see her getting her old humour back, and to see his friend again.

Peter brought the drinks over and they sat and chatted, made small talk and generally passed a pleasing half hour. Gordon got to his feet and checked what they wanted to drink next and then headed over to the bar.

'How are you doing, Gabriela? Are you getting over it all?' Peter's expression showed concern.

'I'm fine. We're fine,' she added.

'I can't image the ordeal, facing Bilyk at his home. It took some nerve. I hear you forced him to speak. You used a bit of persuasion!'

'I needed to find out what had happened to Gordon. I would have killed him. I shocked myself with what I would do to him, Peter. There was a part of me I didn't like.'

'I've been told he was a bit of a mess. You got him to talk?'

'Oh yes, he spoke alright, but I had to hurt him to get him to start. He told me everything then.'

Peter looked at her quizzically and appeared about to say something when Gordon arrived with the drinks. The conversation turned back to less serious topics as Peter's face changed back to its happy self, and he asked about Gordon's house, the rebuild, and their plans. The day passed into the evening and the drinks flowed and the three enjoyed their time and Peter and Gordon reminisced about their times together. Apparently, they had been at school together and got into all sorts of scrapes. Some made Gabriela laugh, and she learnt more about Gordon and his friend.

Eventually, Peter told them he had to leave, but because he had been drinking, he left the car at the hotel and caught a taxi back. He said that he would see them briefly when he returned the next day to collect his car. Gordon and Gabriela only had a flight of stairs to get back to their room. When the door shut, they both felt happy just to be together and to be putting the horrors of the recent weeks behind them.

'So you were a right tearaway at school, Cariño. I see nothing much changes.'

'Peter was worse than me. He always led me astray.'

'You are so easily led, Gordon. It would have all been Peter's fault.'

'Actually, I was a little worried about him for a while. It is good to see how well life has worked out. I joined the military, and he joined the police. Our paths followed similar lines.'

'You have one thing he doesn't.'

'And what might that be?' he smiled as he said this.

'Me!'

He took her in his arms, forever grateful that he had met this wonderful woman, and she responded in kind.

The following morning they received a call from Peter that he was coming for his car and wondered if Gordon and Gabriela fancied a coffee in the cafe in the hotel. They met downstairs and enjoyed a pleasant chat, but in the midst of it, Gordon got a call from Inspector Salisbury.

'Excuse me, I will take this outside. It could be important.'

Gordon walked out of the room and into the car park. Gabriela was alone with Peter and he instantly took the conversation back to Bilyk and her interrogation.

'So he told you everything? There is a rumour he had someone inside the police. Did he say anything about that?'

Peter's attitude was less relaxed than usual and he had an edge

Gabriela hadn't seen in him before.

'He said many things, but I only cared about where Gordon was and what was happening to him. Dana asked him other questions, but once Amahle and I had got where they were taking them, I didn't give it my full attention. He may have said something to Dana. I just don't know.'

Gordon walked back in and Peter changed the subject.

'What did Salisbury want you for?'

'She told me the trial date,' Gordon said as he sat down.

'It will start in a week's time.'

'I'll be so glad when it's all over,' said Gabriela.

'More coffee, anyone?'

'No, I must be going. I'm supposed to be working. It's lovely to catch up with you both. Take care. I'll see you soon.'

He stood up and made his way out of the cafe and to his car. Gordon and Gabriela watched him drive off.

'I want another,' Gordon said, and he went to the counter to order drinks.

Gabriela was looking pensive when he returned.

'What's wrong?'

'Nothing. Nothing really. Peter was telling me that Bilyk had someone on the inside of the police force. He asked if Bilyk had said anything to me about it. I suppose he wanted to know who it might be.'

'It's certainly possible. Bilyk would have had fingers in many pies. What did you say?'

'He said nothing to me, but he might have to Dana. I only cared about where you had been taken.'

'I guess it would be useful if he had named his man. Or woman,' he corrected himself. 'Whoever it is, it won't make any difference to the case, but it is never a good thing. Bent cops are a threat to all the good work the honest police do. He can always ask Dana.'

'Yes, he can. Is he involved in the investigation?'

'I don't know. I guess he must be. What do you want to do today? Fancy a drive out into the country?'

'Sounds a good idea. I'd like to see more before we return to Calpe. It is so very green and different.'

'That's because of the rain. Drink up then. We'll go and get ready.'

GLOVER

Inspector Glover was recovering. There was so much that had happened these last few weeks and he was still getting his head around the madness. His wife fussed over him and told him in no uncertain terms he was going to retire. He didn't want to argue with her. She always won any arguments they experienced in their forty-year marriage, but he wouldn't leave any case unfinished and certainly not this one. Inspector Salisbury was in charge of the investigation and, although it was galling for Inspector Glover to see someone take his place, she produced a tight case that should see Miroslav Bilyk put into prison for most, if not all, of the remainder of his life. She was happy with her achievements and as an officer still with years of service before her, this could well provide the next step up on her career path. She might be content, but Glover was not. He had known for years that Miroslav had someone inside the force feeding him information and keeping him a step in front of any investigations, but then he also had someone in Bilyk's inner circle.

Dana proved to be an excellent officer. She was thorough, ruthless, and prepared to do anything to bring bad guys to justice. She had worked for Bilyk for several years and been part of his entourage. He knew what she had done to earn his trust and couldn't help but be in awe of her dedication, even if it bordered on fanatical. The officer had never been liked, but always respected. He believed she would find the evidence to put Bilyk away, and so it had proven, but it nearly cost her life. She had realised there was danger and wanted out, but it all happened too late.

Glover learnt about Dana's troubles after recovering in hospital.

She had been in the same hospital at the same time, but he hadn't had the opportunity to talk to her since. He knew she and Gabriela Morales had got Bilyk to tell them what was happening to Gordon Bennet and Constable Maisonet. He wondered if they had learnt anything more.

The inspector was on leave and had no further official role to play, but it was like a nagging itch. He wanted to find the mole. Bilyk had remained silent where that was concerned and nothing, it appeared, would change his mind. Even the chance of a shorter sentence was met with a blank. But there was the chance that Dana had discovered something, even if she didn't realise it.

His recovery was slow and so this was the first chance he had. Driving had been an impossibility, but now he could manage it, even if it was tiring. His wife was out tonight and so what she didn't know couldn't hurt her. If it was a waste of time, then at least he could speak with her, see how she was doing. He had learnt what had happened to her and believed she would take longer to heal than he would.

He reflected on his shooting. In honesty, there was little he could recall. One minute he was lighting a cigarette and the next he was in pain, lying on the ground. That was the only thing he actually remembered until he regained consciousness after surgery. He was told what occurred by the officers that found him. Apparently, the gunman escaped, but his two companions died in a shootout in the gorge. He wondered if the man would ever be brought to justice.

He telephoned Dana, and she answered,

'Hello?'

'Hi, Dana. It's me, Inspector Glover.'

'Hi, Inspector. I recognised your voice anyway. How are you doing? I hear you were shot.'

'I'm on the mend. More importantly, how are you? I am sorry I didn't get you out sooner.'

'Slowly getting there. The wounds are healing, slowly, but each day it improves.'

'Good to hear it. I need to speak with you, Dana. Are you free tonight? It's important. I can fit in with you, anywhere, anytime.'

'I'm seeing someone for a short while at eight. Maybe afterwards?'

'Where are you meeting?'

'At the Fox and Hounds at Roundhay. If you want, I could meet you there. How about nine?'

'That's good for me. Thanks, Dana. I want to catch up and discuss something important. Tonight at nine, and the Fox and Hounds. It's a date!'

The inspector smiled. She sounded better than he had hoped. He understood the emotional harm would take longer to heal, but he believed she would, if anyone could, recover. He hoped it might help her come to peace with the world, but he wouldn't bet on it.

At about five to nine that evening, the inspector made his way to the meeting place. He parked the car a little further down the road opposite Canal Gardens and crossed the zebra crossing. He arrived early, as he wasn't sure how close he would be able to park, and he still needed the cane for support. As he was approaching the entrance to the pub, a man walked out that he thought he recognised. He seemed familiar, but he wasn't sure, as it was dark and rain was falling. The man didn't turn and headed up the hill away from the inspector. The inspector entered the bar and looked around for Dana. She was sitting at a table in a secluded nook, and he walked over.

'Hi, Dana. What can I get you to drink?'

'Hello, Inspector. I'll have a gin and tonic, please.'

'I'll be right back.'

He returned a little gingerly with the drinks, as carrying anything with his awkward gait proved challenging.

'Here you are. I managed it,' he said, placing the drinks on the table.

'You haven't fully recovered, Inspector.'

'No. I still have a way to go, but it is improving slowly every day. And you? You look good, but you always did.'

'I see you have kept your charm, Inspector. Even if you are a poor liar. Some wounds take a long time to heal, and some might never do.'

'True. My wife wants me to retire, but I am not quite ready to do so. There is one thing I must do and then I will walk away and spend my days with her. She deserves that.'

'I hope you enjoy retirement. You must travel the world a bit and enjoy yourselves.'

' I suppose I must, but I'm not sure leisure suits my nature. I need to be kept busy, and if I'm not, I fear I will drive my wife crazy,' he said.

'We are cut from the same cloth, Inspector. So what is the last thing you have to do?'

He looked at her and said,

'I have to work out who the rat is. I want to find out who told Bilyk we had someone in his organisation and how Bilyk found out about you, and when I do, I want them to be locked away with all the others for the rest of their days.'

'We have a shared mission, then!'

'I thought you'd say that. Do you have any ideas? Did Bilyk ever say anything? You were with Miss Morales when she questioned him. Did he say anything about who it might be?'

'I'm sorry, Inspector, but no, and you're the second person to ask me that tonight.'

'I am?'

'Yes. Peter Falkirk asked me about it just a few minutes ago.'

'That was who I saw leaving the pub as I was arriving. I thought I recognised the man from behind. So you were meeting Peter Falkirk. I didn't know you two were friends.'

'We're not. It surprised me when he called me. He asked to catch up, and I thought, why not? I always found him rather good looking. I'm not sure why I'm telling you this.'

'That's ok. You are allowed a private life. God knows, you deserve one!'

'Anyway, we just chatted. He asked how I was. After a while, he asked me about my undercover work. As it should be, he didn't know I was embedded in Bilyk's organisation. He seemed quite interested in that field. He told me he had thought about moving into it. I told him about the work generally, but nothing more, as I wasn't supposed to discuss the case.'

'No. I didn't know he would be interested. He would make a good undercover operative. I may speak with him. Only a few of us directly involved were aware of your identity. He's linked to fraud, so he would know nothing about your status. So, did Bilyk say anything?'

'He said many things. Gabriela Morales and Constable Aysi got a lot of information out of him, but they never asked him about the mole. They were searching for Gordon Bennet and Maisonet.'

'Ah well, I hoped there might have been something. I hate the fact that someone is feeding information to villains.'

'Well, Inspector, whoever told Bilyk there was someone in his organisation, they didn't have a name. He started searching, desperate to discover who it was. I could tell something was wrong, as he was distracted and not making the best decisions. He found me out by testing my reaction to meeting Bennet and Constable Maisonet. It was an unusual situation. He had never involved me in the criminal side of his work. They set me up. I think he saw something in the way I responded and he got confirmation when he beat me. In the end, I would have told him anything he wanted to know.'

'From what you've told me, the mole isn't in our circle. They knew your identity, so it must be someone else and I won't rest until I get them.'

'I wish you luck, Inspector. When I see Peter Falkirk tomorrow, I will ask him. He might have heard something, some loose talk around the station. Maybe someone's been asking too many questions.'

'You're seeing him again. Yes, he might have some ideas. Keep me informed if you discover anything. How about another drink?'

'I'd love one, but I'll get them. I'm thirsty and can't bear to wait while you shuffle over there and back!'

They both laughed. She got to her feet and was there and back in the time the inspector would have taken to hobble over to the bar. They enjoyed the drinks, and each other's company.

DANA

They say there is no peace for the wicked and he guessed it was probably true. Peter had struggled to keep his mind clear after all that had happened since Miroslav's arrest. He had sorted any loose ends by elimination, and Bilyk's wife was safely tucked away in his cellar. Now he felt secure that the Serbian would not cause him any problems, at least for the time being, but he was plagued by fears that he had missed something, that the police were biding their time and would shortly arrest him.

Dana had spent time with Bilyk when he was being tortured and interrogated. Had he spoken about his man in the force? Maybe, and the thought of the possibility gnawed at his mind, kept him from sleeping. He hated unfinished business, but he would find out tonight. Tonight, he was meeting Dana and he would discover the truth. That left only one possibility, Gordon's girlfriend, Gabriela. She interrogated Bilyk. It was possible she had got information from him. Maybe she didn't even realise its significance, but whatever, she wouldn't be a problem for much longer.

Dana waited outside The Myrtle Tavern. The pub had been popular for years and its clientele was a mixture of twenty-somethings to baby-boomers. Some walked across from houses around the area, but most drove into the car park. The evening was mild for the time of year and the fallen leaves left a carpet over the ground, rich, brown, with a pungent odour that reminded her of Guinness. She had been waiting five minutes and had decided to remain five more. Dana didn't enjoy hanging around and she was regretting having agreed to meet Peter Falkirk. It was true she found him charming and attractive, but there was something about his authenticity. She couldn't help suspecting he was acting a part. She wondered if this resulted from what had been done to her. Being suspicious of men must be common for those who suffered as she had.

He appeared from out of the night and caught her off guard. She jumped as he spoke.

'Hello, Dana. I'm sorry I'm late, but I had some business to attend to. I truly am sorry. I won't make a habit of it. Shall we go in?'

'I was just about to leave, Peter. I'll forgive you, just this once, but don't do it again!'

'So there'll be an again?'

'We'll have to wait and see!'

She laughed as she said this, and together they went into the pub.

Inspector Glover had spent the next day calling friends in the force. He wanted to know more about Peter Falkirk. Dana's information that he was interested in undercover work intrigued him. The inspector had come across him on several occasions and knew he worked in fraud, but they had never worked together on a case. After a morning of phone calls, he formed a new opinion of the man. It appeared he was a capable officer, confident in his own ability. Some said to the point of arrogance, but one that got results. On the record, that was about the limit of the feedback, but off the record, a different picture appeared. Falkirk was a man with ambition. He liked to mix in affluent circles. Glover discovered he was a childhood friend of Gordon Bennet and that as a teenager he had got into some trouble with the law, but nothing that received anything but a caution.

One current member of the fraud squad was only prepared to talk in person, and the inspector drove to meet with her. The coffee bar in the city was its usual lunchtime buzz, and tables were full, but the inspector saw her sitting in a quiet corner, looking at the menu.

'Hi, Nolene,' he said, as he sat down on the chair opposite. 'I haven't spoken to you in a long time.'

'Hi! God, you don't look well! I hear it was touch and go for a while.'

'You were never one to mince your words, Nolene. Just say it as it is! That's refreshing, and one of the reasons I respect your opinions.'

'I see you haven't lost your charm, you smooth talker. I just hope you have your wallet with you. Lunch is on you!'

'Lovely as ever! Yes, the wallet is fine, and I'll change a habit of a lifetime to buy you lunch. Let me look at the menu.'

The first part of the meeting comprised ordering, small talk and catching up on families. They had spent years working together when they were younger, but circumstances had led to them drifting apart.

They enjoyed their meal and when it was just about finished, Nolene spoke about the reason they were meeting.

'You wanted to know about Peter Falkirk? I thought you would want the truth, which is why we are meeting in person. What I am going to tell you is just my feeling. I can't prove anything, but it may make you think again.'

'I value your opinion, Nolene. Just tell me what you feel.'

'Well, I don't like the man. I know that isn't grounds for anything, but it is based on several things. He isn't liked, but then I can't see you being on the top of many people's most loved list. But it is more than that. No one who has worked with him has anything good to say. There is a feeling he would sell his own mother to get a promotion. I have heard he planted evidence to get a conviction. This may have happened with Marcus Spinx, and I know you led the case. You are straight, but I suspect he played a part in setting up Spinx.'

The discussion took a while to end. Glover heard things that, despite being rumour and not substantiated, gave him a view of Peter Falkirk that was troubling. Nolene's testimony matched the less damning, but widely held, views of others that worked with the fraud squad officer. He left the cafe with a brooding feeling of unease. It was as he was getting into his car that he remembered. Dana was meeting with Falkirk that evening, and he'd been interested in Bilyk's man in the police force. Could he be? The more that he thought about it, the more the niggling grew. Certainly, no one had suggested he was the leak, but when he put the comments together and added them to Nolene's testimony, he couldn't help his suspicions.

Dana had told him that the meeting was out of the blue, and that they had not been close before. Whoever Bilyk's man was, he would be very nervous. He hadn't anything firm, though. Suspicions were one thing, but what could he do? The man needed watching!

The evening went surprisingly well. Peter and Dana relaxed in each other's company and her initial irritation and reservations evaporated as the drinks flowed, the laughter happened and time flew. This was just what she needed, she reflected. Life had been harsh with her, and she enjoyed the new experience. By this time, both were feeling the effects of the alcohol and as they walked out into the cold autumn air, Peter suggested a stroll down to the park to blow the cobwebs away.

She took his arm and walked across the green and then down through the wood towards Meanwood Park. They saw no one else, and it was the chill wind that provided sufficient deterrent to keep the dog walkers at home. Their breath came out like smoke in the icy air and she was pleased she had a thick jacket and Peter's body-heat to help keep out the cold.

They hadn't walked far when Peter stopped and stared out into the night. The sky was clear and there were myriad stars, framed by the naked tree branches.

'You know, I always had a thing for you, Dana.'

His voice was quiet, but in the silence it was clear, and Dana smiled.

'Did you? I didn't think you had any interest in me?'

'Oh yes, I was always interested in you. A stunning woman like yourself is not something to ignore. I hear you captivated Bilyk!'

'I don't want to talk about him,' she said, stiffening.

'Sorry! I understand. He is not a nice man. There's just one thing I need to know. Did he ever mention me?'

'Mention you? No, why should he?'

She was a little shocked at how the atmosphere had changed to match the icy air. She was facing him and he held her shoulders and stared deeply into her eyes, as if searching for the truth.

'You know, I think I believe you! But unfortunately, think, is not enough. I'm sorry, my dear, but I can't take the risk.'

His hands moved on either side of her throat, but this was no loving caress. She was shocked as his hands squeezed tightly, and his eyes showed a cold indifference she had never seen before. She looked into the eyes of death: blank, unemotional and terrifying.

Struggling to break free, she realised how weakened she had been by her ordeal. The man holding her was far stronger, and he was intent on one thing, choking her to death.

She found it impossible to draw in air and she felt her pulse throb in her neck. Spots appeared, blurring her vision. Her struggling and kicking stopped, and despite trying to break his grip with her hands, she began to relax into oblivion. Maybe death wasn't as bad as she expected. She almost felt at peace!

GABRIELA

Gordon looked at Gabriela, and despite the frustration he felt about Marcus Spinx and Miroslav Bilyk, he was relieved that she was safe and that the danger was no longer present. The two ringleaders of crime were behind bars and he hoped they would remain so for a very long time. Inspector Salisbury had kept him up to date on the investigation and told him they had identified all the bodies removed from the lake. The inspector was hopeful that the recent spate of killings was finally at an end. Everything now rested in the hands of lawyers and Gordon and Gabriela's roles were to give evidence in the upcoming trials. Trials, plural, because Marcus Spinx had been charged with Paul Montgomery's death. Ariadne Spinx's murder meant the case against her husband was weakened, but the prosecution held out some hope. Gordon didn't know how he would handle Spinx escaping a guilty verdict, even knowing the man would spend the rest of his life in jail.

The Law would run its course, even if justice wasn't served, but he would find it hard to accept it. He needed to get away from Leeds and he would be so happy to board the plane with Gabriela. Calpe would welcome them back and he had set himself the task of learning the language and then opening his own business. Gabriela was the one to suggest he became a private investigator. He had checked what paperwork was required to operate legally in Spain. It would be a chore, but there were no requirements he couldn't meet. The only possible stumbling block would be getting police clearance. He hoped that Inspector Navarro would forget some of their run-ins and provide approval. They had formed a strange bond over the trouble the town had experienced, and he smiled as he thought about the dour Spaniard. The similarity between Navarro and Inspector Glover had not been lost on him, and both men had earned his respect.

This would all happen in the future, but first they had to see the trials through to their conclusions. The first was Bilyk's. The case was strong, to the point where Bilyk's lawyers had tried to arrange a deal to reduce the sentence, but the prosecution would have nothing to do with it. Proceedings were to start the next week and, depending on Miroslav's plea, they estimated it would last for two weeks.

'I won't be long, Gordon. Dana's text asked me to meet her for a drink. She said she has something she needs to talk to me about.'

'Well, can't I come along?'

'I've told you, it's women's business. She has no one else to talk to. She suffered a lot, and if I can help by giving her some support, it is the least I can do. I promise you can have me all to yourself when I get back.'

'All right, but at least let me drive you there. If you are having a drink, it's better you don't drive.'

'You can do that, darling. I was going to ask you to, anyway. Are you ready?'

He realised he had fallen for one of her plans and smiled. There was nothing he wouldn't do for her.

'Where are you meeting?'

'In the city, down by the river and canal. Apparently, there is a bar she wants to try, and it has become a popular area. '

'I know where she means. It used to be really seedy, but it is being upgraded and warehouses turned into apartments. Come on. What time do you want picking up?'

'I'm not sure. Can I give you a call when I know?'

'Fine by me. Just give me a bit of notice.'

The drive into the city was uneventful, but quite busy, until they crossed the river to the new developments: tall blocks of fashionable apartments, cafes, restaurants, and wine bars. It had managed to keep the atmosphere of the docks, and narrow walkways threaded between the buildings, with only sparse lighting and some fashionably cobbled laneways. Pedestrian ways were the norm, and footbridges crossed the dark waters of the River Aire. This night had the suitable addition of a mist building and the streetlights that there were, added a spectral atmosphere. Being an autumnal night, people were dressed against the chill, and couples hurried to get indoors where the lights, the drinks, the food and the company helped them forget the season that was approaching.

Dana had sent the name of a wine bar and given a time and said to meet her outside. Gabriela was about five minutes early, but she hoped Dana would be there.

It was a short walk from where Gordon dropped her off.

'I'll meet you back here,' he said. 'Just ring and I'll be here as soon as I can.'

She leaned in through his window and kissed him, turned, and headed over the arching footbridge, almost disappearing into the rising fog. Gordon sat there for a while, considering what to do. If she wasn't going to be too long, it wasn't worth driving all the way back to the hotel. He thought about it. The alternative would be to find something to do locally. He could find another bar or cafe and wait until Gabriela was finished.

Peter Falkirk lurked in the fog, out of sight of anyone approaching the wine bar, but from where he could clearly see who approached or left the venue. He was there ahead of time, as he didn't want to risk missing his final victim. He was feeling quite pleased with himself. Just this last loose end to tie up and then he could relax. Even the elements seemed on his side tonight. The fog provided additional cover and added to the melodramatic ambiance. The gods were smiling on him and after tonight he would be in the clear. Bilyk's trial was coming fast and once that was over, he would dispose of the man's wife and get back on with his life. First, he had to get rid of the delightful Miss Morales. It was such a waste. He could have enjoyed getting to know her, if not for Gordon. He was aware of how dangerous his friend was, and that was the only concern he had. How would he react when she was no more? His hope was that his friend would turn to the bottle and return to the self-destructive path he had been on before he met her. Needs must, and his needs meant she had to go.

He waited in the shadows, knowing she would soon arrive. She expected to meet her friend, but in reality, it was her end she was facing. He heard footsteps. It was surprising how quiet this part of the city was. He stared towards the sound and saw a silhouette crossing the footbridge. He wasn't sure it was Gabriela, but it was the right time. Adding to his fortune, the streets were deserted apart from the new arrival. The figure approached the wine bar and looked around. He was certain it was Gabriela. The right size and shape. He watched. She looked at her watch and mist came from her mouth and hung on the still night air. He watched Gabriela walk to the wrought-iron fence and look out onto the River Aire. Lights filled the upper storeys of the apartments, but the fog shrouded the lower levels.

Peter glanced around to check and took a step forward when a hand covered his mouth and he was yanked backwards. Any attempt to cry out was stifled as powerful arms held him. There were two men. That was all he knew, and a gun barrel pressed against the side of his head.

'Now, I wouldn't make a sound if I were you!'

The whispered words left him in no doubt, as they frogmarched him along the dark, fog-filled walkway, away from the wine bar, away from Gabriela and towards his judgement.

Thoughts ran through his mind. Were these police officers? Had they found out? Had he been set up? He found out a few minutes later when they stopped next to a black van and the door slid open and the three got into the back. One man looked into Peter's eyes.

'Mr Bilyk sends his regards. Apparently, you have something of his that he wants back. You are going to take us to her, or I will start removing fingers.'

He pulled out a set of bolt cutters from behind the seat.

'Now, I can ask you ten times, but after that, I'll kill you!'

Gabriela stood in the swirling mist, staring out onto the city, and felt homesick for the first time. She had never enjoyed the cold and the greyness of an English winter was not something she looked forward to. She felt overdressed in the cold climate and the thought of the sunshine, the warmth and the freedom of her home, Calpe, called to her. There was nothing she wanted more than her small house and the familiar things of her town, other than to be with Gordon. Somewhere safe and away from the nightmare of this supposed holiday was what they both needed. Leeds had a rugged charm that matched the folk that lived here. The countryside was magnificent, green and full of a variety of lush valleys, high moors and fells, but it was not her home.

As her mind wandered, she forgot about time and the purpose of her visit, but eventually she remembered and looked at her watch. Where was Dana? It was more than late. She couldn't imagine what had kept her new friend, but she would only give her five more minutes. When the five minutes were up, she phoned Gordon.

'Hi, she hasn't turned up. Can you pick me up now? Great, thanks, darling. I'll meet you where you dropped me off. I can't think what happened to her.!'

She walked back to where Gordon had left her and was delighted to find him standing next to the car, waiting.

'You didn't go back to the hotel then?'

'No. It wasn't worth it, and I'm glad I didn't. I wonder what happened to Dana?'

'I guess we'll find out. Take me home!'

'Home?'

'Well, at least as much home as anywhere here.'

'Your wish is my command,' he said, and they drove away.

GOODBYE AND HELLO

The next day started so peacefully. Breakfast in the hotel restaurant was leisurely and, by now, had become so familiar that the staff knew them by first names. Gordon and Gabriela had spent their time on the witness stand the previous day. This was a little sooner than they had anticipated, but they both wanted to get it all over and done with. Neither felt any great satisfaction, as before the trial had started, Dana's body was discovered in the woods at Meanwood. All involved in the case were terribly shocked and there was a brief delay to proceedings.

The undercover police officer had been strangled and left in the open. There was a lot of supposition as to who might have been responsible, but scant evidence. Gordon and Gabriela spoke with Inspector Salisbury, but there was little for her to go on until Inspector Glover came to her with his suspicions about Peter Falkirk. She listened to the still recovering fellow officer and agreed they should bring in him for an interview.

The difficulty was no one had seen him for a couple of days. He hadn't been in to work and hadn't called in sick. Salisbury and her officers went to his house with a warrant, but there was no answer. When they broke into the house, they found his body in the kitchen. There was obvious evidence of torture and his little finger was missing, but the single bullet hole through his head was the cause of death.

Both Gordon and Gabriela were shocked to learn about both deaths. Peter had been one of Gordon's long-time friends, and despite the rumours that he was Bilyk's man inside the force, he still couldn't come to terms with discovering his friend was a cold-blooded murderer and a corrupt officer. It hit him hard, but then everything that had happened since he returned to his hometown had hit him hard. All the positive memories were now sullied, and he needed to move away as soon as possible. He felt guilt for once again immersing Gabriela in a series of life-threatening episodes. She deserved better, and he wanted to get back to Calpe as soon as they could to start a regular, peaceful, uneventful life.

Despite Dana not being able to give evidence, the case was pretty substantial, and it was as certain as trials could be, that Bilyk would be found guilty. The two of them had decided they wouldn't wait for the verdict and once they had met their commitments, they were returning to Calpe, but first they had another funeral to attend. This was to happen later that morning, and both felt a deep sense of anxiety about another burial. As they looked out of the window, they could see the day was bright but frosty. The sun did nothing to lift their mood, and it just reinforced their need to get away. They had tickets booked for the following day. Inspector Salisbury had okayed their leaving. She had their contact details and they could return if it was necessary. Gordon knew he would have to come back at various points. He was dealing with the final arrangements for the rebuilding of his house and the adjoining ones. They had historic value and had to be rebuilt as near to the originals as possible. This was particularly expensive, but that was what his insurance was for. The contents were less of an issue, and he had agreed on a financial payout, which would add to his contingency funds for his new business venture.

Gordon had decided to sever his ties to his hometown permanently, and he would sell his house when it was completed. He had needed a new start when he first went on holiday to Southern Spain, and now he was determined it would be so.

'Have you finished?' he said to Gabriela, as she drank the remains of her coffee.

'Yes. Let's get it over with. It is dreadful, Gordon, but at least she has found some peace.'

'We've been at too many of these. I don't want to attend another for a very long time.'

Dressed in black, they walked out to their car and drove the short distance to Lawnswood Cemetery. There was a further police guard of honour for yet another one of their number to lose their lives. It was the potential cost that the serving men and women lived with, in order to maintain the safety of the majority of citizens. As Gordon and Gabriela approached, they saw no relatives or friends, just the honour guard, Inspectors Salisbury and Glover and one or two others. It was terribly sad that the closest people to Dana were serving officers and Gordon and Gabriela.

Mercifully, the service was brief, and Dana's casket disappeared. Dana left the world as she had entered it, alone. The two inspectors walked over and they shared their sadness. There was a conversation about the bravery of the officer, the sacrifice, but nothing could hide the sadness of Dana's life and ending.

'She turned up, you know.'

Inspector Salisbury said this as if everyone knew who she was talking about. Realising their confusion, she added.

'Bilyk's wife. She just turned up, back at their house, and she hasn't said where she had been other than away. At least she didn't turn out to be another body. We've seen too many. Far too many!'

'I never thought she was mixed up in this business,' Glover said. 'She will be better off with Bilyk in jail for the rest of his days.'

'You don't have any doubt about the verdict, then?' Gabriela asked.

'I think we have the clearest cut and dried case possible. No. He won't be coming out.'

'I agree,' Salisbury concurred. 'You can rest a little easier. I hear you leave tomorrow?'

'Yes. We need to get back. We have a lot to do, but I will have to return once or twice as the house is being sorted.'

'Well, I only hope the next visits are less eventful. Don't you agree, Inspector Glover?'

'I certainly do. I couldn't handle being shot again. My wife would kill me if the bullet didn't!'

For the first time that day, all four laughed, and they headed off for the wake at the police club.

RETURNS

The case went as everyone expected, and Miroslav Bilyk's future was destined to be a long routine locked behind the walls of a British prison. Gordon and Gabriela were back in Calpe when they heard the verdict. They hoped this was the final ending to the whole sad business. Both had experienced events they hoped never to again. They had so very nearly lost each other, and that was something that shook them, witnessed some terrible events and, for Gordon, his hometown would forever be a place of sadness. One thing hadn't been harmed was their love for each other, and both were eager to get on with life in Calpe. The small Spanish resort town felt like a familiar friend when they were driven from Alicante airport.

Similarly, the small square was just as both had remembered it and the bar, the bookshop, and, most importantly, Gabriela's house welcomed them like old friends. As Gabriela opened the door, the relief and the feeling of being home was obvious. The air was a little stale, but everything was just as they had left it, and they turned and smiled at each other.

'Welcome home, mi amor!'

She pulled him over and kissed him deeply.

'Promise me you won't take me on another holiday like that one!'

'I can't promise anything, Gabriela. Danger seems to follow us, but I will try my best. I have a business to set up. You have a job that awaits you and I just want to enjoy living.'

'I suppose I'll have to make do with that, then. Let's have a shower and then we have some shopping to do. We've nothing in the kitchen but a bottle or two of rioja. You could be an angel and pour a drink?'

Gordon smiled and headed to the kitchen cupboard, whilst Gabriela headed to the bathroom.

Later that evening, there was a knock on the door.

'Expecting anyone?' Gordon looked at Gabriela.

'No. I don't think anyone knows we are here.'

'Well, someone does.'

Gordon walked over to the door and gingerly opened it a little. Standing on the threshold was Inspector Navarro.

'Meester Bennet, welcome back!'

'Inspector Navarro, how did you know we were back?'

'Nothing escapes me, Meester Bennet. May I come in?'

'Of course!'

'Buenas noches, Inspector.'

'Buenas noches, Señorita Morales.'

'Would you like a drink, Inspector?' Gordon asked.

He and Gabriela already had one, but he went to get the inspector a glass, and poured a red wine.

'Cheers, Inspector!'

'Salud!' he replied, and they savoured a few moments of enjoying the deep, rich wine.

'I hear you had a very memorable stay in England, Meester Bennet. The police there tell me they were glad to see you go. Bombings, killings, it appears trouble does follow you, Meester Bennet. You have both recovered, I hope?'

'Thank you, Inspector. We are both well, but you can rest assured that I am not looking for any trouble here.'

'I certainly hope that is the case. I have become quite fond of the two of you, and I wouldn't want anything to happen to either of you. You could tempt me with another glass of this wine. It is quite a good one, I think.'

'Certainly Inspector,' and Gordon got the bottle and refilled all three glasses.

'I was going to come and see you,' Gordon added.

'You were?'

'Yes, I am hoping to set up a business and I will need police approval.'

'I am pleased to hear you are going to earn an honest living. What type of business, if I may ask?'

'I want to set up as a private investigator. I have the right background, and I am sure there will be the odd missing dog, unfaithful wife or husband that someone will pay me to find evidence about. Nothing to concern you. I don't want to step on your toes, Inspector.'

At the news of what Gordon intended, the inspector's face dropped.

'I'm not sure that's a very good idea, Meester Bennet!'

'Nonsense, Inspector,' Gabriela added with a broad grin. 'The two of you have worked so well together. Gordon will be busy helping you keep the town safe. It will be like old times!'

The inspector almost choked on his wine, but there wasn't much he could say.

'So, you'll approve my application?'

The inspector looked uncertain what to say and then became even more flustered as Gabriela sidled up to him, leant in and kissed his cheek.

'Please, Inspector. You know it will be fun having him around. At least life won't be dull!'

She kissed him again and the poor man had no option but to smile and agree to her request.

Gordon smiled to himself. This was just another example of how Gabriela was an invaluable partner in crime.

A TREMBLING OF FINCHES

Marcus Spinx smiled to himself, even though he had not had a lot to smile about until the news that Miroslav Bilyk had been convicted. He was standing, caressing one of his finches and he looked at the beautiful little creature and marvelled at how the world could hold such delicate beauty and yet harbour great evil.

Marcus was realist enough to understand where he stood, but he could still admire innocence that lacked ambition and ruthlessness. Returning the bird to its cage, he went to check everything was ready. Wealth allowed privileges, but when you had to move mountains, you had to have the correct leverage, and that had taken a lot of organising. He was soon to return to court over murder charges. As Ariadne was no more, he was the only one to be charged for organising them. His lawyer had told him she would do her best to get them dismissed, but he didn't hold out much hope. In reality, it was more of an academic exercise. He would most likely die in prison and so there was little they could do to him.

The positive side of this was there was little stopping him from doing exactly what he wanted. What could they do? Lock him up for longer? As that was an impossibility, he really felt a freedom that few experienced. When there are no consequences, then a man can do as he wishes, and he had a list.

Cherry Jung had given him the leverage over Franco and he had made the man dance to his tune. The guard wouldn't want to find himself an inmate in his own prison. Money had assisted, and large amounts of cash had been paid to ensure his requests were met. Miss Jung had slipped the cash to him directly or made private deliveries.

It was all untraceable, and the amounts asked were obscenely large, but Marcus had reserves enough to last his remaining days. To be honest, he was past caring. He would never go hungry. Never have to worry about where his next meal was coming from. It was all planned out before him.

His nights were filled plotting how to exact revenge on the Serbian ex-city counsellor. The verdict had given him some joy, but he still wanted to make him suffer for Ariadne's death. It gnawed at him. He couldn't believe his luck when he discovered Bilyk was to join him in the same prison. Such fortune provided many possibilities, but he had manoeuvred, bribed, begged, cajoled, and used his influence to procure his opportunity.

Franco let him know the arrangements were in place. He knew it would result in an inquiry, maybe reprimands for certain staff, maybe a dismissal, but in the end, it would be viewed as another gross lack of organisational control within Her Majesty's Prison Service. No one would really care. Good riddance to bad rubbish!

Marco felt under his pillow. It was still there, and he drew out the thin cord. It was time, and he went and leaned against the wall, waiting. He felt his heartbeats drum out the anticipation and life had never been so electrifying. Footsteps, slow, a pattern from two sets, approached, and he held his breath. They stopped outside the heavy door.

'Why the hell do I have to share a cell?'

'I just carry out orders, Mr Bilyk. I don't make them.'

It was Franco's voice, and he didn't sound overly happy, but Spinx didn't care.

'I'll bloody well get this sorted. I want to see the Governor! I want to see him now!'

'All in good time, Mr Bilyk. I'll go and see what I can do when you are in your new cell. Look, just go in and wait, and I'll get back to you, but the Governor is a very busy man.'

'Does he know who I am?'

'Oh, yes. Everyone knows who you are, Mr Bilyk. You are prisoner LDS 900911. Are you going in, or do I need to get some help?'

Marcus Spinx couldn't help smiling. He was impressed by Franco's manner. If he saw the night out, he would have to reward the guard. He was making this even more entertaining than he had hoped.

The door slowly swung open, and this partially hid Spinx from the sight of those entering. Bilyk walked in and the cell door slammed behind him. The newcomer's eyes took in the birds in the cage and, for a second, watched the two finches chatter away, hopping on the perch.

He stood transfixed for a moment, and that was all the time Spinx needed. He stepped forward and threw the cord over the head of the man before him. Both ends were wrapped several times around his hands and once over the man's neck, he pulled tight. Bilyk sprang into action, as his reflexes made him drop what he was carrying and his hands clasped the cord. Marcus was prepared and his knee pressed into the small of the man's back and the cord bit tight.

When death is a possibility, even the weakest of men will find superhuman strength. The will to live is primal and Bilyk struggled and Spinx was pulled off his feet and the two men writhed on the bed and onto the floor, but the knee and the cord maintained their pressure and the rope cut into the neck.

Marcus's hands also felt the cord bite into the flesh and the pain was only just bearable, but nothing, nothing, would break his hold. The man in his grasp continued to struggle, but it was a vain hope. His movements slowed, the power was reduced and still Spinx held the cord tighter and tighter.

The birds in the cage were unsettled by the commotion and Bilyk's leg kicked out for the final time, catching the stand and almost tipping the cage over. The two finches fluttered to the bottom of the cage, but as the cage stopped rocking, they fluttered back up to their perch in a blur of wings.

Bilyk on the floor was still twitching, and Marcus maintained his grip. Two birds nestled together as far away as possible, trembling with fear.

'Guess you won't have to share a room now,' Marcus Spinx said, with surprising glee in his voice.

'I'll see you in hell, you bastard! But I won't be joining you for a while.'

Sweat poured off his face. He sat on the floor of the cell and released his muscles and gently unwound the cord from his hands. Blood covered, he flexed them and the blood flowed freely. He turned Miroslav Bilyk over and stared at his lifeless eyes. His face was flushed purple and his eyes bulged, but he was no longer present.

The finches recovered their composure and chirped as if nothing had happened, but Marcus knew his life was changed forever. He got to his feet and ignored the body on the floor. Opening the door of the cage, he reached in and both birds jumped onto his outstretched finger. He could feel their tiny chests pounding with the gentle trembling of their hearts.

'I'll only share my cell with you two. Back you go. I have to call the guard, but I'll give you some seed first. I might be away for a while, but I'll be back!'

ABOUT THE AUTHOR

David M Cameron was born in Leeds, in Yorkshire. He is married with four sons and two grandchildren. David has lived in England, Papua New Guinea and Perth, Western Australia, where he has been for the last twenty-eight years. He has written two novels for children, Wickergate and Soulmare, the Moondial fantasy series for adults, and Dead Men Don't Snore, his first thriller in the Gordon Bennet stories. David also has a weekly blog of his 'Cup of Tea Tales' that tell some of his life's stories on growing up in Leeds during the 1950s.

More information on both David's music and books can be found on his website/blog:

http://davidmcameronauthormusician.com

Printed in Great Britain
by Amazon

18360177R00139